HARLEQUIN'S SUPPORT OF BIG SISTERS

Harlequin began sponsoring Big Brothers/
Big Sisters of America and Big Brothers and
Sisters of Canada in April 1988. Since then,
we have become the largest single sponsor of
Big Sisters Programs and related services in
North America.

This fitting association between the world's
largest publisher of romance fiction and a
volunteer organization that assists children and
youths in achieving their highest potential is a
wonderfully different kind of love story for
Harlequin. We are committed to assisting our
young people to grow to become responsible
men and women.

Brian Hickey
President and CEO

For more information, contact your local
Big Brothers/Big Sisters agency.

D1012622

Dear Reader,

Writing *One to One* was not an easy task, but it was a labor of love. Big Brothers/Big Sisters of America has been matching boys and girls with adult friends for over eighty years. These special friendships provide stability and companionship to school-age children, most of whom live with a single parent.

By telling Tiffany, Christine and Ethan's story in *One to One,* we were able to show the hard work and dedication of the Big Brothers/Big Sisters professionals and volunteers. We also, in a small way, influenced organization policy. When the plot line of *One to One* called for Executive Director Christine Baldwin to have a Little Sister of her own, it was discovered that no guidelines for the matching of an agency director existed. But the wonderful people at Big Brothers/Big Sisters responded to our request for clarification and as a result, there are now official guidelines for the matching of agency executives with "Littles" of their own.

As sisters, we had the privilege of growing up in a large and loving family. We cannot think of a better way, a more personal or meaningful way to make a difference in a child's life, to contribute to his or her well-being, to help mold a successful future on a one-to-one basis, than to be a Big Brother or Big Sister.

May God bless you all,

Marisa Carroll
(Carol Wagner/Marian Scharf)

ONE
TO
ONE

Marisa
Carroll

Harlequin Books

TORONTO • NEW YORK • LONDON
AMSTERDAM • PARIS • SYDNEY • HAMBURG
STOCKHOLM • ATHENS • TOKYO • MILAN
MADRID • WARSAW • BUDAPEST • AUCKLAND

Published September 1992

ISBN 0-373-70515-8

ONE TO ONE

"Ethan, will you marry me?"

She held her breath and waited for his answer.

"Oh, God, Chris," he said. "I'd hoped you wouldn't ask me that question tonight."

"I—I don't understand," she said, feeling bewildered and hurt. The band stopped playing. They were still standing on the edge of the dance floor. If the other guests were watching, Chris didn't care. "Tell me what's wrong. Please."

"It's Jeff. He wants the children back. I'm sorry, Chris. I can't marry you until my son and I have settled what's between us."

"I'll wait. And I'll help."

"I love you, Chris Baldwin," he said very softly, as her last hope faded away. "But I can't ask you to wait when I don't know what's going to happen next myself."

CHAPTER ONE

ETHAN CONNOR LOOKED OUT over the playing field, searching for his granddaughter in the crush of small bodies, narrowing his eyes against the glare of mid-May sunlight. Tiffany had just scored a goal, the winning goal, and one of the other parents sitting nearby slapped him on the back.

"Way to go, Mr. Connor. She's great. We'll be sorry to lose her."

He was sorry to take her away.

Tiffany's dark, bobbed head popped up over the top of the crowd of cheering kids as two of the boys lifted her off the ground. It was a coed soccer team, eight- and nine-year-olds combined, and still Tiffany was a standout player, smaller, faster than the boys, more aggressive and focused than the girls.

"Way to go, Tiff," he yelled, standing to cheer the team off the field.

The child looked a great deal like her mother: elfin features balanced by a strong, stubborn chin, dark hair and dark, intelligent eyes. Ethan often found himself wishing he'd known his daughter-in-law better. He wished he could have made her last pain- and worry-filled weeks on earth easier. He hadn't even been aware how seriously ill she was until the end—when his son had chosen to tell him about her condition.

"Grandpa! Grandpa, did you see my goal?" Tiffany cried, rushing up after the ritual filing past of the opposing team.

It had taken him a long time to get used to being called "Grandpa." He wasn't quite forty-eight years old. Hell, he had friends with kids not much older than Tiffany. It served him right for marrying so young.

"We beat them good. They were a bunch of wimps."

So much for good sportsmanship. Ethan hid a smile. "You were great, kid." He pulled her close for a quick, hard hug. Tiffany didn't like mushy demonstrations of affection—at least, she said she didn't. But Ethan was afraid that was because she'd had so little affection in her young life, not because she didn't crave it.

Where had he gone wrong raising a son who would abandon his own children?

"I wish it wasn't my last game," Tiffany said wistfully. "I'll miss the guys."

"They have a soccer league in Bonaparte," Ethan reminded her. "I checked."

"Just for girls." Tiffany snorted inelegantly. "How can anyplace with a weird name like Bonaparte have a good soccer team?"

"The town was named after the French general, remember, and to tell you the truth, in that part of Ohio they're probably more into softball and football than soccer." He tried never to lie to Tiffany. She'd been lied to too often by her father and, for her own protection, by her mother.

"Great." Her disgusted tone said it all. Tiffany scuffed the toe of her shoe in the dirt. "I still wish we didn't have to move away from Chicago. It's home."

The nine months Tiffany and her brother and sister had spent with Ethan had been the most stable time the eight-year-old had ever known. Once again he felt familiar anger and disappointment at his son's desertion of his children surge into his bloodstream, making his heart pound and his fists clench at his sides.

He pushed down the anger and spoke calmly, matter-of-factly. "It can't be helped." That was as close to a lie as he wanted to come. He could have refused the transfer to Ohio, but not without financial sacrifices he wasn't willing to make. He couldn't afford to drift into middle-age complacency where his career was concerned, not with the likely prospect of raising three children staring him in the face.

"The company needs you," Tiffany said, accepting the high-five congratulation of two more of her teammates as they left the rickety stands bordering the city league playing field. "They can't get along without you," she added proudly.

Ethan laughed. He couldn't help it. She looked so smug and proud of him. He wished he deserved half her praise. "A lot of people in Bonaparte depend on Castleton Soups for their jobs. It's an old plant. It needs a lot of work to fix it up, make it run right."

"And you're the best at fixing up old factories as good as new."

She smiled up at him and he knew beyond a shadow of a doubt he'd done the right thing in promising Tiffany's dying mother that he would keep the children with him as long as they needed him.

"Yeah, I know," he said, ruffling her hair. "I'm the best."

"Did Dad call yet?" she asked as they walked toward the car, switching the subject in one breath.

Only Ethan knew that for Tiffany thoughts of her absent father were always there, just below the surface. Questions about him could pop out at any time, during any conversation. He tried not to let his anger at the resignation he detected in her voice show. It was anger directed at his son, at his own failure as a father, not at his granddaughter.

"Not yet," he said carefully.

"Is he with Maria?"

"I don't think so."

Tiffany had never met her grandmother, Ethan's ex-wife. Their divorce a dozen years earlier had been ugly and painful. Maria never left the artist's colony/sixties-throwback commune in California where she'd lived for the past six, or was it seven, years. He could never remember. Their son, Jeff, wasn't likely to be there, but he sometimes got in touch with his mother. It might be worth a shot to try to reach him through her.

"Will he be able to find us in Bonaparte?" Tiffany asked for the tenth time that week as they climbed into the car. The seats were hot. She yelped as her bare legs touched the hot leather, and jumped back outside again.

"Yes," Ethan said as he knelt to check the back of her legs for possible damage. "Put a towel over the seat, honey," he suggested. "That should help."

"Are we going to pack the little kids' things tonight?" she asked as he started the car. Tiffany's mothering instincts, as far as her little brother and sister were concerned, were always working overtime.

"As soon as we get Brandon to bed." Brandon Joseph Connor was twenty-two months old and quite a handful. His sister, Ashley, was five and almost as grown-up as Tiffany.

"We're moving tomorrow."

She sounded disbelieving and a little scared as she wiggled around on the towel he'd dug out of the sports bag in the back seat.

"Tomorrow."

Tiffany sighed, her serious little face screwed up in a frown. "I suppose I can play softball if they don't have a good soccer team."

"I'LL BE BACK to relieve you as soon as I shower and shave."

Christine Baldwin looked up her tall, blue-eyed, blond-haired son and smiled. "Hurry back, I'm melting in here." The concesssion stand at Veterans' Memorial Field wasn't air-conditioned. In the corner by the steam table where Chris had been working it had to be more than a hundred degrees.

"Hey. Can't you even congratulate the game's MVP with a hot dog or something?" Keith pleaded. Muddy softball cleats tied together by their laces hung over his shoulder. His red-and-black Panther jersey, Chris noted with a sigh, was just as muddy as his shoes—stained with the black clay that made the fields around Bonaparte fertile and productive. "I'm starved and I bet you didn't leave anything simmering on the stove for dinner, did you?"

"In this heat?" Chris asked, slathering mustard and ketchup on a bun before slapping a Home Run frank in its center. Home Run franks were a subsidiary of Castleton Soups, Bonaparte, Ohio's principal employer and the sponsor of the concession stand. Each night of the week a different charitable organization operated the stand, with Castleton Soups providing the food and soft drinks at cost and the group supplying the volunteers, as well as collecting all the profits. It was a public service Castleton's had provided for many years. Chris just wished her Big Brothers/Big Sisters program had enough clout to be assigned one of the league nights instead of the high school teams' summer league games. But game nights were assigned by seniority and their allocation in the United Fund's budget. Her program was new, just four years old, and she was lucky to have snagged six Wednesdays and the County High School Softball Tournament the first weekend of August.

Keith grabbed the sandwich and stuck half of it in his mouth. "Great," he mumbled. There wasn't a kid in Bonaparte who dared admit to not liking Home Run franks or tomato soup.

"Fifty cents," Chris teased, waggling her fingers.

"I'll owe ya," he said, laughing his father's laugh as he sprinted away.

"Good Lord, that boy looks more and more like Jack every day," Chris's friend Miriam Leonard said, pouring the foam off a diet cola and handing the drink to the overweight, matronly woman on the other side of the counter. "Sixty cents, please." Miriam dumped the money in the cash drawer. "There's another fifteen cents for the program." She shook her iron-gray head. "There must be a quicker way to earn money."

"There isn't," Chris said, laughing. "Wishing on a star just doesn't cut the mustard." She watched her tall, handsome son head for his car.

The older woman's gaze followed Chris's. "I can't believe he's going to be a senior in high school next fall."

Miriam had no children of her own. She'd more or less adopted Chris's son and daughter when Chris and her husband, both native to the area had moved back to Bonaparte ten years earlier after working in one of Castleton Soup's West Coast plants. She'd become even more of a friend when Jack had died of leukemia five years later. In fact, it was Miriam who had talked Chris into putting her never-used degree in psychology to work heading up the fledgling Big Brothers/Big Sisters program in Hobart County.

At the time Chris had never expected the appointment to become her life's work.

But it had.

And in many ways, it had been a lifesaver, helping her to recover from her husband's death, keeping her from retreating into a world of grief and loneliness. Being the executive director of what was essentially a one-woman program was nothing if not challenging. It was also hard work. And she loved it.

"How are the wedding plans coming along?" Miriam asked, changing the subject, or at least branching off in a new direction.

Any mention of one of Chris's children usually led to mention of the other. Her daughter, Erika, was twenty, recently graduated from junior college with an associate degree in office management. She was employed at Bonaparte Community Hospital and planning to marry her childhood sweetheart in the spring.

"We've been looking at wedding gowns every weekend for the past month, as you very well know," Chris complained good-naturedly. "I think we found 'the one' at La Belle Bride."

"Oh, heavens," Miriam murmured in sympathy, "that place is *sooo* expensive."

"Don't remind me." Chris made change from a five-dollar bill. She handed the coins and a cardboard container of food and soft drinks across the counter to old Mr. Petersen, who was there watching his great-grandson play in the junior high game and treating the rest of the family to franks and sodas. Chris smiled at the old man and then over at Miriam. "She looked so beautiful, how could I say no?"

Miriam sniffed. "Erika would look beautiful in a feed bag."

It was true. In her daughter, Chris's dark blond hair and brown eyes had been translated into ash-blond curls and dark blue eyes—like her father's—and a tall, willowy figure that wouldn't start to pick up pounds until Erika was a lot older than Chris.

"How much did the gown cost? And the veil?" Miriam demanded with the devastating candor of an old and valued friend.

Chris named a figure that still made her cringe whenever she thought of it. "We're going to have to economize somewhere else. Maybe on the table decorations? What do you think?"

Miriam nodded agreement. "You've always been good at that sort of thing. It'll be a lot more work, though." She smiled at the next customer. "What can I get for you, Mrs. Bailey?"

Thirty minutes later, Keith returned with his latest girlfriend, a redheaded cheerleader and National

Honor Society student. Chris smiled politely at the girl and turned the concession stand over to her son with a sigh of gratitude. "Keep track of what you eat so I can reimburse the kitty," she reminded him as she washed her hands at the sink in the back of the building. "I'll be back to lock up at nine."

"Nine?" Miriam looked at her watch. "Good, that will give us time to go to Carter's and get a salad. I'm starved and I hate Home Run franks." Miriam's husband, Walt, had been the plant comptroller at Castleton's Soups for twenty-five years. It still didn't stop his wife from speaking her mind. "Besides, there are some papers I want you to fill out."

"Papers?" Chris had to walk very quickly to catch up with Miriam's long-legged stride. "Slow down. It's too hot to walk this fast."

"Sorry." Miriam slowed her headlong pace. She looked over at Chris. "You short people are such a pain to walk with."

"Five foot five is not short. What papers are you talking about?" she demanded as they turned onto River Street and headed for the restaurant. Reaching out, she grabbed her friend by the hand. Miriam was five inches taller and forty pounds heavier, but she stopped walking at Chris's touch. "What papers?"

Miriam took a deep breath. "Your application to become a Big Sister." Her round face was flushed with something more than late-afternoon heat.

"My application to do what?" Now it was Chris who was flustered. "What are you talking about?"

"Oh, dear." Miriam looked up and down the street as if looking for assistance. None was forthcoming. "This isn't how I planned to tell you."

"Miriam, quit stalling." Behind Miriam the century-old, red brick county courthouse rose above the trees and blocked out Chris's view of the achingly blue May sky.

"Can't we at least go inside the restaurant and sit down? I'm dying of heat prostration."

"You're going to be dying of more than that if you don't tell me what harebrained scheme you've cooked up now."

Miriam squared her shoulders and launched into an explanation. "You're going to be getting a new applicant for the program on Monday. Her name is Tiffany Connor. Her grandfather's the new plant manager at Castleton's. You know Will Whitson retires next week."

"There isn't a living soul in Bonaparte who doesn't know there's a new soup aristocrat in town." Chris didn't move, continuing to block the older woman's way into the air-conditioned building.

"He's got the power to make or break the plant," Miriam warned darkly. "This facility's forty years old. His recommendations for the future will mean a big overhaul and lots of work for the next generation of Bonaparte's citizens ... or ..."

"Okay, I get the picture," Chris said just as darkly.

"Anyway, he's a nice guy. And Tiffany's a great kid."

"Of course we'll do our best to find a match for her," Chris began automatically. She had six teenage girls and eleven boys of various ages on the waiting list. She could squeeze one more child in. "How old is she?"

"Eight," Miriam responded with what sounded suspiciously like triumph in her voice.

"Eight." Chris felt the silken jaws of Miriam's trap close around her.

"She lost her mother less than a year ago. Her father is...I don't know where he is." Miriam frowned. "She's living in a new town, being raised by her grandfather, who's divorced, and she's lonely."

"That's what we're here for," Chris said more softly.

"She's a perfect match for you." Miriam pressed her point home. "You've always said you might consider taking a Little Sister if she wasn't a teenager."

"I have two teenagers of my own...."

Chris stepped aside to allow several departing patrons to exit the restaurant. Miriam greeted each of them in her friendly way. Chris also nodded hello, and before Chris could stop her, Miriam walked inside.

"You won't have two teenagers in the house much longer," Miriam said, holding the plate-glass door for Chris to follow. "Have you listened to yourself lately? You're either talking about Erika's wedding or Keith's graduation from high school and what college he should attend. It's almost as if your life is going to end a year from today."

"That's not true."

"Isn't it?" Miriam looked at her for a long moment, then led the way to a table.

The restaurant was small and cozy and nearly empty, the early dinner crowd having already left. No one ate supper in Bonaparte much after six-thirty except on the weekend. Miriam and Chris sat near the window and Chris looked out over the broad, muddy-brown waters of the Maumee River, which flowed through the center of town.

"Do I really sound that tied up in my children's lives?" she asked after a minute or two of silence.

"Yes," Miriam said decisively. "You're too young to be settling into waiting to be a grandmother."

"I'm forty-two," Chris reminded her. "One or two of my old high-school classmates are grandmothers already."

"They probably had no choice. Two chef salads and two iced teas," Miriam instructed the waitress without missing a beat. "Not that it's a bad thing, but you're too young for that to be the next major goal in your life."

"Spoken like a woman who's staring the big five-0 in the face."

"Maybe it is." Miriam colored slightly under her tan, then smiled. "A good friend wouldn't remind me of my age."

"A good friend wouldn't tell me I'm dwindling into middle age less than gracefully," Chris shot back.

They both laughed.

"Tiffany will be a great match for you." Once set on her course, Miriam was harder to redirect than the *Queen Mary*.

"At least she's only a potential Little Sister. God forbid you should take it into your head to find me a husband." Chris smiled politely as the waitress set her salad and iced tea in front of her.

Miriam almost choked on a bite of sesame cracker she'd unwrapped from its plastic covering. "I'd never think of such a thing."

"No, of course you wouldn't." Chris grinned to show she'd been teasing.

Miriam looked relieved and headed the conversation back to where she wanted it to be. "When do you want to meet with Tiffany? Monday?"

"Miriam..."

"You have to interview her regardless. She is coming into the program whether or not I can convince you to be her Big Sister."

Chris sighed. "This is ridiculous. I'm not even sure our policy would permit the matching of an agency director."

Miriam reached into the big straw shoulder bag she'd dumped on the floor by their table. "No problem. I checked it out last week when I suggested to Ethan Connor that Tiffany needed a Big Sister."

"And..." Chris couldn't believe she was giving in without a fight.

"And there is no policy against directors having Littles of their own, as long as we don't bypass any of the steps involved in getting you accepted as a volunteer."

"Miriam, I screen the applicants, have you forgotten?"

"No." Miriam presented the papers she'd dug out of her bag with a flourish. "Here's your application and the waiver that allows us to conduct a police check. And you'll need three references, just like anyone else. I've asked Steve Harris, since he's a member of our board and also the director of the family service program, to volunteer his casework supervisor to handle your match."

"Tell me he thought it wasn't a good idea and turned you down flat," Chris pleaded.

Miriam looked smug. "On the contrary. He thinks it's a fine idea. He's already talked to Annie Plotts, the casework supervisor, and she accepted the assignment. Based on your references and the interviews you'll be approved . . . or disapproved . . . just like any other applicant. As far as you and Tiffany are concerned, Annie will function in your position, conducting quarterly evaluations, monitoring any problems that crop up between you. The usual.''

"All right. You've certainly done your homework." She threw up her hands in defeat. "I'll fill out the application. But if I don't feel that Tiffany and I will match, I won't submit it. Her name will go on the waiting list with the other children and I'll match her as soon as possible." She set her lips in a firm line and stared her friend straight in the eye. "Agreed?"

"Agreed. I'm not worried. You two are a perfect match."

"We'll see." Chris was intrigued in spite of herself. She'd mentioned the possibility of taking a Little Sister of her own at various times over the past year. She did sometimes feel left out of the monthly activities she planned for her volunteers and their kids. They always seemed to have so much fun. "It's been ages since I've had to deal with an eight-year-old's problems," she said, half to herself.

"Piece of cake," Miriam said around a mouthful of lettuce and hard-boiled egg.

Chris made a face, remembering some of the crises she herself had weathered as the mother of two youngsters. "Give me a break," she grumbled, stabbing a tomato wedge with her fork, but she smiled as she said it.

TIFFANY CONNOR SAT swinging her legs over the edge of the chair. The seat was hard and it was hot in the little office where she sat. She didn't know how the lady behind the desk could stand it, except that the little fan on the filing cabinet was blowing on her and not on Tiffany, so maybe that helped.

"It's sure hot in here," she said as the lady read over the papers Mrs. Leonard had given her grandfather to fill out.

"I know," the lady said, looking up from the paper and smiling.

She was old but still pretty and Tiffany smiled back, a little, just to be polite.

"The air conditioner's broken. I'm not sure it can be fixed. It's old and I can't afford to buy a new one until next year."

It was June 27. Tiffany was good with dates. "Too bad," she said, and went back to swinging her legs. Her grandfather had made her wear a skirt and blouse to the interview. She hated skirts. She couldn't wait to get back home and put on a T-shirt and a pair of shorts.

"What things would you like to do with a Big Sister, Tiffany?"

The lady pushed back some dark blond hair that had fallen onto her forehead. When she smiled, lines crinkled up at the edges of her eyes, but nicely, not like Mrs. Baden, her grandfather's housekeeper, who was so fat when she laughed her eyes just disappeared into her head.

"Just things," Tiffany said, checking out the toes of her Sunday shoes. They were scuffed and dusty from dragging her feet on the way into the court-house. She was a little ashamed of acting like that now, but at the time it had seemed okay.

"Do you like dolls?"

The lady looked kind of like she wished she hadn't said that. "Not really."

"Music?"

"I like the New Kids," Tiffany said grudgingly. The lady nodded, as if she knew who the New Kids were, but she might be fooling. "Have you seen their new video?"

"Yes."

She'd told Tiffany to call her Chris, but it seemed funny to call someone that old by their first name.

"My son watches MTV when he's home, but most of the time he's out playing softball."

Tiffany sat up straighter in her chair. "I like sports," she said. "Did I remember to put that down on my paper?" She couldn't quite come up with the long word her grandfather had used to describe the sheet of paper that was full of questions for both of them to fill out—*plication,* or something like that.

"It's right here on your application."

The lady... Chris... nodded. *Application.* Tiffany filed the word away for future reference. "I like to shop. My grandpa doesn't. And Mrs. Baden says it's too hard on her feet. Can you look for a Big Sister for me who likes to shop? I have my own money," she added hastily. That probably made a difference. If her mom hadn't died, they could have gone shopping together. Except there'd never been enough money to spend on walking around the mall. And anyway, dinky old Bonaparte didn't even have a mall. The closest town that did was twenty-five miles away. What a bummer.

"I'll make a note of it."

Chris smiled. She had a real nice smile. She didn't look nearly so old when she smiled. But she had almost grown-up kids; she must be nearly as old as her grandpa. Of course, the girls she'd met in Bonaparte, the ones on her softball team, said her grandpa didn't look like any of their grandfathers. He looked like Indiana Jones, one of the girls who had a bunch of older brothers and sisters had said. Tiffany hadn't been sure who Indiana Jones was until she'd seen a poster of him at the video store. He did look like her grandpa, except she'd never seen her grandfather in a hat, or carrying a big whip. "Is there anything else you want to tell me about yourself?"

Tiffany thought a moment. "I'm eight and a half. I'll be in the third grade when school starts and I have a little brother and sister. Maybe if this works out I'll fill out an application for them when they're old enough." She sat back in the chair and folded her hands in her lap. "Can my grandpa come in now, please?"

Chris smiled over her desk at the dark-haired, dark-eyed little girl. How grown-up her expression was. How pleased she appeared with herself for something in what she'd just said. For the first time Chris found herself truly enthusiastic about taking the child for her own Little Sister.

"I think so," she said, buzzing her secretary/office manager/all-round dogsbody, Lena Foster, to show Mr. Connor into the office. "He must have some questions of his own."

"We're going to stay in Bonaparte a long time," Tiffany volunteered, swinging skinny legs, showing Chris that she was relaxing once more. "My grandpa's going to fix the plant so that it makes the most and the best tomato soup in the world."

"My husband used to work for Castleton Soups, too," Chris heard herself say.

"Used to?"

The child was quick.

"He died five years ago," Chris explained.

"My mother died, too." Sadness darkened her eyes to ebony.

"I know. I'm sorry. It's very hard to lose someone you love." Impossibly hard, surely, for a child to lose her mother at such an early age.

"I miss her. And my dad. He had to go away for a while because he was so sad."

Tiffany sounded as if she were parroting words spoken in the past to comfort her, Chris thought.

"We're going to stay with my grandpa until he comes to get us. My grandpa," she said with a great deal of satisfaction, just as the door from the outer office began to open, "is great. He looks just like Indiana Jones."

Chris smiled indulgently as she made a few quick notes on her file sheets. How sweet and how imaginative. Tiffany must really love her grandfather to think the probably balding, potbellied executive looked like Chris's own favorite larger-than-life hero. The door opened all the way. Chris stood up to greet Tiffany's grandfather.

"Good afternoon," he said in a pleasant tenor voice. "I'm Tiffany's grandfather, Ethan Connor." He held out his hand.

"Good Lord, you are Indiana Jones!"

CHAPTER TWO

FOR ONE APPALLING MOMENT Chris was afraid she'd spoken the ridiculous statement aloud. She'd been known to speak without thinking in the past and the consequences had usually been embarrassing, to say the least. Thank goodness, this time she seemed to have been able to keep her mouth shut.

Ethan Connor was staring at her with a quizzical smile on his face. She swallowed to clear her throat and held out her hand. "It's very nice to meet you, Mr. Connor. I'm Christine Baldwin, the executive director of Hobart County Big Brothers/Big Sisters. Won't you be seated?" His grip was strong and warm and he held her hand neither too long a time, nor too short.

"Thank you, Mrs. Baldwin," he said, taking his cue from the name plaque on her desk.

Although Chris no longer wore her wedding ring, she still preferred the old-fashioned title to the ambiguous *Ms.*, an ugly, truncated word that always seemed to be appropriate nowhere except perhaps in old B-Westerns.

"I'm sorry I'm late. It's the beginning of tomato pack and the plant is gearing up."

"No need to apologize. Everyone in Bonaparte is aware when the tomato harvest begins."

Almost all the tomatoes used in Castleton's famous tomato soup were grown within a forty-mile radius of Bonaparte. The plant also made juice and sauce. From July until the first killing frosts, production would be going at full capacity.

Chris wouldn't have been surprised if Ethan Connor had canceled their meeting altogether, but he had not. "Tiffany and I have been having a nice chat."

"I'm glad to hear that." He smiled at his grand-daughter in the chair beside him.

He did look a great deal like Indiana Jones, or more precisely, Indy's real-life counterpart, Harrison Ford. At least at first glance.

Ethan Connor was just about six feet tall, she guessed, with dark blond hair, no gray to be seen, hazel eyes and a sexy, crooked smile. His nose was... commanding... Chris thought, being charitable with her choice of adjectives, but it was balanced nicely by a forceful chin. He was a very good-looking man. For just a heartbeat she let herself imagine what he'd look like in a Stetson and a well-worn leather jacket, trusty bullwhip coiled over his shoulder, before she pushed her fanciful musing aside and got down to business.

"I think it will be good for Tiffany to spend some time with a female friend." Ethan leaned back in the chair, one arm over the back as he ruffled Tiffany's short, straight dark hair. "She spends too much time worrying about me and her younger brother and sister."

There was an underlying note of concern in his voice that Chris wondered if he knew had slipped past his guard.

"Someone has to take care of you, Grandpa," Tiffany replied, as if it were the most natural thing in the world for an eight-year-old to say.

Chris blinked. *Grandpa.* Ethan Connor didn't look like anyone's grandfather as far as she was concerned. He was too young, and face it, too sexy to fit the part. He turned amused, intelligent hazel eyes in her direction. Somehow, without his saying so, Chris realized the affectionate title had made him uncomfortable, too. The thought surprised her. Chris didn't consider herself even vaguely intuitive about anyone or anything...especially men as attractive as Ethan Connor.

"We'll do our best to find Tiffany a match," she said, falling back on familiar routine. She launched into her first-visit speech. "The process of matching our kids and their Big Brothers and Sisters is a painstaking one." She stopped for breath.

"How soon can you find Tiffany a Big Sister?" he demanded before Chris could form another sentence.

She opened her mouth, then closed it abruptly. "Tiffany," she said, after taking a moment to think things through, "how would you like a soda or fruit juice?"

"Okay." Tiffany gave Chris a sidelong glance. "It is hot in here. The air conditioner is busted," she added in an aside to her grandfather.

"Mrs. Foster will take you down to the snack area." Chris buzzed her secretary, and when she appeared in the doorway, she took several coins out of her desk drawer and gave them to her. "Will you take Tiffany down and get her a soda, please?"

"Sure," the older woman replied. "Let's go, honey."

Tiffany started out of the room, stopped and looked back over her shoulder. "I suppose you want to talk about me behind my back," she said flippantly, but there was a hint of wariness in her dark eyes.

"Of course we do," her grandfather said with a grin. "Now scat. And no pop, hear? Get apple juice. It's better for you."

Tiffany made a face. "Okay. I'm out of here." Relieved by her grandfather's ordinary tone and attitude, she scampered off.

"What did you want to talk to me about, Mrs. Baldwin?" he asked, cutting straight to the heart of the matter. "I've already given my permission for Tiffany to join the program. I understand you probably feel there are other children financially more in need of your service—"

Chris cut him short. "We make no distinctions like that. Each child is special, with special needs. We do our best to match each and every one with an adult volunteer they can relate to and become friends with."

"Of course." Ethan settled back in the chair. "I'm sorry. I'm an impatient man. I tend to ride roughshod over anyone who'll let me."

"Please don't apologize." Chris held up her hand. "I don't allow anyone to run roughshod over me where these kids are concerned."

"I get your point."

He smiled apologetically and this smile was every bit as sexy as the first one. "Sorry," she apologized in turn. "You landed smack on one of my buttons. I don't usually get this intense."

"I wouldn't want it any other way where my grandchild's welfare is at stake."

His remark embarrassed Chris. She didn't often let people see how really involved with her work she was. It was a way of distancing herself from the program, from the needs of the children, which she couldn't always fill to her complete satisfaction. She brushed at a fly skimming through the air between them. It landed on the window screen and immediately began to search for an escape route to the outside air. "You see, matching Tiffany has taken me outside my usual guidelines."

"I don't understand, Mrs. Baldwin."

"Please," she said, smiling a little, "call me Chris. 'Mrs. Baldwin' is too formal for such a hot afternoon."

"Chris it is. Do you mind explaining that last statement? I can assure you Tiffany does need a Big Sister. I'm too busy running the plant and too new at relearning a parenting role to give her all the time and attention she needs." A frown darkened his face and regret shadowed his eyes. He nodded toward the paperwork on her desk. "She lost her mother only ten months ago. Her father...my son...abandoned her and her younger brother and sister."

His jaw hardened, the regret in his eyes was replaced by anger as cold and unyielding as lake ice in December. Chris shivered in spite of the heat of the June afternoon.

"They spent two days in a children's shelter in Atlanta before I could get to them and bring them home with me. She is deserving of a Big Sister's time and friendship, Chris." His voice softened almost imperceptibly on her name. "She needs someone who can help her be a little girl again."

The statement went straight to Chris's heart and lodged there. She could do that for Tiffany. And Tiffany would help her remember what it was like to be young again. She could do it if she kept her wits about her, stayed objective. She could enjoy the pleasure of the child's company, give her the benefit of her experience and friendship, without going beyond the guidelines of the program. "Yes, we can do that for Tiffany," she said at last. "Mr. Connor?"

"Ethan, please," he interrupted with another smile.

"Ethan," Chris nodded, but didn't smile back. "What I'm doing now is out of the ordinary. I'm going to submit my own name to the board of directors for consideration as Tiffany's Big Sister. Do you have any objections?" He was watching her closely, a faint frown arching his brows.

"I have no objections," he said in a carefully neutral tone. "I take it this isn't standard procedure?"

"No." Chris stood and walked toward the window. Her office was on the third floor of the courthouse, her view toward the river and the lovely old houses lining the far side. Ethan Connor, she knew, lived in one of those houses. She envied him that luxury, although she was perfectly happy with her own three-bedroom brick ranch near the park.

"May I ask why you've chosen Tiffany, when I assume there are other girls on the waiting list?"

"There are six. And eleven boys. There are always more boys in need of Big Brothers than girls waiting for Big Sisters. But the other girls are teenagers, or at least several years older than Tiffany," Chris explained. "I have two children that age of my own. I'd like to spend some time with a younger child. I coordinate all the group activities, all the fund-raisers."

She smiled a little, looking back over her shoulder. "Sometimes I feel left out. And I have a lot to offer a child. I've just been sitting on the fence. Meeting Tiffany has given me the push I needed."

"How long will the match last?" he asked.

"A year," Chris said, folding her arms beneath her breasts as she leaned back against the windowsill. "At the end of that time we'll all meet and decide whether to continue the pairing. Some relationships just don't work out. Others grow into friendships that last well into adulthood. Naturally, we'll evaluate the relationship at regular intervals throughout the year. Usually the volunteers, the kids and the parents meet with me, separately and together. In this case, we'll meet with the case supervisor from the Family Services program, who will function in my place."

"I understand." Ethan turned his head, listening as Chris was to the sound of Tiffany's piping laughter floating up the open marble staircase, listed in the State Historical Registry as one of the most interesting features of the century-old building. "I hope you do become Tiffany's Big Sister."

"If everything goes well," Chris said, returning to her desk. "I can assure you we won't be taking any shortcuts with the acceptance process. Please don't say anything about my becoming Tiffany's Big Sister until everything is settled. I don't want her to feel pressured about the match in any way."

"That goes without saying." Tiffany appeared in the doorway. "What do you think are the Panthers' chances of winning the league championship this fall?" Ethan asked as he rose to leave.

"I think they're good," Chris said proudly. "My son is the quarterback."

Tiffany came into the room and leaned against her grandfather's leg. "I like football," she said. "Will you add that to my...application?"

"I'll do that right now. Is there anything else you'd like to know about Big Sisters, Tiffany?" Chris asked as she added the information to Tiffany's file. She smiled to herself. If she did become Tiffany's Big Sister, they could go to the Panther games together. That would be nice.

Tiffany thought a moment. "No."

"Then I believe that covers everything for now. We'll be in touch." She held out her hand to Ethan Connor. His handclasp was strong and firm and left Chris's palm tingling. She folded her hands in front of her, surprised at the rush of pleasure she experienced at his touch. "I'll see you soon, Tiffany."

"Okay." Tiffany tugged at her grandfather's leg to hurry him along. "Goodbye," she said.

"Goodbye, Chris." Ethan smiled and left the room.

Chris watched him go, curled her fingers into her still-tingling palm and smiled, too.

"I LIKE HER," Tiffany said as Ethan turned the car onto Front Street and headed across the river bridge toward home.

"So do I." Christine Baldwin was easy to like, her ready smile, her soft dark eyes, her hair that wasn't quite brown or blond, but some shade between the two that reminded him of the colors of autumn leaves.

"Her son is the quarterback of the Panthers. He plays softball and baseball and basketball, too," Tiffany said with just a hint of awe in her voice. "Lisa Wilhelm told me so. Her mother is friends with Chris. Did you know a lot of people in this town are related to one another? Every time I go to the store with Mrs. Baden, she sees someone who's related to her." She shook her head. "She has thirty-five first cousins. She told me so."

"I think that's one of the nice things about living here, don't you?" Ethan probed. "That everyone knows one another and takes care of one another." Tiffany had said very little about her feelings toward their new home in the six weeks they'd been in Bonaparte. She'd declined to play on the girls' soccer league after attending just one practice. "They play like sissies," she'd told him in disgust. But she seemed to enjoy the softball team she'd opted to join instead.

"Do I have cousins?"

"On your mother's side of the family, yes. Your uncle and his children live in Florida." Ethan had the address and phone number of Katherine Fielding Connor's brother in his desk. They had never corresponded.

"Maybe Daddy will take us to visit when he comes to get us."

Ethan couldn't decide if Tiffany's tone was wistful or resigned. She'd stopped asking when her father might return during the past week or so. Ethan wasn't sure if that was a good sign or a bad one. More and more often over the past month, when he'd had time to think about it at all, he'd found himself working out plans for keeping the children with him. What kind of a father was he himself, Ethan wondered, to be thinking of taking Jeff's children away from him? Not a very good one, he decided in disgust, or his son would never have abandoned such great kids in the first place.

"I don't want to go to Florida," Tiffany said as they pulled into the pine-shaded driveway of his house. "It's too far away."

The simple statement tugged at Ethan's heart. It summed up everything that was wrong in Tiffany's young life. He watched his granddaughter climb out of the car and take the front steps two at a time. Everything she needed, everything she deserved, was too far away: a home of her own, parents who loved her and could be with her, security and stability.

A Big Sister could provide her with at least one of those missing pieces, a stable relationship with a caring female role model. Christine Baldwin. A fleeting image of her calm, smiling face flashed before his eyes. She would be good for Tiffany. He believed her when she said she would be scrutinized as thoroughly as any other volunteer. Still, he hadn't gotten as far as he had in life relying on other people's opinions. He'd do a little checking of his own. It shouldn't be hard. Walt Leonard, the plant comptroller, was a likable and talkative guy. He also knew just about everything there was to know about everybody in Bonaparte. Ethan couldn't be too careful where Tiffany's welfare was concerned.

His palm tingled on the steering wheel. He remembered the touch of Christine's soft, cool skin against his fingers. Her hands were small, with slim wrists and delicate bones. He had a feeling she would be good for him, too.

Mrs. Christine Baldwin. The name on the plaque on her desk registered clearly in his memory. It was too bad she was a married woman. But, then, the best ones always were.

TIFFANY DIDN'T WISH on stars. And tonight she couldn't even see them. The moon was right outside her window, or at least it seemed that way, so bright and big it lit up the whole sky. Wishing on stars didn't work. She'd tried it before, a lot of times, such as when her mom was sick and dying. She'd prayed to Jesus and Mary and Joseph and all the saints and martyrs, too, but that hadn't helped, either.

She lay very still, just the sheet on top of her. It was hot in the big upstairs bedroom she shared with Ashley and Brandon, her little brother and sister. It was a big house. Grandpa had said the little kids could have a different bedroom so she could have a room of her own, but she didn't want one. She liked hearing them breathe in the night, knowing they were safe and close by.

They were both asleep now. Brandon was sucking his thumb and Ashley was snoring. Downstairs, the TV was still on. She could hear it through the open windows. Grandpa was watching the eleven o'clock news. She felt very grown-up to still be awake so late at night. She snuggled into her pillow. Everyone was safe. It made her feel good. Maybe someday she'd like a room of her own with a TV set and a telephone, but not yet. She needed to be able to take care of the little kids.

They'd been alone after her mom died and her dad went away. The people at the shelter were nice, but they wouldn't let her stay with Ashley and Brandon. It had been the scariest time of her life. She didn't like to remember it. Grown-ups. You just couldn't trust them to be there when you needed them.

Except her grandpa. He was great. Even if he'd told her in the morning that he might have to work late, he

always called again at dinnertime just to talk, even if
he was out in the plant and it was so noisy they had to
shout to hear each other. She wouldn't mind her dad
being gone so much if he'd just do that once in a
while, call and say hello and talk to her and the kids
for a while. He never did, though.

That's why she never wished on stars.

Except there was one right outside her window now,
just below the moon, that was moving up into the
branches of the tree that grew next to the house. She
closed her eyes, trying not to look at it, but she
couldn't resist. Finally she made her wish. If she was
going to get a Big Sister, she wanted her to be Chris
Baldwin. She liked her. She would be nice to talk to,
fun to do things with. She liked sports. She knew
about baseball and football.

And Tiffany wouldn't be sorry at all to meet her
son. Lisa Wilhelm was always bragging about how
cute he was and what a good baseball player he was.
Lisa only said that to show off. She didn't know anything about baseball. Lisa just liked older boys. Tiffany wasn't going to be nine for a while and she didn't
like boys at all. Besides, seniors in high school didn't
pay attention to third-grade girls. But Keith Baldwin
was cute. She smiled a little to herself as she drifted off
to sleep. If she was Chris Baldwin's Little Sister, he
could show her how to throw an inside curve.

CHAPTER THREE

MAYBE IT DID PAY to wish on stars.

Once in a while, at least.

Tiffany jiggled her toe and watched the patterns the soles of her new running shoes made in the mud on the floor of the courthouse elevator. They were interesting. She'd rather be climbing the steps, holding on to the fancy, curly metal railing, but Mrs. Baden said the marble steps were too hard on her calves. The soles of Mrs. Baden's shoes had great big ridges, hers had diamond shapes and those of the man standing beside Mrs. Baden were smooth, so that just the outlines of his shoes showed in the mud.

She was sorry it had to rain the first day she was going to do something with her Big Sister, but she hadn't wanted to press her luck by wishing for the sun to come out when her grandpa told her the weatherman had said it was going to rain for two more days. And she was prepared. Her brand-new purple raincoat rustled and crackled every time she moved.

And luckily the Panthers would still play football in the rain.

The elevator stopped and the doors opened onto the third floor. Tiffany knew the way to Chris's office by now. She'd been there three times already. So had her grandpa. There were an awful lot of questions to answer before you could get a Big Sister, but she'd done her best. She'd just about jumped off her chair when Chris had asked if she could be her Big Sister. She was even more surprised when she found out that Chris had to be tested and okayed by people before that could happen. A grown-up, the lady who was the boss of everybody, had to get permission to be her Big Sister. Wow!

Chris had asked her what she wanted to do on their first visit together. So she'd hinted she wanted to see Chris's house and maybe meet her family. Chris had said fine, and would she like to go to the Panthers' first home football game of the season?

Would she!

That's when she knew for sure wishing on stars really worked. She was going to have dinner with Chris and her daughter—and meet Keith Baldwin, the cutest boy in the world according to Lisa Wilhelm, even if he was way too old for Lisa to think about as a boyfriend, and Tiffany had told her so. He was also the very best athlete at Bonaparte High School, and for Tiffany that was the most important thing of all.

THERE WAS A KNOCK on Chris's door. Lena didn't work on Fridays. Chris was alone. She called for the visitor to come in, but she knew who it was before the door opened. "Hi, Tiffany. Hello, Mrs. Baden," she said, smiling politely at the short, heavyset woman accompanying Tiffany. Her Little Sister. Chris tried not to look as nervous as she felt. After all, she'd written the agency handbook on first meetings. She knew everything you should and shouldn't do with your new Little.

"Hi, Chris. Am I late?"

The little girl sounded anxious. Chris wanted to make her feel at ease. "You're right on time. And I'm just about finished here." She closed and locked the file cabinet beside her desk, then stood. "Thanks for bringing Tiffany up here, Mrs. Baden. I have one or two errands to run on the way home. Tiffany can help me."

"Shopping?" Tiffany said hopefully, dropping into her usual chair in front of Chris's desk.

"Just the dry cleaners—and the ice-cream shop," Chris added hastily when she saw Tiffany turn up her nose. "We'll drive into Toledo to the mall someday when it's too cold and nasty to do anything else."

"It's raining today," Tiffany pointed out.

She looked ready to defend her point with great determination. For a fleeting second Chris wondered how Ethan Connor was coping with Tiffany and her younger brother and sister with only day help from Mrs. Baden. He had to be under a lot of pressure at the plant. It couldn't be easy with his responsibilities, to be burdened with the care of three small children. Yet Ethan Connor, it seemed, was doing an excellent job of parenting...for a man his age.

Chris considered the phrase. He certainly didn't look the way *a man his age* ought to look or act, at least not to Chris's way of thinking. And she'd been thinking about him much too often over the past few weeks.

She pushed and pulled her unruly thoughts back into order and countered Tiffany's observation on the weather without missing a beat. "We'll miss the football game if we go shopping." She could not let an eight-year-old get the upper hand any more than she could give in to her inappropriate fantasies about her grandfather.

"Yeah. I forgot." Tiffany perked up immediately. "Are you ready to go?"

"All set." The opening game of the Panthers' season had been a lifesaver for Chris. She hadn't wanted their first meeting to be too intense, too personal and intimate for Tiffany's sake, as well as her own. She had to admit for a minute or two she'd contemplated breaking her own cardinal rule by taking her to McDonald's. Chris didn't encourage eating out or going to the movies as regular activities. In many of the children, it raised expectations that their Big Brothers and Big Sisters couldn't continue to fulfill. She always suggested spending time together in ways that didn't involve a lot of expense or special treats. Everyday companionship and sharing of values were the goals she stressed. When she did take Tiffany shopping at the mall, she wouldn't buy her a present. Definitely not.

"Mr. Connor will be waiting at the gates to pick Tiffany up at the end of the game."

Wilma Baden bobbed her head as she talked, just as she always had. Chris had known the woman since she was in high school and was best friends with her daughter. Jenny Baden had married one of the Wilhelm boys from out on the Ridge Road and they had five kids. The youngest, Lisa, was just about Tiffany's age.

"That isn't necessary, Wilma. I can take Tiffany home after the game. Mr. Connor doesn't need to come all the way out to the school for her." She didn't know which would be more unnerving, walking Tiffany to her front door and encountering the man there, in his own home, or meeting him among a crowd of her friends and acquaintances.

"He wants to do it." Wilma Baden smiled, her eyes disappearing in folds of fat. "I think he wants to check out the Panthers for himself."

"My grandpa played football in college," Tiffany informed them proudly. She squirmed inside her bright purple raincoat. "It's getting hot in here. Can we go?"

"Right now." Chris slipped into her raincoat and grabbed her umbrella from the stand behind the door. "You go call the elevator and I'll lock the office. We'll all ride down together."

Tiffany looked mutinous. Chris already knew how much she liked to clatter up and down the broad, shallow flights of marble stairs.

"Can I push the buttons?"

"Yes."

"Okay."

One small hurdle crossed. Chris felt just a little less nervous. Children's problems were more straightforward than teenagers'. That was all she had to remember. For Tiffany, right was still right and wrong was wrong. Later she would begin to question her grandfather's values, Chris's values, test her limits, but not yet. And by the time that happened, Chris hoped to have established a relationship with Tiffany that would see them through the rough times.

"What kind of ice cream are we going to buy?" Tiffany asked in a very leading tone of voice.

The two adults smiled over her head.

"I'm not sure."

The elevator doors creaked open. They stepped inside.

"My grandpa likes black cherry, but I don't."

Ethan Connor liked black cherry ice cream. A small thing to know about him, but very personal some-how, like remembering the color of his eyes, smoky hazel, flecked with gold. And the touch of his hand, warm and strong against her skin.

"What's your favorite ice cream, Chris?"

"Butter pecan. But I usually buy double Dutch chocolate chip for Keith."

The doors creaked shut as slowly as they had opened.

"What do you know!" Tiffany grinned up at Chris as she punched the lobby button with a flourish. "That's my favorite, too."

SHE DIDN'T quite believe it. There he was, Keith Baldwin, sitting across the kitchen table from her, wearing his black Panthers jersey with the red number seventeen on the front. She would give everything she had, her entire life savings, all twenty-seven dollars of it, for a football jersey like that.

"More lasagna, Keith?" Chris asked.

Keith shook his head. "It was great, Mom. I'll have some ice cream, though, and then I have to get going."

"How about you, Tiffany?" Chris held up the pan of lasagna.

It was good, but Tiffany couldn't eat another bite. "No, thank you," she said, remembering her manners. "But I'd like some ice cream, too."

"I'll get it." Chris stood and went to the refrigerator.

"Double Dutch chocolate chip is my favorite kind of ice cream," Tiffany divulged after taking a deep breath. She hadn't been able to think of a single thing to say to Keith yet, and she'd been at Chris's house for almost an hour.

"No kidding?" He looked up from his plate and smiled a little. "It's mine, too."

"I know." Tiffany squirmed with pleasure. "Your mom told me so."

"It has been since I was a little kid like you."

"I'm not a little kid." Tiffany was crushed. "I'm eight and a half. I started the third grade on Tuesday." She bit her lower lip. What a bummer. He was just as bad as boys her own age. They all said stupid things like that just to make you feel bad.

"I'm going to be eighteen in February. To me you're just a little kid." He made it a statement of fact, not an insult, and grinned at her again.

Tiffany was mollified a little. "Yeah, I guess you're right."

Chris set a huge bowl of ice cream in front of him. Tiffany stared, even though it wasn't polite. She didn't think anyone could eat that much ice cream at one time. Especially after two helpings of lasagna, salad and breadsticks. Keith started spooning ice cream into his mouth. It just disappeared out of the bowl. Tiffany blinked, then smiled crookedly, as Chris set a smaller bowl of ice cream in front of her. She took a bite. It was good. Double Dutch chocolate chip wasn't really her favorite flavor. She'd never had it before. But she liked it.

"Tiffany's going with me to the game." Chris sat down across the table from Tiffany. "It's our first outing together."

"Then it's all settled?" Keith asked around a mouthful of ice cream. "She's officially your Little Sister?"

Chris nodded and smiled at Tiffany. "Yes, she is."

"I think," Tiffany said with great calculation, stirring her ice cream into mush, "it means I'm *your* little sister, too." She looked over at Keith's astonished face and grinned.

ETHAN CONNOR STOOD in the shadow of the tall brick pillars that marked the gateway to Veterans' Memorial Field, the home of the Bonaparte Panthers, and waited for his granddaughter to file by. He'd spotted where she was sitting in the bleachers with Christine Baldwin early in the fourth quarter of the game. The Panthers had won their match over a bigger, heavier team from one of the Toledo schools sixteen to ten, and the crowd was in a festive mood. Their spirit was infectious. Ethan smiled to himself as he caught sight of Tiffany's purple raincoat bouncing down the steps of the wooden bleachers. It had stopped raining soon after he'd arrived at the game, but she was still wearing the coat, and looked as if she had no intention of taking it off, even though the early September evening was warm and muggy.

Tiffany walked toward him, holding hands with Christine. Ethan smiled again, but it was a different smile, for a different reason than seeing his granddaughter carefree, basking in the glow of Chris's undivided attention. This smile was for Chris herself. Mrs. Christine Baldwin, wife of the *late* Jackson Baldwin, not a married woman, a widow, and completely uninvolved with any man, if what Walt Leonard had told him was true. She was free and Ethan was interested. That in itself was unusual enough. There hadn't been a lot of women in his life since his divorce, but a few. None of those relationships had meant enough to him to pursue them when they had begun to fade. He'd figured he'd never find a woman he cared enough about again to make an effort to catch her interest. Christine Baldwin was making him rethink that philosophy.

"Grandpa!"

Tiffany had spotted him in the knot of people standing near the gate.

"Grandpa, we won! And Keith threw a touchdown pass. It was great!"

"I know, pumpkin. I got here in time to see it."

"Why didn't you come sit with us?" Tiffany caught his hand and looked up into his face. Her lower lip trembled, her expression threatening to become a pout.

"Because it was easier to spot Keith on the field than it was to spot you in the stands."

"I had the only purple raincoat in the crowd," Tiffany countered, clearly unimpressed with his explanation. "I shouldn't have been that hard to see."

"My poor old tired eyes just couldn't pick you out of the crowd." Ethan laughed and ruffled her short black hair. "Besides, you were spending time with your Big Sister, remember? Hello, Chris," he said, and felt her quick smile touch him with warmth.

"Hello, Ethan." She'd hesitated for just a heartbeat before saying his name. "It was a good game, wasn't it?"

"Your boy's got quite an arm."

"Thank you." Her smile grew wider. She loved her son and she was proud of him. She made no effort to hide the love or the pride.

Ethan felt a familiar, stabbing regret. When Jeff had been the age of Chris Baldwin's son, he'd been willful and rebellious, responding the only way he knew how to the escalating tensions between his parents.

"Would you like a bite of something to eat before I take Tiffany home?" he asked, trying another tack. The crowd continued to flow past them, but Ethan wasn't blind to the sideways looks they were getting. Bonaparte was a small town. He was the new plant manager, and an eligible male, even if he did come burdened with three small grandchildren. If he spent too much time standing here, talking with Chris, people would notice. He kind of liked the idea of their being considered an item, a couple. He could see Chris did not.

She hesitated, looked down at Tiffany, then brought her deep brown eyes back up to meet his. They were filled with resolve.

"No, thank you. I think I should be getting home. And Tiffany, too. She's tired."

"I am not. I'm hungry, though."

Ethan decided not to press his luck. He'd read the literature, listened to the lectures Chris and the screening committee had given him. She was to be Tiffany's friend. Their time together was for them alone.

"Chris is tired. She's had a long day, working, fixing dinner for you and Keith. We'll get a snack at home, okay?"

Tiffany wilted, hung on his hand. She was a very tired little girl.

"Some other time, Tiffany," Chris said gently. She twirled her umbrella by its handle, looking down, watching the tip work its way into the muddy grass.

Tiffany wouldn't meet her eyes, only nodded. Chris looked at Ethan, smiled, sharing the knowledge, the fleeting instant of guilt parents everywhere suffer when their children punish them for small transgressions.

"I'll call you early next week and we'll plan our next visit together."

Tiffany looked up, surveying Chris from the corner of her eye. "When?"

Ethan tensed just a little. Had he conveyed to Chris the urgency of Tiffany's need to be reassured, to pin down every detail, so that no unpleasant surprises caught her unaware, left her alone, afraid? He needn't have worried.

"How about Monday evening? About seven? Will you be done with your homework by then?"

"Yes." Tiffany straightened; her grip on Ethan's hand eased. "I'll be waiting."

"Good. And if I should forget, you call me. My number is in the book."

Ethan liked Chris even more for giving Tiffany that extra added assurance that she wouldn't disappoint her.

"I'll look it up myself."

Chris smoothed her hand over Tiffany's silky, straight black hair. "Goodbye, Tiffany. Goodbye, Ethan."

She didn't hold out her hand. Ethan knew she didn't want to draw more attention to herself, even with such a mundane gesture. Ethan was not so constrained.

"Good night, Chris." She hesitated a heartbeat, two, three, then rested her hand in his. He tightened his grip for the barest fraction of a second, then released her. "Sleep well." He turned on his heel and led Tiffany into the shadows of the parking lot. He didn't look back to see if Chris followed or if her car was parked in the opposite direction along River Road.

He wondered what had made him think she was a restful, peaceful woman when he'd first met her? Her merest touch warmed his skin, heated his thoughts. She was a very desirable woman, intelligent, independent, yet soft and loving. A potent combination, a dangerous one, for a middle-aged man with more responsibilities and concerns than he cared to think about. Chris was there for Tiffany's sake, not his. He should remember that. And perhaps she wasn't interested in any kind of romance. Maybe she didn't want to consider a relationship with a man burdened with three small children.

He'd certainly never expected to be raising three kids at his age, but he was. He looked down at Tiffany's head bobbing along beside him. Her steps had slowed. He swung her up in his arms. "Tired, pumpkin?" he asked as she nuzzled her head in his shoulder.

She only nodded. "It was a great game."

"Yes." His car was parked in a row by itself. Silence grew and lengthened around them. In the distance, lights glinted off the slow-moving river. It was warm and still, but there was a smell of fall in the wet night air.

"I'm glad Chris is my Big Sister," Tiffany said at last, sleepily. "I like her a lot."

"So do I." Ethan took a deep breath and let it out slowly through his teeth. "So do I."

It was funny how quickly fate could sneak up and change things on you. The last thing he'd planned on in this middle-aged reshaping of his life was the possibility of falling in love again...ever.... Yet tonight it didn't seem like such an impossible thing to have happen. Because now he'd met and gotten to know Chris Baldwin. During their conversations regarding Tiffany's entrance into the Big Sisters program he'd come to realize just what an intelligent caring woman she was. She was everything he'd dreamed of in a woman and had never found, not in his wife, not in his love affairs after the divorce.

She was a woman worth waiting for, worth winning, worth fighting for if necessary. She might one day learn to love him, become his lover, his partner, his wife. If he could offer her himself alone. One to one. That was the kind of relationship a woman her age would expect.

That's why it could never be. He wasn't free and unencumbered. In all his discreet inquiries into Chris Baldwin's life, he hadn't been able to come up with an answer for the most important question of all.

Did she want to be a mother again?

CHAPTER FOUR

"GRANDPA'S LOCKED the door again to keep Brandon from getting loose," Tiffany explained with a sigh as she rattled the doorknob of the big old house on River Street. "Baby brothers are such a pain."

"Sisters have been complaining about them for thousands of years."

"Probably since back before the Flood," Tiffany agreed with perfect seriousness. She'd informed Chris they were learning about the Creation and Noah and the Flood in Sunday school after mass.

"I'm sure of it," Chris agreed, hiding a smile. She'd forgotten how entertaining an eight-year-old's conversation could be.

"Of course," Tiffany said with an air of long-suffering, "little sisters are just about as bad."

The porch light came on and Chris blinked in the sudden brightness. Ethan Connor's figure appeared behind the lace curtain that covered the oval of beveled glass set in the walnut door. Chris had always wanted just such a front door, opening onto a wide porch, with wicker rocking chairs and geraniums in pots by the creaky wooden steps. She loved the big old wood-and-brick houses, their backs to the river, their front yards shaded by rows of stately oaks and maples that lined this street. She and Jack had always dreamed of owning one of them someday, but that dream, like so many others they had shared, had died with her husband.

"Hello, Tiffany." Ethan smiled down at his granddaughter. "How did you do bowling?"

"I got a seventy-nine," Tiffany announced proudly. "And I had two strikes."

"That's great. And how did you do, Chris?" he asked, lifting his head to smile at her.

It wasn't quite the same smile he'd given Tiffany. That one hadn't made Chris's breath catch in her throat. This one did. "Not too badly," she managed to say without stumbling over the words.

"Chris bowled a one-sixty-eight," Tiffany said with great satisfaction. "We got third place. It's a certificate for a pepperoni pizza at Elroy's. We're going to use it next week."

"Congratulations."

"Thanks," Chris said, and smiled, too. "It's the best game I've had in ages."

"I'm going to learn to keep score," Tiffany announced, then turned away from her grandfather and tugged lightly on the sleeve of Chris's sweater to get her attention. "Won't you come and sit a spell?"

Ethan laughed, looking perplexed. "'Come in and sit a spell.' Where did you hear that?"

"From Mrs. Baden. She says that to her friends when they come by. It means come on in and talk awhile . . . and have a snack." Tiffany got to the heart of the matter. "We didn't stop for anything on the way home because Chris thought it would be past my bedtime."

"It is past your bedtime," Ethan reminded her.

Chris thought that must be her cue. "Then I'd better be on my way."

"No. Don't go."

"Please, come on in." Ethan's request followed Tiffany's outburst by only a second or two. "Mrs. Baden made chocolate chip cookies today. And I have a pot of coffee that's not too old or too strong. And it's decaf, if that makes a difference."

"All right," Chris heard herself say. "But only for a few minutes. Tomorrow is a school day."

"Don't remind me," Tiffany said darkly as she stepped inside. She wrinkled her nose. "Grandpa, you're making chili again."

"Tomorrow's Mrs. Baden's day off, remember? I thought it would be good for dinner since we have to fix it ourselves."

"It's okay if you don't put too many onions and those yucky green peppers in it." Tiffany danced ahead of them, across the marble-floored foyer and on into the wide hallway leading to the kitchen at the back of the house.

"And to think," Ethan said in a lugubrious voice, "I used to pride myself on my five-alarm chili. Now it's so mild a baby could eat it. And come to think of it a baby does. Or at least a toddler."

A faint note of lingering surprise in his words caught Chris's attention. She wondered just what kind of sacrifices this man had made in his life to give Tiffany and her brother and sister a stable and loving home.

He bent to pluck a red-white-and-blue plastic airplane out of their path and place it on the wide overhanging edge of a stair tread where it no longer posed a threat to navigation, but would still be easy for a little boy to see when he went looking for it in the morning. A small, unthinking act, perhaps, but one that showed Chris how caring and considerate a man Ethan Connor was.

"I hope Tiffany isn't too excited to sleep," Chris said as she preceded Ethan down the hall. She could hear Tiffany banging cupboard doors and rattling glasses ahead of them. "I did worry a little about including her tonight. She's the youngest child we've matched and the others, of course, have later bedtimes."

"Don't worry," Ethan assured her. "She's something of a night owl. And always the first one up in the morning."

"I try to find things to do on Fun Nights that don't last past nine o'clock during the school year."

"It must be a challenge to come up with something new every month in a town this size."

"It is, believe me." Chris's agreement was heartfelt. "At least I know what we'll be doing next month."

"What's that?" Ethan motioned her to a seat at a big scrubbed oak table in the middle of the high-ceilinged, well-lit kitchen. The table looked like an antique, maybe even original to the house, and Chris felt another quick stinging jab of envy, which she resolutely ignored.

"Getting our booth ready for RiverFest, of course. The only problem now is that I'm not certain what we should do. Two years ago we sold buttons and posters. Last year we sponsored the dunking booth, but in October it's hard to get volunteers to sit in the tank."

"I can imagine."

"I wanted to do something different this year."

She accepted a mug of coffee from him with a smile of thanks. His hands were big and square, with a sprinkling of dark blond hair on the knuckles. His wrists and forearms were strong and solid-looking beneath the rolled-up sleeves of his white shirt. He put a plate of cookies down between her and Tiffany. The little girl grabbed two and began dunking half of one in her glass of milk. Chris looked up with a smile, expecting to find Ethan's eyes on his granddaughter. She found him looking at her instead.

"Do you mind if I keep working at the chili?" he asked, gesturing over his shoulder with a flick of his thumb. "I'm just about finished."

"No, of course not." A tiny curl of heat unfurled somewhere deep inside her. She was very much aware of Ethan Connor as a man. It surprised her; it disturbed her. She took a sip of her coffee. It was hot and burned her mouth. "I understand Castleton's is very much involved in RiverFest."

"Castleton's is involved in just about everything that goes on in Bonaparte."

"I'm finding that out, too."

He added several spoonfuls of assorted, carefully measured spices to the mixture already beginning to simmer in a slow cooker on the marble counter—also original to the house, Chris guessed. Then he stirred the chili and took a taste from the end of a wooden spoon.

Tiffany finished her cookie and rested her elbows on the table and her chin in her hand, watching her grandfather cook. "Grandpa won a prize once for his chili," she announced in a voice decidedly sleepier than it had been fifteen minutes earlier.

"Did you, really?" Chris asked, aware she was watching Ethan too closely to be considered only casually interested in what he was doing. She turned to look at Tiffany.

The little girl nodded. "When he lived in Texas, right, Grandpa?"

"At the El Paso plant's annual cook-off five years ago," Ethan confirmed. "I'll show you the plaque sometime."

"A chili cook-off." A small, bright light winked on inside Chris's brain. "We could do that here."

"What for?" Tiffany asked, her mouth once more full of chocolate chip cookie and milk.

"For RiverFest," Chris said, her mind busy turning over the possibilities. "Do you think it would work?"

"I don't know why not." Ethan looked at her with a quizzical smile deepening the lines at the corner of his mouth. "As far as I know, it doesn't require federal approval or a special license from the EPA."

Chris laughed a little self-consciously. She wrapped her hands around her coffee mug and leaned forward, her forearms braced on the rounded edges of the big oak table. "No, I mean, do you think Big Brothers/Big Sisters...the program...could successfully sponsor a cook-off at RiverFest?"

"It's not hard to set up," Ethan said. His brow furrowed into two straight lines as he stared off over Chris's head a moment or two. "It doesn't require a lot of planning. Just decide how many people you'll want on each team, set up your categories, like mild, spicy and, of course, five-alarm. The winner gets a nice plaque or trophy...."

"We could get Castleton Soups to supply the ingredients and the program gets all the proceeds from selling bowls of chili to hungry festival goers. We can get a panel of celebrity judges to award the prize,'' Chris went on, still thinking out loud.

''My grandpa is a celebrity in Bonaparte,'' Tiffany reminded Chris, then yawned loudly.

''Yes, he is,'' Chris agreed with a gleam in her eye. ''Would you do us the honor of being a judge, Mr. Connor?''

Ethan shook his head. ''I'll have to think about it.''

''Please. Do it, Grandpa. Everyone will think you're special then.''

''And that statement puts me soundly in my place, doesn't it?'' Ethan laid his spoon on a plate beside the chili pot.

''I didn't mean to put you on the spot,'' Chris said, rising to leave. Suddenly she felt young and awkward and still very much aware of Ethan as a man. It made her feel uncomfortable. It made her more uncomfortable that he might be amused at seeing her carried away by her enthusiasm for the idea of a fund-raiser while sitting at his kitchen table.

''You haven't put me on the spot, Chris,'' he said, moving to stand behind Tiffany's high-backed chair. ''I'm just trying to decide which will be more fun— judging the contest or entering myself. Why don't you help me choose?''

''Certainly,'' she answered without thinking, before she heard the undercurrents in his voice, before she felt her pulse speed up slightly. She took a deep breath to steady the sudden flutter in her heartbeat.

Ethan tilted his head, his eyes holding her gaze. ''If I promise to give you the secret ingredients of my world famous five-alarm chili, would you and my lovely granddaughter—'' he inclined his head in a negligently graceful bow as he smiled down at

Tiffany's upturned face "—agree to join me as my partners on one of the teams?"

"Sure, Grandpa," Tiffany said, stifling another yawn. "That would be great."

"I don't know." Chris realized the statement was ungracious and too bluntly spoken the moment she said it, but she was more than a little confused by his words and the warmth in his tone. "I mean, it might not be correct. I'm going to be sponsoring the event . . . I don't know . . . I haven't thought about the rules."

"Good," Ethan said, picking up Tiffany's glass and the empty cookie plate. He set them on the drain board. "I'd say that means you can make the rules up to suit yourself."

He looked at her over his shoulder and her heartbeat fluttered again.

"Am I correct?"

Chris felt as if the room had grown very warm all of a sudden. The statement was full of hidden meaning, she was sure. She could answer him as if she hadn't noticed any of the warm, sensual overtones in his words, of course. She could say good-night politely and firmly, run home to the safety of her cold, lonely bed. Or she could acknowledge what was happening between them.

"You have a point, Mr. Connor."

"Ethan," he said quietly but forcefully. "My name is Ethan. I thought we agreed on that the first day we met in your office."

"Yes, we did, Ethan," she repeated dutifully, softly. "And you are correct. If I sponsor the event I make up the rules." She lifted her chin and found with a small rush of pleasure that she'd disconcerted him slightly, as well. *I'm flirting with him,* she realized, *flirting with a man after so long. And liking it, liking it very much.* She smiled.

Ethan sucked in his breath with a slight hiss. "And what have you decided, Madam Chili Chairman?" he asked, returning her smile with a slow, sexy one of his own.

"I'm not sure. I'll let you know when I make up my mind."

"TIFFANY, IT'S nine o'clock. I think you should be getting ready for bed." Ethan stood and stretched, rubbing the back of his head, trying to ease the tension in his neck and shoulders.

"Not yet, Grandpa," Tiffany wheedled. "I want to finish this."

Ethan turned off the TV set, which Tiffany hadn't been watching anyway, and laid the report he'd been reading on the table beside his easy chair. The younger children had been in bed for more than an hour and the house was quiet. He walked over to where his granddaughter was industriously lettering a poster announcing the chili cook-off with fat, brightly colored indelible markers.

"You can finish it tomorrow after school," Ethan reminded her. "You know Chris and Keith aren't planning on putting them up in the store windows until Friday."

"If I don't get it done tonight the little kids will see it and mark all over it before I get home from school," she said, looking up at him, her expression intent and serious, too serious for a little girl. "They'll ruin it."

"I'll put it in the hall closet for you before I go up to bed. They can't get in there."

She stuck out her lower lip and blew her bangs off her forehead while she considered his suggestion. "All right," she said after due consideration. "That'll work." Then she capped her red marker and gathered up the rest to put back in the box. "Chris is counting on me to do these just right."

"You're doing a great job." It had been quite a feat to get the big squares of poster board in the car when he'd picked Tiffany up at Chris's house on his way home from the plant. It was a warm, gusty September night that promised rain before morning and the half-finished posters had behaved more like captive kites bent on escape than announcements for the upcoming fund-raiser.

"Chris says we're going to make a lot of money for the program."

"I'm glad."

"A team from the sheriff's department signed up today," Tiffany announced proudly as she followed Ethan to the big closet under the stairs and watched as he placed the posters neatly against the wall and propped them up with a box labeled Mittens and Ski Masks that hadn't been unpacked on moving day and probably wouldn't be opened until the first cold days of November.

"How many teams does that make?" Ethan asked as Tiffany watched him close the closet door.

"That makes eleven."

"Very impressive."

"Chris says it's because the radio station is entering a team and they've challenged all the merchants and restaurants to enter, too."

The radio station had been running public service spots for the last week. The sales manager had been stationed in Texas for three years when he was in the army and Chris's scheme had caught his fancy.

"And Castleton Soups has three teams. You helped get them to sign up, didn't you?" Tiffany added.

Every sacrifice Ethan had made over the past year was worth it when Tiffany looked at him like that, her love and pride for him shining innocently from her dark brown eyes. "We aim to please," he said a little gruffly, trying to hide his emotion.

"You don't think it's cheating that Mr. Leonard and the others are going to use Castleton Chili, do you?" she asked earnestly as he put his hands on her shoulders and headed her toward the stairs.

"No. It's all good fun and for a good cause." His comptroller, the chief accountant and head maintenance supervisor were planning on heating up a big iron kettle of Castleton's own brand of chili con carne as their entry in the competition.

"But Chris and Keith and I are going to win." He couldn't fault Tiffany for her competitiveness. She got it from him.

"You sound mighty sure of yourself."

"I am. Because you're going to give us the secret to your special ingredients."

"Shhh." Ethan swatted her lightly on the behind and she scooted up the next three steps with a hop, giggling behind her hand.

"You can't tell anyone I'm doing that. What if there is a tie and the official master of ceremonies—" he made a sweeping mock bow "—was called on to cast the tie-breaking vote and it leaked out to the press and public that I had a vested interest in one certain team of contestants winning the five-alarm category?"

"I'll never tell," Tiffany promised, crossing her hands over her heart with a gesture every bit as theatrical as his own. "I swear on my oath of honor. Anyway, there won't be a tie." She grinned and flounced up the stairs. "Last Wednesday when Chris and I made a batch of chili with your special spices just to practice, Keith and his friends from the football team came to eat it and they said it just about set their mouths on fire!"

"No kidding." Ethan touched his finger to his lips to remind his excited granddaughter that her small brother and sister were asleep. Tiffany lowered her voice.

"Those guys were whooping and hollering and running around Chris's kitchen like Indians, drinking soda and sucking on ice cubes and pretending to cry it was so hot." Tiffany sighed, a far-off, very feminine look in her eye. "It was great fun."

"You like spending time at Chris's house, don't you?"

"Of course. She's my Big Sister."

He supposed those words said it all for Tiffany.

Ethan leaned against the door frame of the children's bedroom as his granddaughter went into the bathroom to brush her teeth and get ready for bed. Chris had made it clear from the beginning that her interest and her responsibility lay with Tiffany alone. He'd thought they were beginning to connect on a personal level that night two weeks ago when she'd brought Tiffany home but obviously he'd been wrong.

Or had he?

Two days later she'd asked him officially to be master of ceremonies for the cook-off, a voting judge only in the event of a tie. He'd agreed reluctantly and

wondered if he'd been out of circulation so long that
he'd only imagined her response to him that night in
his kitchen. He certainly hadn't imagined his response to her. Then she had asked him for the secret
ingredients to his chili recipe as a special favor to her—
because she and Tiffany did want so dearly to win—
and he'd grinned like a teenager and, without a second thought, handed over the recipe he'd never let
another human being see.

At that moment it had occurred to him that he was
falling for Christine Baldwin in a big way. A woman
who, as a matter of principle, wouldn't have anything
to do with him as long as she was involved with his
granddaughter.

It was a challenge that at any other time he would
have accepted without a qualm. But now he wasn't so
sure he could handle the added complications of a
difficult romance. He owed Tiffany and Ashley and
Brandon as much of his time and emotional energy as
he could provide. For the first time in his life he admitted he might have bitten off more than he could
chew. The Bonaparte plant was in bad shape, but it
could be salvaged, made to run efficiently and at less
cost to Castleton than pulling up stakes and relocat-
ing somewhere else, but it would take time and work,
lots of hard work.

Ethan lifted his hand to the back of his neck and
rotated his head, trying to ease the persistent ache that
somehow had moved up along his jaw. He must be
getting old. The task that lay ahead of him plus the
added responsibility of Tiffany and the other children
were momentarily daunting. He'd failed pretty badly
at fatherhood the first time around. How could he be

ONE TO ONE 63

sure, given the complicated circumstances of his life, that he wouldn't fail just as badly again?

At least he had one ally in his quest. A fleeting image of Christine Baldwin's smiling face flashed before his mind's eye, and all his doubts and worries backed off into a small dark corner of his mind.

He didn't feel old at all when he thought of Chris. He felt like a man half his age, ready to take on all the dragons in the universe if it would impress the woman he'd chosen to love.

Love. That was a pretty strong word for his feelings at this point. For a lot of years after his divorce he'd been convinced he wasn't capable of loving a woman again. Now he wasn't so sure.

Tiffany came out of the bathroom in her pajamas and he pulled his thoughts away from Chris and learning to love again with more reluctance than he cared to admit. "All ready for bed?" he asked, falling back on age-old parental ritual.

"All set." Tiffany tiptoed into the big front bedroom she shared with her brother and sister and walked immediately to Ashley's bed and straightened her covers. Moving on around the room, she adjusted the night-light so that she could see Brandon's round, blanket-covered fanny sticking up through the bars of his crib and pulled the curtains open over the two big double-hung windows so that she could see the sky and the lights of the town across the river before she crawled into her own bed.

Ethan sat down on the side of her bed. "Good night, sweetheart," he said, patting her shoulder.

"Night, Grandpa." She smiled up at him and wiggled down into her covers like a little mole. "D'you suppose Chris will take me with her to put up the posters if I ask her to?''

''I don't see why not.''

''Friday isn't our regular night together.''

She sounded more sleepy than worried to Ethan. ''I don't think that matters,'' he reassured her.

''No, I suppose it doesn't. You won't mind if I leave you alone with the little kids?'' She frowned, trying to stay awake until she'd solved this new problem in her life.

''We'll be fine,'' he assured her. ''Go to sleep.''

''Okay.'' She rolled onto her side.

Ethan stayed where he was a moment longer. No matter how attracted he was to Chris Baldwin, he was going to have to be very careful in how he conducted himself with her. Nothing he said or did could jeopardize the fragile, growing friendship she was establishing with his granddaughter. Nothing. Not even if he'd decided he might have found the one woman in the world he could share the rest of his life with.

CHAPTER FIVE

FOR THE FIRST TIME in three years it looked as if the October weather intended to cooperate for the full three days of RiverFest. It was sunny and warm in the afternoon, pleasantly cool in the evening, the sky that particularly clear shade of blue that seems to come only at the turn of the year.

Chris pushed up the sleeves of her pale yellow cotton sweater, then lifted her hand to her eyes as she watched Ethan Connor work the crowd. He was good, at ease with the portable microphone in his hand, witty and cajoling as he encouraged passersby to sample the various categories of chili available. The judging had taken place an hour or so earlier, but the winners weren't to be announced until later that evening. Chris thought they stood a pretty good chance of winning in the five-alarm category. She'd seen Father Carmine mopping his bald head with his handkerchief after he'd finished eating their entry and that was a good sign.

Of course she couldn't discount the volunteer fire department's efforts. They were so certain their chili was the best they claimed they needed to keep a fire extinguisher on hand in case the chili burst into flame of its own accord.

Miriam Leonard and Steve Harris were taking money. Keith and a couple of his high-school friends were busing the picnic tables under the oak trees at the edge of the parking lot where their booth was set up. Three or four of the children, along with their Big Brothers and Sisters were passing out napkins, plastic spoons, chunks of buttered sourdough bread and fruit drinks to their customers. All the volunteers were working two-hour shifts during the afternoon, and so far no one had failed to show up and throw her whole schedule off. She was keeping her fingers crossed, though; they still had four hours to go.

Tiffany came up to her, carefully balancing a cup of iced tea in both hands. "I think my grandpa's getting thirsty, talking so much. He likes iced tea so I got this for him."

"How thoughtful, Tiffany." Chris took a quick look around. Everything seemed to be going smoothly at the moment; no crisis appeared imminent. "I'll walk over with you."

"We brought you something to drink, Grandpa," Tiffany announced as they approached the pickup truck whose bed served Ethan as a podium.

As always when she heard Tiffany address the man as "Grandpa" Chris felt a jolt of amused surprise deep inside. To her eyes, Ethan Connor was the last man on earth one would expect to be anyone's grandfather. His red-and-white striped cotton, long-sleeved shirt strained across his shoulders and lay flat against his stomach. His jeans were soft and well-worn, hugging still-slender hips and thighs, and he had a very nice behind.

"Thanks, honey. This is dry work." He turned off the portable microphone, laid it aside and jumped down off the back of the pickup.

As he took a long swallow of the tea, Chris watched the smooth play of muscles in his neck and throat when he lifted the cup to his mouth and drank. She'd seen him only in passing, spoken to him only briefly since that night he'd invited her into his kitchen for coffee, but he'd been in her thoughts—and lately in her dreams—a great deal.

"Would you like me to get someone to take your place behind the mike?" Chris asked, appalled she hadn't thought to ask him if he wanted a break earlier. He'd been working the crowd steadily since before noon. She glanced at her watch. It was almost three o'clock. "I'm sorry. I've taken advantage of you."

He brushed her apology aside with the wave of his hand. "Forget it. I'm having a great time."

He looked tired, though. There were new lines around his intriguing hazel eyes and a slight tenseness in his jaw she hadn't noticed before. "Maybe Walt Leonard could take over for you...."

"Don't bother. He's doing a great job peddling Castleton Chili for the good of the cause, or haven't you noticed?"

"I've noticed." Chris grinned. "I would never have guessed he'd sell so much canned chili with all these homemade recipes to sample." Walt and his team had shown up with a huge old iron kettle they'd dug up somewhere, built a fire on the gravel parking lot, hung the kettle from a tripod and immediately began ladling out bowls of chili to festival goers.

"The citizens of Bonaparte know where their loyalties lie," Ethan said, grinning.

"That's true. And let's face it. In Bonaparte a lot of people aren't quite brave enough—" she grinned, too

"—or foolish enough to sample some of the entries. I've seen the amount of chili peppers that went into several of those pots."

Ethan rested his hips against the side of the truck. "I think at the end of the day you'll find you're doing very well."

"We are doing well—the program, I mean," she added hastily.

"You are the program, I think," Ethan said very quietly. He crushed the empty cup in his hand.

"No." Chris shook her head. "I'm only the conduit. My volunteers and their kids are the program." He must have sensed her embarrassment, her reluctance to talk about what her job really meant to her at such a time.

"Let's all take a break. What do you say?"

"I want a snow cone," Tiffany said, grabbing the opportunity with both hands.

"I can't leave," Chris began.

When Ethan saw Chris was going to protest he put his arm under her elbow and began to steer her away from the booth. "Yes, you can. The crowd's thinned out. It's time for the classic boats parade. Let's get Tiffany her snow cone and go watch it." He waved at Steve and Miriam, who were conferring at the money table. "I'm taking Chris to watch the boats. We'll be back in thirty minutes or so."

"Take your time," Steve hollered back. "We'll mind the store."

Chris felt foolish protesting anymore, so she simply started walking in the direction of the riverbank, her thoughts in a whirl, her senses fully alive to the light touch of Ethan's hand on her elbow through the thin cotton weave of her sweater.

Tiffany hopped along beside them, searching the crowd for the snow-cone vendor. "Grandpa, do you know who won our contest?" she asked slyly. "Will you tell us so we don't have to wait until dark to find out if we get a prize?" She made the word *dark* sound as if it couldn't possibly come before the end of the century.

"No, I don't know who won. And I wouldn't tell you if I did."

"Grandpa." Tiffany whirled around, skipping backward so that she could address her grandfather face-to-face. "You have to know. You're the head judge, the master of ceremonies."

"Head judge is an honorary title. I only got to cast a vote if there was a tie, remember?"

His tone of voice made Chris turn her head to glance up at him. He was watching her and smiling that beguiling, sexy smile that invaded her thoughts, waking and sleeping, more often than she cared to admit.

"And there weren't any tie votes for me to break, so I don't know who won any more than the two of you do."

"Chris, you should have let Grandpa be a real judge," Tiffany said accusingly.

"Or you could have let me be on your team."

Ethan's tone was light and teasing, but it still sent chills of awareness shooting through her. "I...I thought," she began helplessly.

"You didn't think my being on the team would be any help to you at all, did you?"

That wasn't what he really meant and they both knew it. She was uncertain about spending more time with him. It showed in her words and in her actions, and she didn't seem to be able to do anything to hide it.

"That's not fair," Tiffany pointed out, still skipping backward. "You gave us your secret recipe. If we win, it's because you helped us."

"Turn around and walk facing forward, Tiffany," Ethan admonished. "You almost ran into old Mr. Petersen and made him spill his beer." He sounded perfectly normal, parental, not as if he'd been carrying on a conversation with her but a breath earlier that was full of hidden meaning and secret needs.

"Oh, look, Tiffany, there's the snow-cone man." Chris welcomed the vendor's appearance as an excuse to look away from the warm golden lights in Ethan's hazel eyes. When she broke eye contact he looked away, also.

"Okay. Give me some money."

Ethan did as his granddaughter demanded. "What do you say?"

"Please and thank you," Tiffany blurted and danced away.

"She's so excited," Chris said, defending her Little Sister's rudeness and changing the subject at the same time.

"That's no reason for her to be allowed to be a menace to navigation or to forget her manners."

When he took his hand away from her elbow, Chris felt relieved and bereft at the same time, a jumble of contradicting sensations that left her more confused than ever about her feelings for the man beside her. "Tiffany is acting exactly like any other almost-nine-year-old acts in situations like this. Don't tell me you can't remember how excited you were as a boy when the circus came to town?"

"My dad was in the army and we lived in Wyoming when I was Tiffany's age, so it was the rodeo coming to town. But you're right. I remember. I remember very well." He laughed. "My friends and I were way past being mere hazards to navigation who forgot to say please and thank-you. We were holy terrors."

"See." Chris laughed, picturing the ornery, blond-headed boy he must have been in those days. "It's not so hard to recall being a child if you put your mind to it. I'll bet," she said teasing a little, "you even had a flat-top haircut."

"Don't remind me. Anyway, I'd rather concentrate on the present than remember the past." He looked down at her and he wasn't smiling, he wasn't teasing. He was very serious. Chris glanced hastily away.

"Oh, look, there's an open spot along the bluff fence. I hear the boat whistles, so the parade's starting. We have some very lovely restored boats here in Bonaparte. You really ought to see them. Have you lost sight of Tiffany? Oh, good, here she comes." Chris shut her mouth. She was babbling like a silly, love-struck girl. The thought brought her up short. Love-struck? Impossible.

"She's got a blue snow cone," Ethan grumbled. "Mrs. Baden will have a fit if she dribbles it all down her front."

"Mrs. Baden will cope." Chris led the way to the top of the low bluff so they could view the small flotilla of classic wooden boats cruising by on the blue-brown water below.

Ethan watched her go, the brush of her hair against her shoulder, the swing of her hips beneath her blue cotton skirt. "And so will I," he said under his breath, "but, lady, you make it damn hard to do what's right."

"GRANDPA! Grandpa, look. See our trophy!"

Tiffany came bouncing up to where Ethan was standing at the edge of the crowd surrounding the bandstand. She was holding Chris's left hand with her right hand and waving the trophy above her head with the other.

"We won second place! The firemen got first place and their trophy is bigger, but Chris says that she'll put this one right on her desk where everyone will see it and it will have my name on it!"

"That's great, sweetheart. I'm proud of you." He reached down and swung her up into his arms for a hug. A momentary twinge of pain in his chest made him wince, but he forgot it immediately when he saw Chris's flushed, smiling face. "Congratulations."

"Thanks. We couldn't have done it without your help."

"Shhh. I told you it has to be a secret."

Chris put her finger to her lips, her eyes sparkling. "Wild horses couldn't drag it out of me. Especially since you were crafty enough to give us a bag of already-mixed dry ingredients instead of the recipe itself."

"A good chef doesn't give away all his secrets, even for a worthy cause."

"Mom! Tiff! We did it!"

Chris's son came bounding through the crowd of people standing at the edge of the portable dance floor waiting for the Fifties and Sixties dance, the highlight of the evening's entertainment, to begin.

"I heard the announcement come over the loudspeaker in the parking lot. "Where's the trophy? Let me see it."

Tiffany thrust the small wood and gold-colored metal trophy forward for his inspection. "Hey, not bad. A leaping flame on top. What weighty symbolism. Did you pick out the design, Mom?" he asked with a cheeky grin.

"As a matter of fact, I did."

"What's symbolism?" Tiffany jumped up and down impatiently as Keith inspected the small, inexpensive trophy. "It's got fire on top because this is the five-alarm trophy and it means the chili was *hot*."

"That's what I said, squirt."

"No, it wasn't."

"Hey, it doesn't matter. Our team got second place!"

Keith picked Tiffany up and swung her high in the air, far higher than Ethan had managed just a few moments earlier. He heard her squeal of delighted laughter, saw the excited smile on her face when she looked down at the handsome teenager, and realized his granddaughter had found a new hero. The knowledge made his heart jerk out of rhythm with a pain far different from the stitch in his side. Then Keith set Tiffany on the ground and whirled his mother off her feet with another exuberant hug and Ethan wished he'd thought to do the same.

He'd been thinking about holding Chris Baldwin in his arms a lot the past few weeks. And not just holding her, either, kissing her, loving her. It was becoming an obsession, but a very pleasant one.

"Keith! Enough." Chris laughed breathlessly.

"Mother, here you are. We've been looking all over the park for you."

A very pretty, blond young woman and a tall, very thin dark young man hailed Chris and came walking quickly to her side.

"Well, now you've found me." Chris smiled at the couple and turned to introduce them. "Ethan, this is my daughter, Erika, and her fiancé, Michael Schroeder. Kids, this is Tiffany's grandfather, Ethan Connor."

"Hello, Mr. Connor," Erika said with a dimpling smile. She held out her hand. "It's nice to meet you at last. We think Tiffany's a great kid."

"Thanks. So do I."

"Sir," Michael said politely.

His handshake was firm and strong. He was wearing an Ohio State T-shirt and red-and-gray striped shorts, so Ethan felt safe in commenting on the Buckeyes' chances of making it to the Rose Bowl. He guessed correctly and Chris's future son-in-law was immediately launched on a detailed analysis of his favorite team's post-season prospects.

"No more football," Erika Baldwin interrupted without a qualm after about three minutes of Michael's monopolizing the conversation.

"Jeannie and Brian are expecting us to meet them at the main gate in five minutes. We're going to have to leave now if we want to be on time."

"Oh, sure." Michael smiled at his strong-minded bride-to-be, then held out his hand once more. "Nice to meet you, Mr. Connor."

"Yes, nice to meet you." Erika smiled at Ethan again, but it wasn't Chris's smile; Keith had inherited that. He suspected Erika resembled her late father, in looks and possibly in temperament.

With a wave of her pink-tipped fingers, Erika took Michael's arm and walked away.

"Whew." Keith gave an exaggerated sigh of relief. "Mike's an okay guy, but don't ever get him started talking about football, Mr. Connor. He never shuts up."

"I'll remember that," Ethan said, straight-faced.

"We're used to it," Chris said, equally serious, although her eyes twinkled with laughter. "Although I must admit it takes some getting used to. He showed up on the doorstep the day Erika turned sixteen and was allowed to start dating, and they've been together ever since."

"A match made in heaven," Keith quipped. "Hey, Mom, I have to take off."

"Aren't you staying for the dance?"

Keith rolled his brown eyes heavenward. "Mom, I got you a Beach Boys CD for Christmas and I never say a word when you play Dave Clark 5 stuff while you're washing the car, but I'm not wasting a Saturday night at a Fifties and Sixties dance."

"I get the picture," Chris said dryly.

"I just stopped to let you know the cook-off site has been policed to within an inch of its life and restored to its former pristine glory."

"In other words, you cleaned up the parking lot."

"Isn't that what I just said?" Keith spread his hands in a gesture of appeal.

Tiffany had been listening to their bantering with a rapt expression on her face. Now she broke out laughing. "Why don't you just say what you mean instead of using big words that no one else understands?'' she demanded.

"I do use words grown-ups can understand, squirt."

"Don't call me squirt." Tiffany bristled and raised her beloved trophy in a menacing gesture.

"I think it's time we headed home before you give Keith grounds for lodging an assault complaint," Ethan said, reaching out to catch hold of Tiffany's wrist and ease the trophy out of her grasp.

"Tell him not to call me squirt."

She sounded hurt, and sulky and very much like a tired little girl. Ethan looked down at her frowning, blueberry-stained face and realized he would have to take her home soon. He should have sent her with Mrs. Baden and the two little children an hour ago, but she'd been having such a good time and she was so excited about learning who'd win the chili cook-off that he'd relented and let her stay.

"I'll tell you what, Ms. Connor," Keith said, seeing the same signs of fatigue and bad temper on Tiffany's face that Ethan had just noticed. "I'll take you home in my car so you can show the trophy to your little sister and brother before Mrs. Baden puts them to bed. How's that?"

"I don't know." Tiffany looked torn.

"C'mon, Tiff, help me out," Keith said, holding out his hand. "Otherwise I'll have to stick around for an hour or two and wait for my mom to get tired of dancing the Funky Chicken or the Mashed Potatoes or whatever it was they called it, and get ready to go home. Someone has to go with her because she's got the money from the cook-off locked up in the sheriff's booth and we can't let her walk around alone with it."

"Someone might knock her on the head with a baseball bat and steal it," Tiffany said, instantly diverted.

"Something like that," Keith agreed, nodding.

"If I go with you my grandpa can take care of Chris and see that she gets home safely. He's very good at that."

Tiffany looked up at him with a smile of such complete trust that Ethan felt, for a moment, as if he were more of a hero than Batman and Superman combined. He opened his mouth to veto the idea, then shut it again. The opportunity to spend time alone with Chris, to hold her in his arms, even on a crowded dance floor in full view of half the town hadn't come his way very often. He decided to take advantage of Keith's offer.

"It is getting late, sweetheart. Why don't you let Keith take you home? You'll just be in time to help Mrs. Baden tuck Ashley and Brandon into bed."

"Will you be home before it's too late, Grandpa?"

"The dance is over at eleven. I'll stop in your room and give you a kiss if you're still awake."

"You'll give me a kiss even if I'm asleep," Tiffany said, and smiled. "Okay, I'll go with Keith. But I know you just want to dance a slow dance with Chris. I'm little, but I'm smart."

"You are very smart."

"And mouthy. Come on," Keith said, giving her a little jerk. "Let's go."

"Don't be late," Chris said.

She was avoiding looking at him, Ethan noted. He felt somewhat uncomfortable himself. He hadn't realized how difficult it would be to conduct a courtship under the watchful eyes of two generations of offspring.

"Football curfew is midnight. I'll be home on the stroke of twelve, just like Cinderella."

"Cinderella was a girl," Tiffany sniffed, hanging on Keith's arm with both hands.

"Okay. Just like Prince Charming, then," he said, walking away. "Who, I might add, more than one senior girl has told me I resemble."

"Yuck. Senior girls are dopey," Tiffany scoffed, having the last word.

"Well, that's settled." Chris turned back to Ethan after watching the pair walk away. She didn't look at him directly, but at a point just past his left shoulder.

People walked by them in both directions, the very young and very old heading away from the bandstand and the dance floor, those in-between in age arriving to try to recapture the past for a few hours by listening to the music of their youth.

"Would you like to dance?" Ethan asked as the band began the set with a medley of Righteous Brothers hits.

The moon was just coming up over the treetops and the air smelled of the river and falling leaves and dusty grass.

"I don't know...." Chris bit her lip.

Ethan saw her eyes flicker over the crowd of people. People she'd known all her life, who'd known her husband, who would speculate endlessly at seeing her dancing with another man and form their own conclusions, no matter how far from the truth those conclusions might be. "Chris," he said softly, but with a hint of challenge in his voice, "you don't have to dance with me."

"I'd love to dance with you," she said with a sudden smile.

Ethan felt as young as he'd been when he'd heard the Righteous Brothers sing "You've Lost that Lovin' Feeling" for the first time.

She held out her hand. "I never could resist that song."

THE MOON WAS a cool silver ball floating high above them, growing misty at the edges as a thin veil of cirrus clouds began to whisper across the sky. The warmth of the early October afternoon had long ago disappeared. The air was damp and chilly. Chris pushed her hands deeper into the pockets of her oversize yellow sweater. She was grateful for its warmth, grateful, too, for the warmth of Ethan's arm around her as they walked toward her car, parked on the street just beyond his house.

"I hope it doesn't rain," she said, glancing once more at the hazy sky. "The Lions' Club chicken barbecue and the children's pet parade are both scheduled for tomorrow."

"What happens if it does rain?" Ethan asked.

"They'll have them anyway." Chris shook her head. "I ought to be ashamed of myself. Here I am worrying about what's going to happen tomorrow instead of enjoying the success I had today."

"It's a pretty common personality trait, I believe."

Ethan sounded amused and Chris looked up at him from the corner of her eye. "You're making fun of me," she accused.

"No. On the contrary. I admire your drive and commitment."

For once Chris didn't shy away from the praise for herself and her hard work. "We did do well today, didn't we?" She patted the bank deposit bag tucked safely inside the zippered tote hanging from her right shoulder. "Six hundred and thirty-seven dollars. And even better, pledges from three people to apply as volunteers. All three of them are men," she finished happily.

Ethan laughed. "You sound very satisfied by that last comment."

Chris laughed, too. "As executive director of the Hobart County Big Brothers/Big Sisters program, I am. Very satisfied. I need Big Brother volunteers so desperately. I have twelve boys waiting for matches right now."

"And what will you do with the money."

"Buy an air conditioner," Chris said without a moment's hesitation.

"It's October," Ethan pointed out. "You won't be needing an air conditioner any more this year."

"But I will next June, and by then I'll have found fifty other places the money should be spent. No. My mind's made up. I'm going to Murphy's Hardware first thing Monday morning and order one while I still remember how stifling it gets in my office at four o'clock on a hot August afternoon."

They walked in silence for a minute or two.

"How long have you been director of the program?" Ethan asked, stopping at one of the scenic turnouts along the riverbank to watch the moonbeams shimmer across the dark water.

Chris leaned her arms on the wooden railing that edged the walkway, very much aware of the man beside her. "It will soon be four years," she said, amazed at how quickly the time had passed. "I took over from the original director when the program was two years old." She was quiet for a moment. "My husband had died the year before, my children were growing up and I was at loose ends. Now I can't imagine doing anything else."

"You're a very special woman."

Ethan was no longer looking at the moonlight on the water. He was looking at her. Chris could feel his gaze on her, though she didn't turn her head. "No, I'm a very ordinary woman. I have a job that fills a very special need. There's a difference."

"I disagree."

He reached out, touched her hair, grazed the line of her jaw with the tip of his finger. Chris shivered, not from the cold but from the pleasure of his touch. It filled her with heat and light and sparks of longing. She'd told everyone she was content to slip quietly into middle age, but she was wrong. When Ethan touched her she felt young and alive, desirable and desiring. The realization surprised and dismayed her.

"It's getting late. I...we should both be getting home," she said, not only because it was true, but because she could think of nothing else to say. She hadn't been in this situation—alone with a man, a vital, virile man—for so long she was unsure of herself and her feelings.

"You don't have to run away from me." Ethan's voice was low and husky. He stepped closer, took her in his arms.

Chris's momentary indecision disappeared. This was what she wanted, too. "I have no intention of running away." She put her arms around his neck and wondered a little dazedly what he would do next, what she should do next.

Ethan pulled her closer, fitting her body to the hard length of his, resting his chin on the top of her head. "I've wanted to hold you in my arms like this for what seems like a very long time."

She leaned her cheek against his chest. She felt the smooth cotton of his shirt, the hard contour of muscles below, the steady rise and fall of his breathing.

Was he going to kiss her?

It seemed likely, the next logical step, and she wanted him to, wanted him to very badly.

He tipped her face up with his knuckle. "Chris?" His expression was shadowed by the branches of the maples overhead. His face was a study in contrasts: light and dark, hard lines and smooth skin, rough voice and soft words. "What are you thinking?"

"I don't know."

"Do you know I want to kiss you?"

"Yes," she said, and smiled nervously. "I want that, too. The problem is I'm not sure I remember how. It's been a long time for me, a very long time."

"It's easy," he said with a low, warm chuckle. "Like riding a bicycle. Once you learn you never forget."

"I've always thought whoever said that probably never stopped riding a bicycle long enough to worry about it."

She wasn't being coy. She hadn't been kissed in a long time. She'd forgotten how marvelous it was to be held in a man's arms, to feel his mouth on hers, to respond with every fiber of her being to the magic of his touch.

"Let's give it a try. I promise I won't let you fall."

Ethan lowered his head to hers. He tasted the corners of her lips, coaxed her mouth open as his tongue slid inside ever so slightly and her arms tightened around him, answering the reawakened needs of her own desire.

"I want to keep seeing you," Ethan said as he lifted his mouth from hers.

Chris began an automatic protest. Her first responsibility was to Tiffany. Didn't Ethan realize that? She couldn't jeopardize her fragile rapport with the child by becoming involved with her guardian. He stopped her words with another kiss.

"I want to be with you as Ethan and Chris, not as Tiffany's grandfather and her Big Sister. I think you want that, too."

"Yes," Chris said so softly the words were barely audible above the rustle of falling leaves. "I'm just not certain how best to handle the situation. None of my volunteers has ever become involved with a parent...."

"We'll play it by ear. We're both adults, Chris. Surely we can work this out, have something for ourselves without taking anything away from Tiffany."

He held her a little away from him, his hands on her shoulders. The warmth and strength of his touch caressed her skin through the weave of her sweater. "I don't know. I'll have to think about it," she said, unable not to speak the truth of her thoughts. "You've caught me off guard. I...I hadn't planned to get involved with any man."

"Especially not me." Ethan pulled her close once more, held her for the space of a handful of heartbeats, then let her go. "Poor Chris, the Connor family has turned your world upside down, haven't we?"

"Yes," she admitted with a shaky little laugh. "And I wouldn't have it any other way."

"Come on," he urged, "before I forget my good intentions and kiss you again. It's getting cold and Tiffany's probably waiting up for me."

He moved slightly away from her, giving her space, giving her a chance to collect her scattered thoughts. "She's such a little mother hen," Chris said, then smiled, taking his hand, unwilling to be completely separated so soon.

"She's had a tough couple of years." Ethan's tone was suddenly very serious. "Her mother's death was tragic and unexpected. She was ill barely six weeks. The end came so quickly I couldn't get to Atlanta until a day and a half later. The kids spent two nights in a county children's shelter."

"Surely your son..." Chris spoke without thinking. She didn't know anything about Tiffany's father—Ethan's son.

"My son couldn't stand to see his wife suffer, or so they told me. He left the hospital immediately after Katherine's death without telling a soul where he was going. That's why it took so long for the authorities to notify me. He hasn't been back since. For all intents and purposes, he abandoned his children."

Ethan tried hard to keep the anger and frustration out of his voice, but Chris knew it was there, below the surface. "I'm so sorry," she said, and she meant it. She couldn't imagine being so estranged from her own children. It didn't bear thinking of.

They walked silently through the shadows, following the sidewalk in a long curve that moved away from the river and brought them back to the street in front of Ethan's house. In a few more steps they passed beneath a streetlamp, and as they did so, a small figure in a long white nightgown hurtled down the steps and threw herself into Ethan's arms.

"Grandpa! Grandpa! I'm glad you're home."

"Tiffany, what are you doing outside in your nightgown so late at night?"

"He's back, Grandpa," she said, curling one arm around his neck as Ethan knelt to take her in his arms. "He's back!"

Chris couldn't decide if she sounded excited or anxious, or a mixture of both emotions.

Tiffany wiggled in her grandfather's arms and pointed to a tall, slim figure coming toward them along the darkened sidewalk. Beside Chris, Ethan seemed turned to stone.

"Hello, Dad," the man said, extending his hand. "Long time no see."

"Hello, Jeff." Ethan's tone was wooden.

Chris didn't need to hear the words. The two men were too similar in looks and coloring to be anything but father and son.

Tiffany's father, Ethan's prodigal son, had returned, and Chris had no idea what would happen next.

CHAPTER SIX

TIFFANY SAT UP in bed and folded her arms over her stomach. She glanced at her clock. It was after eleven. The moon was shining too brightly in her window for her to go to sleep, and besides that her stomach hurt.

She supposed she shouldn't have eaten that last popcorn ball at Chris's house. It was keeping her awake. Or at least that's what Mrs. Baden would say was the matter with her. Tiffany wasn't so sure. The candy had been so much fun to make that it didn't seem right it should be keeping her awake now.

No one Tiffany had ever known before actually made Halloween candies for Trick or Treat night; but it seemed people in Bonaparte did, including her Big Sister. Chris was in charge of making popcorn balls for her neighborhood, she'd explained when Tiffany's dad had dropped her off for the evening. If Tiffany wanted to help, that's what they would do with their time together.

Tiffany couldn't think of anything she'd rather do and she'd said so. They'd put butter on their hands and molded the warm, sticky syrup and popped corn into balls and put them in plastic bags. Chris colored the syrup yellow and orange and they put pieces of candy corn in some of them. That was Tiffany's idea because it was the same color and sitting in a bowl on the counter beside her. Chris thought they turned out great and Tiffany was glad she'd suggested it.

Then they washed their hands and pasted little stickers with Chris's name and address on the outside of each bag so that kids' parents would know where the candy had come from and not throw it away. Tiffany thought that was a neat idea because she remembered her grandfather sorting through her trick-or-treat candy the previous year in Chicago and taking out everything that wasn't wrapped, then putting it down the disposal. She was glad that wouldn't happen to their popcorn balls. She was proud of them.

By the time they were finished she'd eaten two, plus some regular popcorn and candy corn and licked the spoon and bowl. Now she was sorry she'd made such a pig of herself. Her stomach hurt a lot.

"Maybe Grandpa's still awake?" she whispered out loud. She liked to talk to herself, especially at night. It made her feel less lonely. "He knows what to do to make your stomach stop hurting." She didn't want to still be sick tomorrow, because it was Halloween and she had a really great vampire costume that she wanted Chris and Keith to see.

She got out of bed and padded out of the room, first checking to see that Ashley and Brandon hadn't kicked off their covers. She passed her father's room, but didn't stop. He'd be asleep, she reasoned, or reading, and he didn't know much about fixing stomachaches anyway, at least not that Tiffany remembered.

Her momma had always done that because her daddy was too busy, or working too hard, or something. Sometimes he just wasn't there at all, like when Momma died. Tiffany shivered and hurried on down the stairs, not pausing at her grandfather's bedroom door because the living-room lights were still on and that meant he was awake, maybe watching TV or working on a report.

He'd make everything right. Tiffany smiled a little and quickened her steps.

"Grandpa?"

Ethan gave a start of surprise at the unexpected sound of his granddaughter's voice. He glanced at his watch, surprised to find it was almost midnight. "What's wrong, sweetheart?" he asked, pushing his chair away from the desk and the schematic drawing of the new assembly line layout he was studying, so that Tiffany could climb onto his lap.

"I can't sleep," she mumbled, resting her head against his shoulder. Ethan tightened his arms around her slim body and held her close.

"Bad dreams?" He kissed the top of her head. She smelled clean and sweet, like sugar and spice and everything nice, as the old saying went.

"No dreams."

"Good." There had been nightmares now and again in the couple of weeks since Jeff had arrived. More often than before, but not with the alarming regularity of the first few months after her mother's death.

"The moon's too bright," she complained, "and my stomach hurts."

"I can't stop the moon from shining unless you let me pull the blind on your window," Ethan reminded her.

"I know that." Tiffany squirmed around on his lap to get more comfortable. "It's really my stomach. I don't think I should have eaten that second popcorn ball at Chris's."

"That might be the problem, all right. I imagine we can find something in the medicine cabinet to help your stomach without too much trouble, though."

"Good," she said, wiggling harder. "Can you stop working and go get it for me right now?"

"Okay. Do you want me to carry you, or can you walk?"

"I'll walk," Tiffany announced, scorning his offer. "Maybe a glass of milk would help me, too," she suggested slyly.

"I don't suppose it would hurt," Ethan agreed, hiding a smile. "Why don't you hop down and let me get this stuff out of the way. I'm going to call it a night."

Tiffany slid off his lap and watched with interest as he took off his reading glasses and shoved them in his shirt pocket, cleared his desk by sweeping the pens and erasers into the top drawer and rolled up the drawings, to replace them in the big cardboard cylinders where they were stored.

"You're working awfully late tonight, Grandpa. Is something wrong?"

"Nothing's wrong, sweetheart." Ethan took her hand and led the way toward the kitchen. He was never sure if Tiffany was just a born worrier or if the traumas of her young life had scarred her more deeply than he'd thought. He looked down at her dark head, bobbing alongside him, and decided it was more than likely a combination of both, and only time and love would make it right. "Since Castleton's has decided to remodel the plant here, we need to get working on the new assembly line as soon as possible. We don't want to be shut down next summer when the tomatoes start to get ripe again."

"I know that." Tiffany tossed her head. "Chris and I talked about it tonight while we were making popcorn balls. Erika and Michael were there. Michael said his dad thinks you saved the town single-handed. If Castleton's had moved away, to Mexico or somewhere, everyone would have lost their jobs, and businesses would close and pretty soon Bonaparte would be a ghost town," she finished with relish.

"Did he really say that?"

"Well, no. But Keith said that's what could happen."

"Keith exaggerates." The situation hadn't been that bad when he proposed the retooling and remodeling of the Bonaparte plant to his superiors six weeks earlier, but with a few more years of decreasing productivity and profits, it might have been.

"Chris said that, too. But she's glad Castleton's is going to fix up the plant because so many people really do depend on you for their jobs."

Ethan had been listening to her chatter with only half an ear. Now he began to pay more attention. Chris's opinions were of interest to him, even filtered through the imaginative mind of an eight-year-old. He hadn't seen Chris alone since the night of the chili cook-off and dance at RiverFest. Jeff's unexpected arrival had coincided with the home office's final decision to go ahead with the capital improvement plan he'd proposed. Between pressures at work and unresolved tensions at home, he'd been too busy to find time to spend with her.

He took the bottle of antacid out of the cabinet above the sink, putting thoughts of Chris Baldwin firmly out of his mind. He was much too familiar with the sleepless hours and restless erotic dreams that resulted from unfettered fantasies of the two of them—alone—together.

"Here, take this." He offered Tiffany a spoonful of the familiar pink liquid.

His granddaughter made a mutinous face as she looked up from pouring a glass of milk. "I don't like that stuff. It tastes yucky."

"It will fix your stomachache. Take it," Ethan ordered. "You can wash it down with your milk." He'd learned from painful experience that reasoning with a tired, cranky child was a hopeless task. Old-fashioned discipline was the key to success in a situation like this. He only wished he'd figured that out twenty years earlier, when it might have done Jeff some good.

"I want something to eat," Tiffany complained, rubbing her fist across her eye. "My stomach aches and it feels hungry, too."

"That's because you've got indigestion," he explained patiently. It was a condition he'd become very familiar with himself the past few weeks. "The medicine will help in just a little while."

"I want something to eat," Tiffany insisted.

"Why don't you make the kid a snack, Dad."

Ethan hadn't heard Jeff come downstairs. He was wearing gray running shorts and a Northwestern T-shirt that looked as if it had seen better days. It probably dated back to his freshman year at the college, the only one he'd completed successfully.

"Snacking is what brought her down here at this time of night with a stomachache," Ethan said.

"I have indigestion, Grandpa says," Tiffany explained, glancing anxiously at both of them. "But I feel hungry."

"How about some milk toast," Jeff suggested, sauntering into the room with the loose-limbed grace of a born basketball player. But he'd never played basketball except for pickup games. He didn't like the discipline and effort necessary to be a member of a successful team. "I remember that's what Great-grandma Connor used to fix for me when I visited her and got a stomachache." He smiled down at Tiffany, but it was a quizzical smile, detached and a little wary, the way he might have looked if he'd been caught unexpectedly in the same situation with a friend or neighbor's child, not his own firstborn.

"What's milk toast?" Tiffany asked Ethan accusingly. "You never made it for me before when I was sick."

"It's toast in a bowl with sugar and warm milk poured over it. To tell you the truth, I'd forgotten all about it. My mother used to fix it all the time for us when we had stomachaches. Do you want to try some?"

"Yes." Tiffany nodded. "It sounds good."

Ethan got out a pan while Jeff hunted around through several cupboard drawers for the bread. It was like him to have lived in the house for more than two weeks and still not know where the bread was kept.

"Second drawer on your left," Ethan growled, angry with himself for letting his irritation show. It wasn't Jeff's fault he'd inherited so much of his mother's casual attitude to the mundane details of everyday life. A lot of people probably thought it was at least an advantage, if not a downright commendable personality trait. Unfortunately Ethan wasn't one of them.

"Okay, okay. Don't get bent out of shape. There's no law against midnight snacks in this town, is there?" Jeff asked with a wink for Tiffany, who laughed as he popped the bread in the toaster.

"For all I know there might be. It's a school night," Ethan said in a theatrical whisper, looking fearfully over his shoulder, determined to keep things light, for Tiffany's sake if not for Jeff's.

"Maybe we'd better douse the lights." Jeff grabbed a box of short, fat emergency candles he'd obviously spied while rummaging through the kitchen drawers and shoved as many of them as he could into a coffee cup. He set the cup in the middle of the big oak table.

"They aren't burning," Tiffany pointed out, her hand on the light switch. "We need a match."

"Matches? Where are the matches?" Jeff looked puzzled.

Ethan bit his tongue rather than point out they were lying right alongside the emergency candles. Instead he picked one of the stubby candles out of the cup and lit it by holding it against the flame of the gas stove where he was heating milk.

"Hey! Great!" Jeff crowed as he lit the other candles and stepped back to admire the effect. Tiffany shut off the overhead light and plunged most of the big, high-ceilinged kitchen into darkness.

"This is just like...I don't know...hiding out from the bad guys or something," Tiffany whispered very loudly, a look of excitement on her face, her stomachache forgotten.

"It's great." Jeff buttered the toast with a flourish, tore it into pieces, dropped the pieces into a bowl and sprinkled them with sugar.

Not a lot, Ethan was relieved to see. He didn't want to be the heavy again by pointing out the last thing Tiffany needed that late at night was another dose of refined sugar.

"Now for the hot milk. Is it ready, Dad?"

"Ready." Ethan poured the steaming milk over the toast.

Tiffany poked at it a couple of times with the tip of a spoon, then took a small bite. She chewed thoughtfully. "Not bad. It could use some more sugar, though."

Ethan took a spoon from the top drawer and took a taste. "Maybe just a sprinkle. What do you think, Jeff?" He looked directly at his son for the first time. Jeff's expression was hidden by the leaping shadows of flames from the fat, stubby candles, but he was smiling, and the tilt of his head reminded Ethan of his wife early in their marriage before everything had gone dark and sour.

"Just a sprinkle," Jeff agreed. "We don't want you bouncing off the walls the rest of the night."

"This is great," Tiffany said, wielding the sugar shaker with, for once, a sparing hand. "Why don't you try some, too?" She looked up expectantly, a drop of milk at the corner of her mouth. A pink, pointed tongue darted out and licked it away.

"Sure," her father said, putting two more pieces of bread into the toaster. "I always loved to eat this stuff at Great-grandma Connor's. I used to pretend I had a stomachache just to get some."

Tiffany looked at Ethan. He shrugged. "Why not?" he said with a grin. "I like it, too." Maybe it would help him sleep tonight. He was tired and in no mood to lie awake for hours pondering questions for which there were no answers.

He watched his son and granddaughter eat. Tiffany was laughing happily at Jeff's jokes and funny faces, and for the moment he seemed content. But by tomorrow that contentment could turn to restlessness and the urge to move on.

Jeff was a carpenter and a furniture maker, and a good one, Ethan conceded. It was a skill that lent itself to an easygoing, no-strings-attached life-style, the kind his son preferred. From past experience Ethan knew Jeff wouldn't hesitate to leave Bonaparte when wanderlust beckoned again. And Tiffany and the younger children would suffer for it, as they had in the past.

Ethan had no doubt Jeff loved his children. He just didn't think the younger man could be trusted to raise them. He had no idea what might happen to Tiffany's fragile, developing sense of self-worth if her father disappeared on her again. Ethan didn't want to find out. He had legal custody of all three children. He didn't intend to give them up.

But was he being fair to Jeff?

The nagging doubts about his own ability to judge the situation dispassionately would not be silenced so easily. He loved his grandchildren. He wanted them for his own. He would do whatever he felt necessary to keep them with him.

Even if it meant alienating himself completely from his son.

"TRICK OR TREAT!"

Chris swung open the front door and lifted her hand

to her throat, feigning terror. "Heavens, you are the scariest-looking vampire I've seen tonight!"

"Do you really think so?" Tiffany twirled around in a circle to show off her long black cape to best advantage. She grinned malevolently. "How do you like my fangs?"

At least Chris assumed that's what she'd said. The plastic fangs sticking out over Tiffany's lower lip and the heavy "Transylvanian" accent made the words hard to decipher.

"Your costume is great, Tiff." Chris knew she'd made a mistake saying her Little Sister's name so early on. She'd intended to keep up the pretense for a while longer, but the nickname had just slipped out.

Tiffany spit the fangs into her hand and gave Chris a hard stare from dark-rimmed eyes. "How did you know it was me?"

"Not from your costume and makeup," Chris said hurriedly, angling for a chance to redeem herself. "They're great. But...I recognized your grandfather and brother and sister standing out by the sidewalk."

"Oh, yeah."

Tiffany seemed satisfied by the explanation. She whirled around, looking over her shoulder to watch her cape swirl out behind her.

"Brandon's still asleep and Ashley's afraid to come up here without Grandpa. I told him they could wait in the car, but he said no, he'd bring them in. You know how stupid little kids are."

She sounded like a grown-up sister, Chris thought, amused and annoyed at the same time.

"I wanted *you* to see me first."

"You certainly gave me a fright," Chris admitted. She shifted the big plastic pumpkin of treats she was holding until it rested against her hip and she could wave with her other hand. "Ethan, hi. Come on in."

"Yeah, Grandpa," Tiffany seconded the invitation. "Come on in. My dad," she added by way of explanation, "is passing out treats at our house. He said Grandpa should take us trick-or-treating because he knows the neighborhoods a lot better."

"That seems like a good idea," Chris concurred. She, for one, was certainly glad they'd decided on that particular division of duties.

Tiffany tipped her head to see into Chris's pumpkin. "Hmmm, fruit drops. They're not too bad. They're good for Brandon. He doesn't have real big teeth. Popcorn balls are hard for him to chew."

Chris knew her cue when she heard it. "There's one for each of you hidden safely away in the kitchen." She smiled at Ethan, aware she was talking about nothing of importance but unable for some unknown reason to stop. "We've had more than two hundred trick-or-treaters tonight. The popcorn balls were gone in the first ten minutes."

"I hope Jeff didn't run out of treats," Ethan said, smiling back. "I'm not in the mood to be washing soaped windows."

He was dressed in a brown pullover sweater and jeans. As always when she first saw him, Chris was struck by how handsome and vigorous he was. Brandon was draped over his shoulder, his Teenage Mutant Ninja Turtle mask hanging down his back, his face buried in the curve of Ethan's neck. He was indeed sound asleep. Ashley, a fairy princess in pink lace and silver glitter, clung to his arm with both hands and peeped at Chris from behind Ethan's leg.

"What do you say, honey?" Ethan prompted with a smile.

But it was a tired smile, and not for the first time, Chris noticed the deep lines running from nose to chin, which hadn't been there in the summer when they'd first met. He looked worried about something and she longed to comfort him.

"Trick or treat," Ashley said, and thrust out her orange-and-black sack.

Chris dropped a sealed envelope of fruit drops into it and added one for Brandon. "Busy day?" she asked, stepping back so that Ethan could enter the house. They were very close, but they didn't touch. How could they with three children at their knees? she thought resignedly.

"Every day's a madhouse since we started the plant renovations," Ethan said, shifting Brandon's weight as Ashley let go of his hand and followed her sister into Chris's kitchen to check on the whereabouts of the promised popcorn balls.

"I can imagine." Chris looked at the sleeping child in his arms and felt a momentary pang of sweet longing as she remembered the feel and scent of her own babies asleep in her arms. "Would you like to lay him on the couch and join me for a glass of cider?"

"Fresh cider?" He looked interested.

"Yes. As a matter of fact my cousin has a press. This was squeezed just yesterday. I can guarantee it."

"Great." He glanced down at the sleeping toddler. "I think our carapaced crime fighter has called it a day."

"He's worn-out, poor little guy." Chris sat the pumpkin-shaped bowl of treats on the foyer table and moved into her thankfully just-vacuumed living room, where she laid a soft woven afghan on the sofa. "Put him here."

Ethan gestured to the mask dangling below Brandon's left ear. He was a sturdy little boy with his father and grandfather's dark blond hair and square, aggressive jaw. "Would you mind taking that off him?"

"Of course not."

He looked at her nubby-weave, off-white couch uncertainly. "Maybe we should lay him on the floor."

"Why?" Chris asked, although she was pretty sure what the answer would be.

"We're right in the middle of potty training and he hasn't got his night diaper on."

Chris laughed. She'd just been thinking, in one tiny corner of her brain that refused to remain silent on the subject, that Ethan looked very much like Indiana Jones tonight. And now here he was, the physical twin to a larger-than-life adventure hero, worrying over the possibility that Brandon might have an accident on her living room sofa. So much for the romantic fantasies of a forty-two-year-old woman who ought to know better.

"What are you laughing about?" Ethan asked, frowning harder. "Sitting on a couch that's been wet on is a pretty sobering experience, let me tell you."

"I know." She reached out to pat his arm, still smiling, but the touch of her hand on the hard muscles beneath his sweater erased the smile from her face and tightened the breath in her chest. Maybe her fantasies weren't so far from reality after all. "It isn't anything that hasn't happened in this house already." She went on talking as if nothing had changed between them, but she felt Ethan's arm tense beneath her light touch and she knew he'd felt the electric response between them as strongly as she had. "Don't give it a thought."

She must be losing her mind—or her heart—Chris decided as she heard herself speak. It was a true statement, but not as far as this particular living room furniture was concerned. It was less than two years old. The kind of furniture she'd dreamed about for years while her own two kids were growing up; the kind of furniture middle-aged women with no small children in their lives chose for their living rooms. She'd waited years for furniture like this. And now there was a partially potty-trained two-year-old asleep on it and she didn't mind at all.

CHAPTER SEVEN

ETHAN PARKED HIS CAR on the street in front of Chris's single-story brick ranch. It was almost six-thirty, already twilight now that it was November, but still balmy and warm. It was one of those last precious Indian summer days that belied the onset of a long, damp northern Ohio winter.

"Stay put, you two," he cautioned Ashley and Brandon. "I'll go get Tiffany and then we'll go home and have supper, okay?"

He glanced over the seat of the car at his grandchildren. Ashley was looking at the new picture book she'd picked up at the library after kindergarten and Brandon was making finger marks on the car window. He was strapped into his car seat and should be safely corralled for the length of time it would take to fetch Tiffany, and possibly, with any luck, exchange a few words with Chris.

"Okay, Grandpa." Ashley smiled. "But hurry up. I'm starved and the chicken smells good." He'd stopped on the way home and picked up fried chicken and all the trimmings. It was Mrs. Baden's day off. Ethan didn't feel like cooking and it would never occur to Jeff to start dinner for the rest of them.

"Chicky leg," Brandon hollered. "Me, too." *Me, too* was his favorite phrase. He applied it indiscriminately, no matter what else he said, on the theory,

Ethan suspected,that in most cases he wanted what everyone else was asking for, even if he didn't know what it was.

"I'll hurry," Ethan promised. "Be good." In the past year of second-time-around parenting Ethan had learned you could never overemphasize good behavior.

He walked up the sidewalk and rang the doorbell. No one answered. He rang it again. Still no response. Then he heard the shouts and laughter coming from the fenced backyard. Ethan glanced uncertainly over his shoulder at the car. Only the golden top of Ashley's head could be seen, still looking at her picture book, although the daylight was nearly gone. Brandon's chubby hand waved behind the glass, but Ethan couldn't see the child's face. They seemed quiet enough.

He walked swiftly to the gate attached to the garage, which gave access to the backyard. Once inside the fence he heard Tiffany squealing with laughter and he quickened his pace.

A huge old maple tree in the corner of the yard had dropped its leaves in a thick carpet on the grass. Erika and Michael were sitting on the bench of a wooden picnic table, rakes at their sides. Keith was scooping up an armful of leaves from a big pile at the edge of the wooden deck that ran almost the entire length of the house. Chris stood at the corner of the low deck, laughingly watching from a safe distance, her hand on the railing, light from the house gilding her dark blond hair, mounds of blooming mums at her feet. She didn't hear Ethan come up behind her. Neither did Tiffany. She was dancing around Keith, screaming with feigned terror as she attempted to make him drop the armload of brightly colored leaves. He ignored her clutching hands as he began to stalk his target.

"Let Chris alone, you rat," she giggled. "Don't you *dare* dump those icky wet leaves all over her."

Tiffany was opening up, blossoming like a rain-drenched flower under the nurturing of Chris's gentle affection, the companionship of her family. He'd made the decision to enroll Tiffany in Big Brothers/Big Sisters rather offhandedly, he realized with the clarity of hindsight. Now he understood just how truly important a decision it had been.

And he realized something else. His feelings for Christine Baldwin must not be allowed to interfere with Tiffany's progress. Chris saw that more clearly than he did, had done so from the beginning. He wasn't a trained psychologist. He couldn't be certain his wooing of Christine might not seem like a betrayal to his granddaughter, who considered her Big Sister her friend alone.

Tiffany had had so many disappointments in her short life, lost so much, that her happiness and well-being should always come first in his thoughts. Unfortunately he was only mortal and high ideals sometimes gave way to more human needs and desires. He was falling in love with Chris Baldwin and he couldn't help himself. However, he would have to walk a fine line in his courtship of the Widow Baldwin, a very fine line. Nothing must jeopardize Tiffany's fragile new friendship with this remarkable woman, including his own search for someone to love.

"Keith Jonathon Baldwin, don't you dare throw those leaves at me," Chris warned, still laughing. "We've spent hours raking them up. If you start throwing them now, they'll end up all over the yard."

"Too late, Mom. Erika and Michael aren't worth harassing. They're deep in another important discussion about altar flowers. Jeez, all they think about is *the wedding.*" He shook his head, moving toward his mother with a shuffling gait, shoulders hunched like a movie monster. "You, on the other hand, pretty lady," he whined in a fair imitation of Peter Lorre, "are a perfect target."

Tiffany spied Ethan as he stepped out of the shadow of the garage. Her dark eyes grew round with surprise. "Chris! Look out—"

"Quiet, squirt!" Keith ordered, grinning wickedly.

Chris was backing away from the deck, directly toward Ethan. He couldn't help but watch the sway of her hips beneath the snug denim of her jeans, the curve of her breasts beneath the cotton of her sweatshirt as she turned slightly toward him, and he longed to hold her in his arms. If she continued to move in his direction and didn't look back over her shoulder, he might get the opportunity to do just that. He stood still, hands at his side, and waited.

"But, Keith—" Tiffany jumped up and down, hanging on the teenager's arm "—Chris is going to walk—"

"Walk into what?" Chris scoffed. "There's nothing behind me but the garage door, through which I will momentarily escape in the blink of an eye."

"Tiffany's right, Mom. She's on your side, remember," Keith said in a voice that rang with counterfeit concern. "There's someone behind you...."

"Good grief, do you actually expect me to fall for that old trick?" Before the last word had left her mouth, Chris took another step backward, whirled around and came up hard against Ethan's chest.

He was ready for her; his arms came around her waist and he took her weight, steadying them both.

Her eyes flew to his. Surprise and embarrassment—and, he hoped, pleasure—tinged her cheeks with scarlet.

"Ethan! Where did you come from?"

"You don't sound very pleased to see me," he said, taking the opportunity to tease her a little while Tiffany was still distracting the others with her spirited attempts to keep Keith from showering them with leaves.

Chris sucked in her breath as their lower bodies touched. "Then you don't know me as well as you think you do. I'm very glad to see you."

She lifted her arms to his shoulders but made no attempt to leave the confining circle of his arms. Ethan felt his body stir with desire and knew she felt it, too, when her eyes locked with his and she leaned into his embrace ever so slightly.

"I've missed you these past weeks. Are you very busy at the plant?"

"Up to my ears," he said, marveling at the nuances of sensuality and passion that could be found beneath the surface of such mundane conversation.

"You look tired."

Keith was coming closer. Tiffany was hanging on his arm, slowing his advance only slightly. Ethan began to wish his skinny little granddaughter was six feet tall and weighed two hundred pounds.

"I am." He knew he should release her, but she felt too good in his arms, too damn good. There was a streak of dirt on her nose and her hair was tangled about her face by the wind, but she was still the most beautiful woman in the world in his eyes.

"You should slow down, get some rest." She tilted her head, looking very concerned.

He wanted to kiss the tip of her nose, the soft curve of her chin, her lips, her breasts. "It isn't worries about the plant that's keeping me awake at night," he said, and let her see in his eyes how much he wanted her.

"Ethan, we shouldn't be standing here like this, talking like this. Not here. Not in front of the kids."

"How are we standing?" he asked, unable to let her go so quickly.

"You know."

He shook his head. "How?"

"Like lovers," she said in exasperation. "Like Erika and Mike. Except they wouldn't do it in front of me." She gave him a push. "They'll start asking questions I don't have answers for." She gave him a tiny, but very special smile. "Yet."

Before Ethan could think of an answer to her provocative statement, Keith's entire armload of damp leaves showered down around them as Tiffany shrieked with joy.

"Grandpa, you have leaves in your hair," she chortled, dancing over to Ethan.

Chris stepped out of his arms so quickly and so smoothly Ethan didn't think her children noticed that she also did so with reluctance. He reached down and gave Tiffany a hug.

She returned the affectionate gesture and began to brush maple leaves from his hair and the shoulders of his blue oxford cloth shirt as he knelt beside her. "Grandpa, you are a mess."

"Whose fault is that, young woman?"

"It's Keith's fault," Tiffany answered, not fooled at all by her grandfather's attempt to look suitably stern and angry.

"You're an accomplice, squirt," Keith advised her. "Before and after the fact." He reached over and plucked a leaf out of his mother's hair. "Sorry, Mom. I just couldn't resist."

"You're forgiven. *If* you have these leaves raked up before it gets completely dark," Chris said, picking pieces of leaf off the sleeve of her faded red sweatshirt.

"Deal. But don't waste a lot of time getting supper ready. I'm starving."

"Me, too," Tiffany inserted pointedly.

"I didn't have a chance to go to the market. The office was a madhouse today and I'm still trying to get my budget proposal ready for the board of directors meeting next week." Chris frowned slightly, her dark arched brows drawing together. She bit her lower lip.

Ethan thought again how pretty she looked with her red lips and rosy cheeks. He wished he'd been able to hold her in his arms longer than the space of a heartbeat or two, much longer. "I'll heat up the vegetable soup I made Sunday, and maybe grilled cheese?"

"Okay." Keith didn't seem too enthusiastic about the proposed menu, then he brightened. "We'll have the pumpkin pie Grandma Ferrell sent over for dessert."

"That should fill any empty spots you might have left," Chris agreed.

"Can I stay?" Tiffany wheedled.

"'May' I stay, squirt. Don't they teach you no good English in third grade, huh?" Keith joked.

Tiffany shot the teenager a dark look. "May I stay?" she asked very prettily.

"Of course you may stay if you have your grandfather's permission."

"I'm afraid not, Tiffany," Ethan said. "I don't know where your father is. Ashley and Brandon are with me in the car now and we haven't eaten, either. It will be past their bedtime before I can get back here to pick you up. Perhaps some other day," he added as he saw the disappointed look on Tiffany's face.

"Why don't you all join us?" Chris asked before Tiffany could launch a protest. "As you heard, it's going to be a very simple meal but there's plenty to go around."

"Yes, Grandpa, please," Tiffany begged, drawing the word out to extraordinary length.

"We'd be happy to stay," Ethan said before his newly formed resolutions forced him to decline the invitation. He was coming to the conclusion that if he was going to have any time to further his cause with Chris he was going to have to take advantage of all opportunities, no matter what they were. Including potluck supper with his three small grandchildren and Chris's grown children in attendance.

"All right," Tiffany crowed, clapping her hands. "This is gonna be great. I'll go let the brats out of the car," she offered none too graciously. "It's just like a party."

She hadn't mentioned her father once, Ethan noticed. Jeff was still a very peripheral figure in her life. He glanced at Chris and saw her watching Tiffany with concern and understanding in her beautiful brown eyes.

"We won't be coming to the party quite empty-handed," he told Chris, shrugging off the heavy mood his thoughts threatened to bring down on him. "I have a fifteen-piece bucket of blue-ribbon recipe fried chicken . . . and all the fixings . . . in the car."

"Great," Keith said as he began raking leaves at a furious rate. "I may be able to make it through the night without going out for pizza after all."

"I'll get things started in the kitchen." Chris brushed at her hair, looking momentarily self-conscious. "I hope you won't be disappointed with the meal, Ethan."

"I hope you aren't regretting the invitation."

Chris smiled and the hesitation disappeared from her face and from her eyes. "Of course not."

"Good, then I'll get the chicken and make sure Tiffany isn't having any problems with her brother and sister."

"And I'll get the lovebirds over there to help me bag these leaves so the whole yard doesn't have to be done over tomorrow."

"Such a smart boy," Chris said, laughing, as she reached up on tiptoe to give her tall son an approving pat on the head. "Give me twenty minutes and we'll be ready to eat."

"Not one second more."

"TIFFANY, DO YOU WANT another piece of chicken?" Chris asked, indicating the platter with one drumstick and two wings remaining on it.

"No." Tiffany caught her grandfather's eye and hurriedly swallowed the food in her mouth. "I mean, no, thank you, but I would like a piece of pie." She shot her grandfather a defiant glance.

"Me, too," Brandon echoed. He was sitting on top of a copy of the JCPenney catalog and *Webster's Unabridged,* covered by a pillow, and still his little snub nose was only about six inches above his plate. "Me, too."

"Why don't you come over here and sit on my lap, buddy, and we'll share a piece." Ethan leaned over and plucked the toddler from his seat, setting him comfortably on his lap.

"How about everyone else?"

"Pie?" Brandon asked, turning his head to search the table for the promised dessert. "Where's pie?"

"It's coming. Wait until we get the table cleared." Ethan folded his arms around the little boy and gave him a playful squeeze.

Brandon erupted in delighted laughter as his grandfather leaned down and tickled the side of his neck with his nose. Chris watched silently, noting the similarities between the two, recalling the warm happy memories of Jack playing with Keith and Erika when they were that age. She also remembered, unbidden, the pleasure of lovemaking that had resulted in such wonderful beings. She wanted to make love with Ethan, soon and often.

"Pie!" Brandon squealed as Ethan settled him back against him. "Now!"

"How about everyone else?" Chris asked, pulling her thoughts away from the dangerous shoals of fantasy.

"None for me. Or Mom, either," Erika stated firmly. "Needing to lose five pounds before we start to shop for her dress for the wedding has been her primary excuse for procrastinating," she added. "I have a fitting for my gown one week from today and mother's coming along to get a dress for herself.''

Oh, no, Chris groaned inwardly. She wished her grown children's table manners were as good as the little ones'. Why couldn't Erika have waited until they were alone to raise the subject of a mother-of-the-bride dress?

"Mother, you haven't answered my questions," Erika said, interrupting Chris's thoughts. "I need to know if a six o'clock appointment at La Belle Bride next week is too early for you."

"Wednesday is my day to spend time with Tiffany. You know that," Chris reminded her daughter gently. Her stomach was doing little flip-flops. Usually she enjoyed this kind of spur-of-the-moment entertaining. She was good at it. When she had to plan too far ahead she always made far more work out of the occasion than was necessary. But tonight was something of a strain, and not only because of Erika's bad temper.

Entirely too many of her thoughts had been taken up by Ethan Connor's presence at her dining-room table. She hadn't been able to keep herself from watching him eat, from noticing the interaction between him and his grandchildren, from fantasizing about being in his arms, about kissing him again... and more, much more.

"Erika," she said more sharply than she'd intended, "will you and Michael please clear the table while I get the pie and coffee?" It was high time she got her mind back on serving dessert.

Erika set her lips in a tight line but did as she was asked. Chris gave a silent sigh of relief and got up from the table. When she returned to the dining room with pie and coffee she paused a moment in the doorway. They seldom used the room these days except for holidays, when Chris's parents, her two brothers and their wives and children filled the house. It was nice to see all the chairs occupied at the big cherry table that had belonged to Jack's grandmother and would someday be passed on to Keith and his wife, just as the matching solid cherry bed and dresser in the guest room would someday belong to Erika and Michael. It didn't matter that the lusters on the chandelier were dusty, that they were eating off paper plates and using plastic soup bowls. The room was filled with warmth and laughter and good times...at least, it had been until ten minutes earlier.

She cut and served the pie and poured the coffee for the adults, all the time aware of her daughter's bad temper and Michael's resulting uneasiness. "My fitting will take about twenty minutes. The store closes at eight. That will give you almost two hours to pick out a dress." Chris sighed and laid down her fork. Erika wanted her to pick out her mother-of-the-bride dress very badly so that Michael's mother could begin shopping for hers. She'd simply been too busy to oblige her daughter. Now, with the holidays rapidly approaching, time to shop for a dress would become harder than ever to find.

"Your fitting for what?" Tiffany asked around a mouthful of pumpkin pie, sublimely unaware of the undercurrents of tension swirling around the table.

"My wedding gown," Erika said, and didn't elaborate.

"Do you already have one picked out?" Tiffany sat up a little straighter.

Ethan looked at his granddaughter, then across the table to Chris. One eyebrow lifted a fraction of an inch. Tiffany's indifference to fashion was notorious. Wedding dresses, it would seem, were an exception to the rule.

"Yes," Erika said, but with less ice in her voice. "It has a princess-style beaded bodice, puffed sleeves, a skirt with lace edging about eight inches wide and an absolutely gorgeous train with cutwork appliqués and lace inserts."

Tiffany nodded, enthralled, as if every word Erika said made perfect sense to her.

"And it cost enough to feed a small third-world country for a week," Keith inserted irreverently.

"Hush," Chris said, relaxing a little as the tension diminished.

"Your dress has a train hooked on it?" Tiffany asked with a puzzled look.

But Erika was already launched on a description of the ceremony and paid no attention to the question in the little girl's voice. "The wedding colors are going to be mint green and peach, with just a hint of blue and yellow and pink, very springtime, you know," she continued, assured that at least one of her listeners was as interested in the subject as she was herself.

Tiffany leaned forward, her elbows on the table, the last bite of her pie forgotten.

"I want Mother to try on some dresses before the selection is picked over. She's been putting me off for weeks," Erika finished.

"Wednesdays are not good for me," Chris reminded her, but gently.

"It's the only evening the store is open late, Mother. Afternoons aren't good for either of us and Saturdays are just impossible in that place. Every teenager going steady for the first time is in there pawing the gowns. The clerks are always so sharp. I don't like to go on Saturday."

"I agree with you—Saturdays are out." Chris shuddered at the memory of her first trip to the bridal boutique on just such a Saturday afternoon.

"It's all right if you go on Wednesday," Tiffany announced suddenly. "I don't mind." But it appeared as if she did. She picked up her fork and began poking at her pie, not glancing up again.

Erika eyed Chris, then turned back to Tiffany. "Mother, why don't you ask Tiffany if she'd like to come along and watch my fitting?"

"Would you like to come, Tiffany?" Chris asked, sensing a solution to the impasse, one so simple she didn't know why she hadn't thought of it earlier, except for the fact that it seemed her brain only worked at about half speed whenever Ethan was around.

"Okay." Tiffany looked up, grinning but still puzzled. "I can't wait to see how Erika can walk around with a *train* hooked on to the back of her dress."

"SO THAT'S WHAT A TRAIN on a dress is," Tiffany said as she perched gingerly on one of the spindly-legged gilt chairs at La Belle Bride. "I knew it couldn't be a *real* railroad train, but I never heard of one on a dress before," she explained to Chris, enjoying the joke on herself.

"One hundred years ago women wore dresses with long skirts and lots and lots of material every day," the saleslady said in a pleasant British accent. "They had trains and bustles, too."

"Bustles? What are they?"

"Big bunches of material pulled up in back of the dress and draped over a kind of frame."

"Didn't that make your butt stick out pretty far?" Tiffany asked innocently.

Erika snorted with laughter as she twisted this way and that in front of the wall of mirrors that fronted the small dressing room.

"Well, yes, it did," Chris agreed. "But that was the fashion then and people thought they were very beautiful."

"How could they move around in clothes like that?" A bustle must look something like Erika's dress did now that the saleslady had hooked all the folds of the train up in back so that she could at least walk around without people stepping on her skirt, Tiffany thought. She had never seen anything like Erika's wedding gown. It was elegant and beautiful. Still, she simply couldn't imagine wearing anything like that on a day-to-day basis. "How could you play catch or kick a soccer ball?"

"Ladies didn't do anything like that back then," Erika told her, and groaned. "Mom, this strapless bra is killing me." She hitched up the front of the offending undergarment and frowned at her image in the mirror. "I'll never last all day in this thing. It's torture."

"Just be thankful it's not a whalebone corset," Chris said with a grin. "You look lovely. Is that the veil you've decided on?"

"I really do like this one." Erika lifted her hands to her hair and surveyed the effect of the fingertip-length veil of white Illusion and its matching headpiece of iridescent beads against her mane of ash-blond hair.

"Your daughter is going to be one of the loveliest brides I've seen in a long time, Mrs. Baldwin," the saleslady said, stepping away from the small podium where Erika was standing and twisting this way and that, smoothing her hands over the rich satin of her skirt, lightly touching the heavy beading on her bodice. "Would you like to see the back, my dear?"

"Yes, please."

The woman held up a large hand mirror and Erika surveyed the back of the gown as critically as she'd eyed the front.

"You look like a princess," Tiffany breathed. "That is the most beautiful dress I've ever seen."

"Yes, it is. But help me out of it, please," Erika said, motioning to the hovering attendant. "It's my mother's turn and we're not leaving here without a dress for her."

"Oh, dear." Chris shrugged and gave Tiffany a helpless, "here we go" look. She leaned close. "Will you help me choose?"

"Sure." Tiffany didn't want to admit it, but she'd never had so much fun shopping for girl things before. Chris was great to be with. She didn't make you feel silly for not knowing something like what a train on a dress was.

Tiffany wondered briefly if that was the kind of thing she would have talked about with her mother if she'd lived. Probably it would have been. The thought made her shiver a little, but it was a good shiver, making her feel all quivery inside. Mother. She'd never thought of Chris as her mother, but it wasn't a bad idea, not a bad idea at all.

Chris liked her grandfather. All the ladies liked her grandfather. She wasn't so dumb or such a little kid that she didn't notice things like that. But the difference was that her grandpa liked Chris back.

And it wasn't as if old people didn't get married. In fact, it wasn't as if her grandpa was so old in the first place, not really. He was only seven years older than Lisa Wilhelm's father. And he was just the right age for her Big Sister.

It didn't occur to Tiffany as she watched Chris trying on dresses that if she told anyone her thoughts they might think it strange that she was setting up as matchmaker for her grandfather, rather than for her father. Tiffany didn't see it that way. She loved her father, but he was never there. She couldn't trust him to be around when she needed him. Her grandfather was always there for her when she was scared or mad or happy or sad. He never let her down, and she wanted to stay with him forever and ever. And if she could have Chris into the bargain she'd be the happiest girl in the world.

Chris did a lot of fussing about how expensive the prices were and where would she ever wear something like that again, but it really didn't take her very long to pick out a dress. It was very pretty, too, a soft, pearly gray with a long skirt that swirled around just above her ankles and a jacket that sparkled with beads just like the ones on Erika's gown.

"Mother, it's you," Erika said, clapping her hands.

She looked a whole lot more like herself, Tiffany observed, in the sweatshirt and jeans she'd put on after taking off the fairy princess wedding dress.

"Isn't she a knockout, Tiff?"

"You look so...elegant...." Tiffany said, coming up with a word she'd heard Erika use more than once.

Chris didn't look like herself anymore, either, in that dress. She looked . . . like a queen.

"It's a lovely dress, but so ex—" Chris never got a chance to finish the word.

"Mother, I only intend to get married once. Splurge a little."

"You do look lovely, Mrs. Baldwin. And the dress is just right for all those other special occasions."

The saleslady sounded so nicey-nice Tiffany wrinkled her nose. Why didn't she just tell Chris she looked great and let it go at that?

"It's a little too big in the shoulders," Chris said, frowning, but in a nice way.

You could tell she thought she looked pretty in the dress, too, Tiffany decided.

"We can take care of that in just a wink. I'll get my book and make you an appointment to try on the dress again just a few weeks ahead of the big day. That way if there's any change in your weight we can make adjustments then."

"Don't gain weight over the holidays, Mother. That dress looks fantastic just the way it is."

"The wedding isn't for almost five months. With my luck I'll probably gain forty or fifty pounds by then," Chris moaned as the saleslady helped her step out of the dress. "You know how I tend to gain weight when I can least afford to." She patted her hips as she smoothed her skirt down and finished buttoning her shirt.

"You look great, Mom. You know everyone thinks you're a lot younger than you are. Anyway, I'd hate it if you were like Michael's mom. She's skin and bones and looks a hundred years old, when I know for a fact she's only five years older than you are."

"Six," Chris corrected her.

"Meow," Erika replied, and they both laughed.

Tiffany wasn't really paying any attention to what they were saying. She'd seen something on a rack near the back wall. Dresses for little girls, a whole bunch of them, and one of them, one of them just called out to her. She reached up and lifted it down. It was pale purple, like flowers on the lilac tree in the yard outside their apartment in Chicago. It had a square collar trimmed with lace, short sleeves edged the same way and a full skirt topped off with a darker purple sash. "It's beautiful," she said as the alert saleslady lifted it down for her inspection.

"Try it on, Tiff. It's only a little after seven. We have time."

"Go ahead, Tiffany," Chris said, her reflection in the mirror smiling straight into Tiffany's dazzled eyes.

"It looks to be just your size," the saleslady said, gesturing toward the change rooms. "And best of all—" she added the clincher "—it's on sale."

CHAPTER EIGHT

"GRANDPA! Grandpa! Look at my dress!" Tiffany yelled even before she pulled open the front door of her grandfather's house. "Chris bought it for me."

Chris followed her into the house more slowly and with some reluctance to face Ethan Connor.

She wasn't sure how she was going to explain her purchase of the lilac dress for her Little Sister, either to him or to herself. She had violated one of her own cardinal rules for a successful Big/Little relationship: do not buy presents. She stressed that point to all her volunteers. A match needed to be based on friendship, caring and shared interests, not on the giving and the anticipation of receiving gifts.

Chris had written that directive herself, and believed in it wholeheartedly. Until today. Until she'd seen gawky, awkward, tomboy Tiffany transformed into a budding soon-to-be young woman before her eyes. There had been no power on earth, including her own good sense, that could have kept her from buying the dress.

Ethan had been sitting at his desk just inside the carved walnut archway that separated the foyer from the high-ceilinged living room. He stood up as Tiffany rushed across the foyer with her new dress, safely encased in a plastic bag, floating out behind her.

"See, Grandpa! Isn't it beautiful? Chris bought it for me to wear at Christmas and to Erika's wedding. She says it can be my birthday and my Christmas present from her and Keith and Erika. Isn't it beautiful?" she repeated, twirling around with the dress held in front of her.

"It is beautiful."

Ethan, however, wasn't looking at his granddaughter or her new dress. He was looking at Chris. It was hard to meet his gaze. The question she saw in his hazel eyes told her without words that he was thinking of her disregarded directive just as she had been moments earlier.

And coming, perhaps, to the same conclusion. Her feelings for Tiffany were going beyond the guidelines of a responsible match. More and more often she'd found herself reacting as a parent in day-to-day situations she'd encountered with the child. They had been, admittedly, minor instances, and she'd ignored the warning signals going off in her brain when they had occurred. After today she'd no longer be able to ignore those warnings.

Chris wanted to nurture and protect Tiffany Connor. She was beginning to care for the child in a way that went beyond friendship, that went beyond the parameters of the program and bordered on love.

Admitting that presented another difficulty. How inextricably bound up with her desire for Ethan were her feelings for Tiffany? Chris had never encountered such a situation in her work. While some of her matches produced lasting friendships between adult and child that occasionally carried over to include the child's parents, no one had confessed to falling in love with their Little Brother's or Sister's legal guardian!

She wasn't certain how to broach the matter to Annie Plotts, the caseworker assigned to oversee their match, when she and Tiffany were scheduled to meet with her for their quarterly evaluation, or even if she should bring up the subject at all.

"I'm going to try my dress on for you."

Tiffany had been rattling away at a tremendous rate and Chris realized she hadn't heard a thing the child had said. Ethan was helping her to slip the plastic cover from the dress and take it off the padded hanger.

As Tiffany rushed to the stairs with her prize, she met her father coming down. "Daddy, did you hear? See my new dress. Chris bought it for me."

She stopped on the second step from the bottom, looking up into her father's face. Chris looked at him, also, and her heart sank. Tiffany's father, if not her grandfather, objected to the gift. She could see it in the tight set of his jaw, the narrowness of his eyes, blue eyes, not hazel like Ethan's. She could see all the uncertainty he felt about his position in Tiffany's life, the hurt pride and stubbornness of the young and sometimes foolish. She knew what Jeff Connor was going to say before he spoke.

"I think a dress like this is much too expensive a gift to accept from Mrs. Baldwin, Tiffany." His voice was gentle, but firm.

Ethan took a step forward. "Jeff," he began.

But his son cut him short. The look he gave his father was not gentle, but filled with grievances, both old and new. "I didn't have anything to say about your enrolling Tiffany in this program, Dad. I do have something to say about what gifts she does and doesn't accept. If she needs a new dress, I'll buy it for her."

"I certainly didn't mean to insult you, Jeff," Chris said stiffly, moving back a step as Tiffany and her father descended the staircase.

"You didn't insult anyone. At least not anyone with half a brain," Ethan said. There was anger in his voice, in the tense set of his jaw and stiff shoulders, but it was anger held firmly in check for Tiffany's sake.

The little girl was watching both men anxiously, her dark, troubled eyes going from one face to the other as she chewed on her lower lip.

"Is that my lesson in remedial parenting for today, Dad? Learn to accept gifts from a stranger with grace and poise?" Jeff bowed mockingly in Chris's direction. "Thank you, ma'am, but I'm afraid we can't accept your too generous gift."

"Daddy?" The irony in his voice may have been lost on Tiffany, but not the meaning of his words. "Don't make me give back the dress. I'm going to wear it to our Bigs and Littles Christmas party and to Erika's wedding in the spring. I'm going to hold a basket with long colored ribbons and pass out little packages of birdseed for the guests to throw at Michael and Erika when they come out of the church. Pastor Willman doesn't like you to throw rice. It's too hard to clean off the church steps," she added ingenuously, repeating what Erika had told her earlier. "Don't make me give it back."

"Jeff, don't be a fool. Can't you see how badly Tiffany wants the dress? Chris is her friend. She wanted to give the child a gift she would enjoy, that's all."

"The dress was a very good buy, Jeff," Chris said quietly and evenly, although she was shaking inside.

The last thing she'd imagined, despite her own self-doubts about the suitability of the gift, was that Tiffany's father would refuse to allow her to accept it.

"It was fifty percent off," Tiffany announced solemnly, clutching the dress to her chest. "I'll get a lot of use out of it, won't I, Grandpa?"

Appealing to her grandfather seemed only to harden her father's opposition. Chris began to wonder what kind of antagonism existed between the two men, what old problems were resurfacing now that they were living under the same roof.

"I'll buy you another dress just as nice as this one," Jeff offered with a smile.

But his eyes were still angry and Tiffany saw that. She only shook her head and held the dress more tightly. "I want this one. There aren't any others just as nice."

"Jeff, for once think before you act," Ethan said, quietly but with a thread of steel in his words. "Don't take your hostility toward me and Chris out on Tiffany."

"She's my daughter. I can provide for her."

"I know that." Ethan sounded more weary than angry this time. "But she's under my guardianship, remember. Chris is her very special friend. The only feminine role model in her life since her mother died. I have no intention of forcing Tiffany to return a gift given in the spirit of that special friendship, and if you care for her one-tenth as much as you claim to, you won't, either."

Chris was grateful for his words. *A token* of their special friendship. That's what she had meant to show by buying the dress for Tiffany. They had been paired for almost three months. Their relationship was stable and growing stronger with each passing week. She didn't need to berate herself endlessly for wanting to give her Little Sister a gift. But she had been wrong to do so without permission.

"I'm sorry my buying Tiffany the dress has upset you, Jeff. I won't buy any more gifts for her in the future without consulting you first. That was my error, but don't punish Tiffany by refusing to let her keep the dress."

"There's no need to apologize," Jeff said, sounding less belligerent but still wary.

Then he smiled—the same marvelous smile Ethan possessed. Chris understood now, a little, why he probably had gotten his way all his life.

"I'm touchy about the kids. It's been a rough couple of years for all of us," Jeff said.

"Of course," she said, not really in sympathy with him but determined not to let it show.

"I want to be able to give them the best of everything, but until I get settled in and line up some work, I can't."

"We all want the best for our children." Chris pushed her hands into the pockets of her coat. What else could she say? Should she say? Jeff Connor looked spoiled and immature despite his twenty-eight years. She could see why Ethan didn't believe his son should have the care of the children.

"And the best thing for me right now is to see Tiffany model her new dress." He smiled down at his daughter with what appeared to be genuine, if casual, affection.

"Will you wait for me, Chris?" Tiffany paused with one sneakered foot on the bottom step.

"I'd like to, Tiffany, but remember, I know how nice you look in the dress and it's getting late. I have to go over the draft for next year's budget proposal before I go to bed tonight, so I think I'll say goodbye right now."

"Okay," Tiffany said, trying not to pout. "I'll see you next week, won't I?"

Chris refused to glance at Tiffany's father for permission. "Wild horses couldn't keep me away. We'll plan the refreshments for our Big and Little Christmas party next month, okay?"

"Great." She started up the stairs. "Come on, Daddy. Are the little kids asleep already? I want them to see me in my dress, too." She looked back over her shoulder. "Are you coming, Grandpa?"

"In a few minutes. I'll walk Chris to her car."

Tiffany's father looked back over his shoulder, also, but said nothing.

"You don't have to escort me to the car, Ethan. I'm parked directly in front of the house." Her words were a polite fiction. She wanted to be with him, alone, even if for only a few minutes, even if it meant standing in full view of anyone in Bonaparte who cared to drive past his house.

Ethan didn't answer, just grabbed a jacket from the oak halltree and held the beveled glass door open for her. She was apologizing again before it had closed behind them.

"Oh, Ethan. I'm so sorry I caused an argument between you and your son. And that Tiffany had to be a witness. I shouldn't have bought the dress. I broke my own rule...."

"Chris, stop. You aren't responsible for Jeff's bad manners or the problems between us."

"I'm sorry there are problems."

"It isn't something that happened overnight. Jeff's as bullheaded as—"

"As his father?" she asked with a smile.

How lovely she looked in the pale November moonlight filtering down through the branches of the leafless maples bordering the street. It was cold, with the smell of snow in the air, but he didn't care except to note the bright spots of color it had brought to her cheeks and the tip of her nose. It had been almost a month since he'd kissed her along the riverbank and that was a month too long.

"Yes." He walked past her to keep from reaching out and taking her in his arms. He lifted his arm and rested it high above his head on one of the round white pillars that supported the porch roof. His fingers automatically curved themselves into a fist. With his other hand he began to massage the stiff muscles at the back of his neck. He was tired, more tired than he could ever remember being in his life. On days like this, when there were problems at the plant and confrontations with his son at home, he felt every day of his forty-eight years. "His mother and I both spoiled him when he was little and then we fought over him when the marriage went sour. It's no wonder he turned out the way he did."

"He'll grow up someday. Everyone has to sooner or later."

"He's not eighteen, Chris," Ethan said wearily. "He's twenty-eight years old. He's the father of three children. It's time he realized that, accepted his responsibility for them and settled down to raise them right. Or get out of their lives."

"Ethan, I know this is a difficult time for you."

She spoke slowly, choosing her words carefully. She was such a restful woman, Ethan thought, listening to her tone of voice as much as her words. Restful and desirable, which, he supposed, was something of a contradiction in terms. "You have every right to be concerned for the children's future."

"You're sure as hell right I do. I don't want them jerked back and forth in a tug-of-war the way Jeff was between his mother and me. But I won't give them up just to have him take off again and desert them the way he did after Katherine died. Tiffany still has nightmares about being taken to the shelter and separated from her brother and sister."

"You can't know for certain that he would do such a thing again."

"I can't trust him not to." Ethan rested his forehead on his fist for a brief moment. "He's decided to stay in Bonaparte. Permanently, he says. I'm not sure I want that. I'm certainly not ready to give the children back to him. Not till he's proven he's capable of caring for them."

"You don't sound as if you believe that will be soon."

"Do you want to know the God's honest truth?" He didn't look at her. He'd never told another human being what he was going to say.

"Yes."

"I don't think my son will ever be a stable, committed parent. I don't think he has it in him, and I wonder every day of my life if it's my fault."

"It's not your fault." Chris's voice was strong and firm, completely assured. "No one who's seen you with Tiffany and Ashley and Brandon could believe that."

"We learn from our mistakes."

"Then perhaps Jeff will, too."

Ethan swung around. Chris was standing just behind him, only a few feet away. "I wish I could believe that." He could smell the faint essence of her perfume or her shampoo, he wasn't sure which. She'd stuck her hands in her coat pockets and hunched her shoulders against the chill night air. Her coat was a rich tobacco brown that made her hair glow with the warmth of beaten gold in the stray moonbeams that found their way onto the porch. She was biting her lower lip thoughtfully as she considered just how much advice to give him.

Ethan didn't want her advice, not now. At this particular moment in time he wanted Chris herself with a fierce aching need that he hadn't experienced in a dozen years.

"Let's not talk about my son or my grandchildren anymore."

"But Tiffany..." She looked up at him, her brown eyes dark with concern, and something more, some emotion less easily described. "The dress caused..."

"Hush." He held out his hand. "The dress was a lovely gesture, nothing more."

"I want to believe that. I'm always so sure of myself when my volunteers and the kids come to me with problems in their matches. But when it comes to my own with Tiffany..." She stepped closer, letting him take her in his arms. "I'm confused. I want to do what's right for her, you know that."

"I've never doubted it for a moment. When Jeff cools down he'll realize that, too."

"I hope so. I—"

He silenced her with a kiss. He'd meant it to be light and friendly. It wasn't. The instant his mouth touched hers it was spontaneous combustion. He pulled her into the saddle of his hips as he leaned back against the pillar behind him. Her lips tasted warm and sweet, the inside of her mouth was molten honey.

God, the things she did to him made him think he could take on the world, solve all his problems in the blink of an eye. She curled her arms around his neck, pressed herself tight against him, kissed him back until his blood pounded through his brain and his head whirled. The world could end and he wouldn't care as long as she went on kissing him, pressing close, moaning softly in the back of her throat.

"God, you're sweet," he said, tasting her lips, the curve of her chin, the velvety softness of her eyelids. "I want you. All of you, not just bits and pieces, not just stolen kisses and public embraces."

"Don't talk," Chris whispered. Her voice was husky, her hands eloquent of her desire as they roamed across his back, beneath the heavy wool of his jacket. "Just kiss me. I need you to kiss me. I need to remember how it feels."

He was more than willing to oblige her. Their lips met and held. He let his hands smooth over her back and hips, shape her waist, glide upward to cup her breasts beneath her open coat. He molded their firm softness with the palms of his hands and wanted more, to touch her naked skin, to feel her beneath him, to sheath himself in her softness and heat.

"Ethan, please."

Chris broke off the kiss so abruptly he was stunned. He searched her face for signs of anger or distress, but found none. Her eyes were round with wonder, her lips parted, swollen from his kiss. She was smiling slightly, a marvelously beautiful, feminine smile that made him want to drag her back into his arms and start kissing her all over again.

"No," she said, reading his mind. She lifted her fingers to his lips. "I'm not ready... for this." She let her fingers trace lightly along the line of his jaw. "I don't often... Actually, I never get carried away like this. It's a little frightening, the way I feel when I'm with you. If we don't stop I have no doubt in the world we'll end up..."

"Where?" Ethan chuckled, trying hard to control the rapid, almost painful gallop of his heartbeat. "In bed?"

"Nothing so refined," she said, taking a deep breath, laying her head against his chest. "We'll end up right here on the front porch of your house."

"Or rolling around in the yard," he said, helping to defuse the sexual tension that sparkled and fizzed between them like champagne. Their relationship was volatile and complicated. He had to move slowly or he'd frighten her away, and that was the last thing he wanted.

"Or camped out in the back seat of my car. Ethan, I don't conduct myself that way." She was very serious all of a sudden.

"I never for a moment thought you did. I've never been into one-night stands myself."

"We're going to have to move very slowly, for Tiffany's sake, as well as our own."

"I know." He slipped his hands around her neck and pulled her close once again. "For now, this will have to be enough. I have as many demands on my time as you do. We're both mature adults. We can wait for our time together." His palms caressed the slender column of her throat as he spoke. Her hair lay across the back of his hands like silk. Her skin was soft as satin and her breasts brushed against his chest with each breath she took. "We can wait." He repeated the words to convince himself as much as her.

Chris took a deep shuddering breath. "I'm not so sure about that." She reached up and framed his face with her hands. "I'm not so sure." She tugged gently, insistently, and he lowered his head to kiss her just once more.

Suddenly the porch light blazed on overhead like a sixty-watt sun. The front door flew open and Tiffany catapulted onto the porch. She was wearing her new dress and a pair of Nikes. Her father was standing just behind her, a look of surprise on his face. Her brown eyes grew round as saucers.

"Grandpa! What in the world are you doing kissing Chris?"

TIFFANY HUGGED her knees to her chest. She pulled her nightgown down and tucked it under her toes. It was cold in her room tonight. The moon was sliding in and out behind the clouds. Her grandpa said it might snow tomorrow or the next day. She wished it would. She liked to play in the snow and it would make it seem as if Christmas was coming faster.

But watching the first snowflakes of the season wasn't the reason she was still awake so late at night. She was worried. She didn't like her grandfather and her father arguing over things. She didn't like her father being mad at Chris for buying her a present. She didn't even know for sure whether she liked the idea of Chris kissing her grandpa on the front porch.

Maybe that would make her dad madder still and he would try to take them away from Bonaparte. She didn't want to leave her new friends at school and especially not her Big Sister . . . and her grandfather.

Why did everything have to be so complicated? she wondered, resting her chin on her knees. Why did her dad have to keep wanting to go away all the time? Why couldn't he just like to stay in one place with people he loved the way she did?

Why?

That was the reason she couldn't sleep. Because she'd figured out that answering questions that started with that one little three-letter word was the hardest thing there was in the world. It was harder than the nine-times multiplication table and harder than long division because it just kept coming back. Even if you finally got the answer to one hard why question, there was always another one to take its place.

CHAPTER NINE

THE STRAINS of a familiar Christmas song wafted by on the sea breeze as a carload of holiday revelers drove past. Ethan leaned down and picked up a battered conch shell from the sand and threw it into the surf. His Christmas spirit was conspicuous by its absence. He glanced at his watch, narrowing his eyes against the bright Florida sun. Jeff and the kids had been gone almost thirty minutes. He wondered if he should go after them. It was a long walk to the ice-cream stand and Brandon had been tired before they'd started.

This wasn't the way he'd envisioned spending the holidays, visiting his dead daughter-in-law's family along the Gulf Coast. But he felt he owed it to his grandchildren to give them this chance to learn to know their mother's relatives. And he didn't want Jeff taking them to Florida alone.

He couldn't say that their precarious father/son relationship had deteriorated in the two months Jeff had been back in his life, but it wasn't getting any better. Jeff talked about settling down for good, about starting his own business, about looking for a place of his own big enough for the kids. But he never did anything about it and the uncertainty about their future was beginning to take its toll on Tiffany's fragile new serenity. If it wasn't for Chris Baldwin's continuing steadying influence, Ethan was afraid his granddaughter would regress into the timid nervous creature he'd rescued from the children's shelter just over a year ago. He'd give his life, if need be, to see that never happened.

It was the primary reason he'd accompanied Jeff and the kids to Florida. The other was simple economics. There was no way his son could afford to give his children a visit to their Fielding cousins and grandparents.

Ethan started walking along the beach in the direction of the ice-cream stand. The dazzling white sand stretched out ahead of him like sugar spilled from a sack. It wasn't hot along the Gulf Coast, but comfortably warm, and the kids were enjoying the sunny weather. The entire month of December in Bonaparte had been cold and wet, sometimes sleeting and sometimes snowing, but always cloudy. Everyone said they were lucky to get away.

And he understood the need for Katherine's aging parents to spend time with their grandchildren. He wanted them, in turn, to see that he was doing his best to make sure Tiffany and her brother and sister were never hurt again as they'd been hurt in the past.

Across the road from the beach a store window was decorated with fake snowmen and red-nosed reindeer, while mannequins, up to their ankles in confetti snow, modeled the very latest in abbreviated swim wear. Everywhere he looked palm trees sported strings of red and green lights. It was garish and disorienting, but no one seemed to notice, or care, except him. He was learning how depressing it could be to spend Christmas away from friends and loved ones, familiar surroundings, family traditions. His widowed mother lived in Arizona. Each year she traveled to

Ethan's sister's home in Tennessee. All the members of his scattered family that could get there did. He hadn't realized how much he had been looking forward to being there himself, to taking the children sledding in the mountains, to arguing politics good-naturedly with his slow-talking, slow-moving brother-in-law, until he'd had to cancel the trip.

He also hadn't realized how much he was going to miss Chris Baldwin.

Ethan spotted Jeff and the kids walking toward him in the hard sand along the water's edge. They made quite a procession. Tiffany was dragging a protesting Ashley by the hand and Jeff was wearing a scowl and carrying Brandon in his arms. Even from as far away as he was, Ethan could see chocolate ice cream smeared across his grandson's face, dripping off the cone and down the front of Jeff's white shirt, as well as the little boy's. Ashley was crying, loudly and insistently, for them to go back. Her cone was empty, and from the way she kept looking back over her shoulder, Ethan surmised her ice cream was lying behind her on the sand. Tiffany was stomping along with her too-old, mother-hen frown on her face. Ethan's heart sank. Even this ordinary routine outing for ice cream with their father seemed to have gone awry.

"What happened, sweetheart?" he asked as Tiffany broke rank and rushed up to him, eager to air her grievances.

"Everything," she said succinctly. "It was a disaster." She scuffed her flip-flop in the sand, making a depression that filled with water even before the others arrived.

"What happened?" Ethan rose from his kneeling position, feeling exasperated at, and sorry for, his son at the same time. Jeff looked as though he was just about at the end of his rope. His face was red from sunburn and embarrassment. His shirt was ruined and he didn't seem to know what to do next.

"Tiffany's right. Everything happened. It was too long a walk. I let Brandon have chocolate when both the girls told me he'd make a mess. Ashley insisted on skipping along the sand and almost stepped on a horseshoe crab that had crawled up out of the water...."

"It was awful. Ugly. I hate it," Ashley said with a fresh bout of tears. "My ice cream fell in the sand and Daddy won't get me another one." She finished the litany of complaints with a hiccupping sob.

"I tried to give her my cone," Tiffany said self-righteously, "but she wouldn't take it."

"I want pink bubblegum ice cream," Ashley wailed, rubbing her eyes with her fists. "Not that stuff you had." She was still holding her empty sugar cone.

"Good Lord, Ashley, stop bellowing. Dad, what should I do?"

Ethan looked at his son. Jeff really didn't know how to deal with his overtired, crying children. Had Katherine had to deal with three babies completely on her own? Would Jeff ever learn anything about parenting?

"Let's get them cleaned up." Ethan pointed to the rental car in the parking lot just behind him. He reached into the pocket of his shorts and gave Jeff the keys. "Get one of the beach towels or something out of the beach bag. There's a clean shirt for Brandon in there, too. Give him to me and we'll wait for you here. When everyone's tidied up and we've got the sand out of our shoes, we'll go back to the motel. It's almost four."

"Damn, I forgot we're supposed to go to that church program with Katy's family tonight. What if this bunch is still whining and crying by then?"

"They won't be," Ethan said patiently as he took Brandon's soggy sugar cone and tossed it into the water to be instantly dive-bombed by a couple of hungry gulls. There was no point in making an issue out of Jeff's lack of foresight in walking the children so far on a warm afternoon when it was going to be a long, tiring evening for them. It wouldn't have occurred to Jeff even if he had bothered trying to think that far ahead. "Everyone is going to take a nap before we leave for the church."

"I'm too old for naps—" Tiffany began.

But Ethan cut short her automatic protest. "Anyone who doesn't take a nap this afternoon doesn't go to Disney World tomorrow. End of discussion." The world-famous amusement complex was about a two-hour drive from the Fielding home. Tickets for his three grandchildren and their cousins were a treat provided by Katherine's parents. Mickey Mouse and Donald Duck, Space Mountain and the Magic Kingdom. Ethan shook his head. It would be a very different way to spend Christmas Eve day.

"Okay," Tiffany capitulated. She scuffed her flip-flop deeper into the sand. "It's sure hard having to do everything with babies." She stuck out her tongue at Ashley, who only started sobbing again.

"Tiffany, go along and help your father." The only way to stop this kind of incipient anarchy was to nip it in the bud. Ethan sat Brandon down where the very edge of the waves from the Gulf could curl over his toes. Immediately he plunged the child's sticky hands into the water, which kept him from ruining Ethan's shirt the way he'd ruined Jeff's.

"Grandpa, what if something crawls out of the water and bites him," Ashley sobbed, obviously remembering her fright over the ugly but harmless horseshoe crab.

"Nothing's going to bite him. Don't you want to wade a little before we leave. We probably won't have time to come back to the beach again while we're here."

"No." She shook her head violently. "I don't like to swim anywhere that I can't see the bottom. I like Grandma Fielding's swimming pool." She put her arms around Ethan's neck, still teary eyed, and the disaster he'd just avoided with Brandon's chocolate-covered fingers occurred instead with pink bubblegum.

"Go," Ethan ordered his smiling son, who was watching the proceedings. "And let this be a lesson to you." He frowned down at the pink stain on his gray shirt but didn't loosen Ashley's clutching fingers as she climbed up on his knee. "Vanilla only. And set them down somewhere to eat."

"You're good at this business, Dad." The smile left Jeff's face. He looked thoughtful. "You were good at it when I was a little kid, too."

Ethan glanced up at his son. "I tried to be." He ducked as Brandon splashed water all over them.

Ashley immediately began to howl at the unexpected wetting.

"I see that. Now."

"I'm glad."

"Grandpa, make him stop," Ashley wailed, burying her face in the curve of Ethan's shoulder. "The water's cold!"

"I'm going," Jeff said. The fragile moment of rapport washed away with the next receding wave. He turned and headed for the car at a trot, Tiffany at his heels.

Running away again. Ethan cradled Ashley in his arms, protecting her from another deluge of cold salt water as he ordered Brandon to stop splashing and wished for the hundredth time that day alone that he was back in Bonaparte.

"HAS IT STARTED to snow yet?" Lena Foster asked, poking her head inside Chris's office door.

Chris turned away from the window, her arms folded under her breasts. She shook her head. "It's still raining. And the weather report on the radio a few minutes ago said it isn't going to get below freezing. I'm afraid we aren't going to have a white Christmas after all."

"Keeping Christmas is in your heart," Lena said, coming all the way into Chris's office. "So I guess sleigh bells and snowball fights and sledding on the riverbank can be there, too, this year."

"At least you won't have to get out and shovel the walk before your guests arrive for Christmas dinner tomorrow," Chris said, smiling, although her smile felt a little frayed around the edges. This Christmas was going to be different. She could feel it in her bones—and in her heart, as well.

"Is there anything else you want me to do this afternoon?" Lena asked, dropping into one of the matching low-backed chairs in front of Chris's desk.

Lena's hair was sticking out in tufts of curls all over her head, just as it usually did, but there seemed to be more gray threaded among the red than there'd been the last time Chris had noticed. Lena was eight years older than Chris, fifty on her next birthday. Life was passing too quickly, Chris decided. Or was it just that she noticed such things more during the holidays, at the end of another year?

"No. What isn't finished can wait. What do you say we call it a day a little early?"

Lena gave a sigh of relief. "I was hoping you'd say that. I have a thousand things to do today before Lumpy's family descends on us full force tomorrow." Lena's husband had eight brothers and sisters, all of whom lived within a fifty-mile radius of Bonaparte. Lena's big old frame house on Elm Street was the only residence capable of containing all of them.

"Then let's close up shop." Chris walked the few steps to her desk and bent to open the top drawer. She took out a small, gaily wrapped package. "Merry Christmas, Lena."

"Chris! We swore not to exchange presents this year," Lena said, her plump face puckering into a frown. "I don't have anything for you."

"I don't want anything. But I couldn't resist picking this up for you when I saw it in Tiedtke's last week." Lena was busy opening the package, still clucking disapproval at Chris's underhanded tactics.

"Oh, Chris, it's lovely." She held up the small porcelain figurine of a bluebird. "How did you know I've wanted one for my collection ever since we spotted a pair of them in the backyard last spring?"

"It could be because you've mentioned it at least a dozen times since then."

"Thank you very much. I'll treasure it. And it might be too late for me to buy you something for Christmas, but just remember, as far as I'm concerned, your birthday is fair game."

"Don't even mention it," Chris said with mock horror. "It's less than three months away."

"I know," Lena said smugly, but her face as she examined her bluebird was full of joy. "I hope I can find something for you just as special."

"Hey, Mom, is there anything you need from the Wal-Mart store?" Keith was talking even before the door to the corridor closed behind him, or before Chris and Lena could see his face for that matter. He walked into the office and dropped into the chair beside Lena.

"I don't think so," Chris said, sweeping a stack of papers off her desk and putting them in a drawer. "I think everything is ready for tomorrow." She let her mind race through a mental list of tasks that she needed to complete before her family arrived after church services the next day. "What have you forgotten?"

"They're having a last-minute sale on Bart Simpson dolls. Tiffany's flipped out over the little guy... and well, you know she brought that Detroit Lions poster by for me before she left for Florida. I sorta... since they won't be back from Florida... you know." He looked uncomfortable, as if he wished he'd kept his mouth shut.

"She'll like that very much. Bart Simpson is her hero."

"Cowabunga, dude," Keith said, imitating Tiffany imitating the animated character's favorite saying. "She's an okay little kid."

"You're an okay big kid." She smiled at the faint wash of dark red that colored his neck and ears. "Actually, Lena and I just decided to call it a day. Will you be home by six? If we eat dinner a little early, we'll have time to open our gifts before candlelight services start at eight."

"Okay. But then I'm going over to Terri's to give her her gift. Is that okay?" Terri was Keith's latest girlfriend.

"Of course. Michael and Erika are leaving after church to go to his parents. They have midnight services, so it will work out well."

"Great. Got it all planned down to the minute just like usual. You never let Christmas get out of control, Mom. You ought to work for the government. Maybe this country wouldn't be in such bad shape if you did."

"Get out of here," Chris said, laughing. "And drive carefully. Everyone will be in a hurry and it's raining harder by the minute."

"Not to worry. 'Bye, Mrs. Foster. Merry Christmas."

"Merry Christmas, Keith." The corridor door slammed shut behind him. Lena stood up, holding her bluebird in one hand and the empty box, wrapping and ribbon in the other. "Sounds like your Christmas Eve is going to be busy." She began walking toward the door.

"For a little while," Chris said thoughtfully. "Then it will be very quiet." And she would be very much alone. Funny, even after Jack had died she'd never thought about being alone at Christmas, until this year. Until she realized her children were growing more independent, making commitments on their own. Before, if she'd thought about it at all, she'd assumed she and Jack would grow old together, sharing a glass of wine in front of the fireplace in the family room, watching the lights sparkle on the tree, someday putting together all the intricate, expensive, batteries-not-included toys that grandparents always buy for their grandchildren. She'd never thought about being alone.

And even now, twilight on a dreary, cold Christmas Eve, she still wasn't thinking of being alone. She was thinking of Ethan Connor and his grandchildren. She doubted any teenage girl in the throes of her first love could spend any more time mooning over the object of her affections than Chris did thinking about Ethan since he'd gone to Florida. And Tiffany. She missed her just as badly. She'd kept her promise to herself and didn't buy Tiffany another present, but she hoped her Little Sister remembered her when she wore the lilac dress on Christmas Day.

"I'm leaving." Lena appeared in the doorway, putting on her coat as she spoke. "Thanks again for the gift and have a very merry Christmas. I'll see you bright and early on Friday."

"Merry Christmas, Lena. You go on. I'll lock up. I have a few more things to file before I leave."

"You're sure you don't need help?"

"Positive. Go, before the supermarket closes and you don't have something absolutely vital for dinner tomorrow."

"Oh, dear, you're right. I have a list a mile long." Having reminded herself how many tasks she still had to accomplish, Lena sailed out the door.

Down the hall Chris could hear the faint sounds of revelry as the courthouse employees' party in the county auditor's office got into full swing. She would be welcome to join them. She didn't. Instead, she sat down at her desk, leaned back in her chair and watched the rain fall as the winter afternoon turned to dusk.

The phone rang at her elbow and she almost didn't pick it up. It was four-thirty-five on Christmas Eve. Who could possibly want to transact business now? But Chris had never been able to ignore a ringing phone.

"Big Brothers/Big Sisters of Hobart County. Mrs. Baldwin speaking."

"Chris?"

Tiffany's voice sounded as if she were only across the room and not twelve hundred miles away.

"It's Tiffany. Grandpa said I could call and wish you a Merry Christmas."

"Merry Christmas to you, Tiffany. It's so good to hear your voice." Chris smiled without even realizing it. "I was just getting ready to leave the office. I'm so glad I didn't miss your call."

"We would have tried you at home next," Tiffany said. "Grandpa said I could keep trying till we got through to you. Is it snowing?" she asked before Chris could reply to her first statement.

"It's raining. We're not going to have a White Christmas—only a wet one."

"It's nice here," Tiffany informed her. "We went to Disney World today, but Ashley got sick on the Teacup ride and barfed all over my dad. We had to come home early. I didn't get to ride Space Mountain."

"Oh, dear," Chris said, hoping her smile didn't communicate itself in her voice. "I hope Ashley's feeling better now."

"She's taking a nap. Both the little kids are. We're going to my Grandma Fielding's to eat dinner and open presents. I wish we were home."

"But you're very lucky to be spending Christmas in Florida. Just think how many people would love to change places with you."

"I know," Tiffany said, but there was a decided lack of spirit in her voice. "I just miss all of you."

"We miss you, too, but you'll be home in only a few more days. In the meantime you should be enjoying the sun and warm weather."

"We went to the beach and hunted for shark teeth," Tiffany said, her tone brightening once again. "I found six!"

"Big ones?" Chris asked, settling back in her chair, unaware until that moment just how very much she had missed her Little Sister.

"No. But I told my cousin, Sam Fielding, to buy me a real shark's jaw for my Christmas present. They have them all over down here."

"I don't think you'll need to worry about getting duplicates of such a unique gift."

"I'm going to take it to show-and-tell when I go back to school."

"You'll be the envy of all your classmates."

"I know."

Tiffany sounded very pleased with herself.

"Wait a minute, Chris."

There were rustling sounds on the wire as Tiffany put her hand over the receiver. Chris could hear her muffled voice protesting even through the barrier.

"Chris?"

"I'm still here."

"Grandpa says I have to tell you goodbye. He says thousands of other people want to use the telephone to say Merry Christmas to their friends."

"That's true." Chris found herself reluctant to end the conversation.

"I figured it was. Grandpa usually knows what he's talking about."

Another muffled exchange took place between Tiffany and her grandfather. Chris waited patiently, her lips curving into a smile.

"Chris?"

The voice wasn't Tiffany's. It was masculine, rich and full. Chris's heart began to beat a little faster. She tightened her grip on the phone.

"Ethan?"

"Yes."

"Merry Christmas."

"Merry Christmas."

"How...how are you getting along down there?" She was having trouble coordinating her thoughts and the beating of her heart. She couldn't think of anything to say, could only remember the touch of his mouth on hers, the feel of his hand on her breast. Her breath quickened and her pulse began to race.

"The weather's great." He could see her if he shut his eyes, almost feel the satiny softness of her skin, smell the fresh flowery scent of her hair.

"Tiffany says you've been to the beach." He probably looked great in swim trunks with those broad shoulders, flat belly and long strong legs.

"Yes. And to Disney World." God, how he wished he could have Chris by his side to watch the sunsets over the Gulf, to spend the cool tropical winter night in his arms, to greet the sunrise with their lovemaking.

There was a short pause as both of them confronted their thoughts. Over the long-distance wire ghostly sounds, voices, snatches of conversation so distant they were felt as much as heard whispered in Chris's ear. She took a deep breath, tried to think rationally. "I miss you," she said before she could censor her thoughts. "I wish you were here."

"My sentiments exactly," Ethan said in a perfectly ordinary voice because he wasn't alone.

There was another disruption on Ethan's end of the line. "Tell her—" Chris could hear Tiffany's excited voice in the background "—that I'm going to look for a shark's jaw for Keith before we come home. Maybe they'll have them marked down for an after-Christmas sale."

"Did you hear that?" Ethan asked.

Ethan might be able to hide his smile from Tiffany, but he couldn't hide the amusement Chris heard in his voice. He loved his grandchildren so very much. He was a good man, a good parent. Chris wished she knew what was best for all of them.

"That child is a born bargain hunter," she said, letting a smile in her voice hide the uncertainty in her heart.

"Are you sure it's not a trait she acquired from her Big Sister?" Chris laughed out loud, and Ethan felt such a strong jolt of longing to be with her that it nearly took his breath away. He loved her; he wanted her for his wife. And soon. Very soon.

"Not guilty. At the risk of sounding like a throwback and a traitor to my sex, I think it's in the genes.

Oh, dear," she said, dismayed, "someone's knocking at my door. I think the courthouse employees' party has spilled over into the hallway and is threatening momentarily to invade my office."

"I'd better let you go." It was the last thing he wanted to do. He would talk all night if he could keep on hearing her voice.

"Yes." Don't hang up, she silently implored him. She would talk all night if she could keep hearing the sound of his voice.

"I'm sure you have plans." Next year they would spend Christmas together if he had to move heaven and earth to make it happen.

"Certainly," She laughed infectiously. "My family frowns on too much spontaneity at Christmastime. We have the next thirty-six hours planned down to the minute."

Ethan chuckled, and Chris was happy her little joke had pleased him.

"Somehow that's not surprising. I'd better let you go. Goodbye, Chris." He didn't say "I love you." Not out loud, not yet.

"Goodbye, Ethan. Merry Christmas." She didn't say "I'm falling in love with you." Not out loud, not yet.

CHAPTER TEN

"THIS IS WHERE my dad came in dressed like a clown," Tiffany explained, pushing a color snapshot of her ninth birthday party within six inches of Chris's nose.

They were curled up on the sofa in Chris's family room, afghans spread over their knees as they watched the fire dance in the grate and listened to the frigid February wind rattle the windowpanes. The house was quiet, no TV or radio. Keith was at basketball practice and Erika was visiting Michael's parents. In the weeks following the holiday rush, Chris and Tiffany had enjoyed several such quiet evenings.

"You know, I didn't even recognize him at first, his costume was so good. He had a big red nose and a horn that he tooted for yes and no instead of talking and he walked real funny." She giggled. "It was great. He's a radical clown. He can juggle balls and everything. Here's a picture of him doing that. See?" she said, proudly handing Chris another photograph from the envelope she was holding.

"Very impressive," Chris agreed with a smile. "It looks like it was a fantastic party. Who took all the pictures?" She didn't need to ask; she knew already, but she was becoming obsessed with the need to talk about Ethan, to learn even the small everyday details of his life.

"Grandpa," Tiffany confirmed, handing her another half-dozen shots of ten small girls playing traditional birthday games—the same games Erika had played at her ninth birthday party—of happy faces watching Tiffany open her presents, of small hands clapping as she blew out the candles on her cake. "I wish you had come to the party. I wish you could have seen everything for real, not just in pictures."

It wasn't the first time Chris had heard that particular lament this cold, snowy Wednesday. "I'm sorry to have missed the party—you know that. But I had to attend that seminar in Detroit. It's part of my job. I explained all that to you before I left, remember?"

Tiffany nodded a little sullenly. It had been the first time Chris had been unable to keep one of her promises to the child and she'd felt badly about missing her Little Sister's birthday party, but there was no help for it.

"I know all about loyalty and responsibility," Tiffany said grudgingly. "Grandpa told me about them. It's why he has to spend so much time at that stupid plant trying to get all the new stuff to work just right."

She twisted around on the cushion and looked at Chris. Her expression was earnest as she concentrated on trying to explain her thoughts.

"Grandpa's worked for Castleton Soups for twenty years and he owes them the best work he can do. That's the loyalty part."

Chris nodded, encouraging without words.

"It's his job to see that the plant gets fixed up and that it runs good. That's what he gets paid for. That's the responsibility part, right?" She tilted her head and smiled up at Chris.

"I think you understand the meaning of the words very well, Tiffany," Chris said with a smile of her own. "But sometimes the hardest part of understanding is trying to live up to those meanings."

"Especially when you want to do something else. Like go to your very own Little Sister's birthday party," she said slyly.

Chris laughed aloud; she couldn't help herself. "Exactly."

Tiffany's smile disappeared and a frown pulled her straight black eyebrows together. "Responsibility isn't much fun, is it?"

Chris chose her words carefully. "Sometimes, no, it isn't. Why do you ask?" Something was bothering her Little Sister and Chris had an idea she knew what it was.

Tiffany looked down at the photographs in her hand, her lower lip caught between her teeth. "And loyalty means having to do things sometimes that you don't want to do, because you gave your word."

"Yes, I suppose that's one way to look at it." Chris leaned forward and put her arm around Tiffany's shoulder. The little girl didn't pull away, but laid her head on Chris's shoulder.

"Taking care of me and Brandon and Ashley isn't much fun, I guess. Maybe that's why it's so hard for my dad to stay with us all the time."

Chris's heart clenched painfully in her chest. It hurt her very much to hear the forlorn note of longing in Tiffany's voice. She wanted this child to be happy, safe and cared for, confident and eager to meet life's challenges. She'd do anything to keep her from being hurt, anything. The vehemence of her emotions startled Chris. When had she started to feel like Tiffany's mother and not just her Big Sister? Was it too late to turn back emotionally? She was very much afraid it was.

"I don't know what your father thinks about such things, Tiffany," she said softly, choosing her words with care. "I wish I did understand him better. Then we could talk about it more if you wanted to."

"It's okay," Tiffany said with heartbreaking maturity. "Sometimes I think he doesn't know why he acts the way he does either. It's just that—"

She stopped talking abruptly and stared into the fire. Her shoulders stiffened, and Chris felt new tension tighten muscles all over her body.

"Tiffany, sweetie, what's wrong? You can tell me, remember. I'm your Big Sister. That's what I'm here for."

"Do you think my grandpa's only taking care of us because he's so good at those things? At loyalty and responsibilities?" She began talking in a rush. "Suppose he thinks that me and my brother and sister are just like his job. That he has to keep us because he promised my momma that he would."

Chris was at a loss. What could she say that wouldn't sound trite and condescending? How could she convey to Tiffany her certainty that Ethan loved her and the other children more deeply than they could ever know? Was it her place even to do so? What consequences might such a statement hold for Tiffany in the future if she was forced to choose between her father and her grandfather? For the first time Chris truly understood, with her heart as well as her intellect, the kind of dilemma other volunteers of hers had found themselves in from time to time. What should she do?

She cuddled Tiffany's angular little body closer, smoothed her hand over her hair and decided what to say. She picked up the last of the pictures of the birthday party and held up one for the child to study. She put her reasoning, questioning mind on hold and answered the little girl from her heart.

"Tiffany, what do you see in this picture?" It was one of the few party photos in which Ethan appeared.

"Me and Grandpa," Tiffany said in the same tone she might use to answer her teacher in school.

"What are the two of you doing?"

"I'm giving him a great big bear hug because he got me a Maggie Simpson doll for my birthday present. See, she's got that cute little pacifier stuck in her mouth and everything. I've wanted one ever since Christmas, to go with my Bart doll that Keith got me."

"How did your grandfather know what gift you really wanted?"

"Because we always watch the TV show together. He thinks it's the greatest, too. We laugh about it every week."

"And he remembered and bought the doll for you. Not because he had to buy you a present. Not because you were his responsibility. But because you are *you* and he loves you very much. Now look at the picture again. What else do you see?"

Tiffany studied the photo thoughtfully for a long moment. "Grandpa is hugging me back," she said finally, triumphantly. "He hugged me so hard I thought we would squish my new doll flat between us. It was a great hug."

She continued to look at the snapshot, but Chris felt the child begin to relax against her. "Do you understand what I'm trying to tell you?" she prompted.

"You don't hug people that hard just because you feel loyal to them," Tiffany answered after the tiniest hesitation.

"Of course not. You hug them that hard because you love them to pieces," Chris said, clearing her throat to loosen the sudden tightness of unexpected emotions.

"Yeah, you do," Tiffany agreed, satisfied at last. "You know something?" She squirmed around to kneel facing Chris with her arm propped along the back of the couch. "I'm going to give Dad and Grandpa a great big hug like that as soon as I get home. I'll see if they can guess what it means. But not Ashley and Brandon," she added after considering the matter. "I'll just give then ordinary hugs. They're brats."

"What about me?" Chris asked, fishing shamelessly for one of Tiffany's special hugs for herself. "Can I have a real great bear hug, too."

"Sure," Tiffany said with a grin as she launched herself at Chris, pushing her backward into the cushions. wrapping her arms around her neck and squeezing for all she was worth. "You asked for it."

"I sure did," Chris said breathlessly, hugging her back.

"Now," Tiffany announced, letting her go. "Enough hugging. I'm starved."

"Starved? We only ate dinner an hour ago."

"I am," Tiffany insisted. "Do you have any more of those sugar cookies we baked last time left in the freezer?"

Fifteen minutes later Chris and Tiffany were sitting at the kitchen table eating cookies and drinking hot chocolate with little marshmallows while they discussed the varieties of flowers that Erika would be using in her bridal bouquet. Tiffany was leafing through one of the sample books the florist had provided and Chris was sketching the design of the bridesmaids' bouquets on a paper napkin for her Little Sister, when Keith came stomping into the kitchen through the garage door.

"Jeez, it's miserable out there," he complained, shedding his gym bag, hat, coat and gloves into a pile on the floor. "It's a great night for a blizzard."

"Blizzard?" Tiffany looked up, immediately interested.

"Blizzard?" Chris echoed with far less enthusiasm. She glanced out the patio door but could see nothing beyond the pale rectangle of light shining onto the snowy deck.

"Mom, didn't you hear the weather report on the six o'clock news?" Keith propped himself against the door to the utility room and began to pull off his boots.

"We haven't turned on the TV since Tiffany got here," Chris admitted. She smiled at Tiffany. "We had lots to talk about. Is there really a bad snowstorm on the way?"

"Not on the way," Keith announced. "It's here. The barometer's falling and the wind's starting to pick up. It's raining now, but that's supposed to change over to snow before midnight. Coach let practice out an hour early because the streets are getting bad."

"Oh, dear," Chris said frowning at the cold windy darkness beyond the patio door. "I think we ought to get Tiffany home before her grandfather starts to worry."

"It's too early for me to go home. I get to stay until nine, remember," Tiffany wheedled. "I haven't finished my cocoa and we haven't made plans for activity night next week yet, either. We won't have anything to do if we don't plan it now."

"By nine o'clock the streets are going to be all iced over."

Keith moved into the kitchen in his stocking feet and leaned his hip against the counter. He looked very much like his father had at that age, Chris thought, tall and lean and so very serious about things that interested him. Meteorology was one of the areas of study he was seriously considering pursuing in college, so Chris knew his comments about the weather were well grounded in fact. "I think we should take the squirt home now." He looked and sounded very grown-up, the man of the house. Chris felt a little knot of sadness form in her throat. Soon he'd be out on his own, starting his own life, and she'd be alone in this house, a house that had never been empty before.

"Does that mean there won't be any school tomorrow?" Tiffany asked, pulling Chris out of her thoughts. "We have to play dodge ball in gym tomorrow. I don't like it. I'd rather stay home and play outside in the snow."

"If this storm is as bad as they say, you won't be playing outside tomorrow. The wind will still be blowing the snow around so bad you won't be able to see past your nose." Keith frowned, looking worried.

But Tiffany didn't notice. "A real blizzard," she said, sounding awed and excited. "I've never been in a real blizzard before."

"Well, I have. Once when I was little like you there was one so bad we didn't have school for a week."

"A week," Tiffany squealed, impressed.

"That isn't quite as much fun as it sounds, Tiffany," Chris said. "Keith didn't tell you that all those missed days had to be made up at the end of the school year."

"In the summer?" This time it was Tiffany who frowned. "I guess you're right. It wouldn't be so much fun if you think of it that way. Oh, well, maybe this will be just a little blizzard and the only day we'll miss school is tomorrow. I still don't want to play dodge ball in gym."

"If you'd been out driving a car on those streets you wouldn't be wishing for any more snow, squirt."

"Okay," Tiffany said, but she didn't sound convinced. "I know," she announced, looking pleased with herself. "Why don't we wait long enough to get you something to eat?"

Chris glanced over at her Little Sister and found her already on her feet, going to the cupboard for a plate and glass, urging Chris to get the remains of the pizza they'd shared for dinner out of the oven. "Fifteen minutes won't make that much difference. Keith can eat while we get our coats and boots on, okay?"

"I don't know." Chris found herself slightly at a loss for words.

Tiffany was smiling at Keith, motioning him to his seat at the table. "Keith can drive us over to my house. That way I won't worry about you driving home in a snowstorm and maybe getting the car stuck," she said, smiling at Chris.

"That's a possibility," Keith agreed, looking amused as he sat down at the table, "given Mom's driving record on snowy streets."

"One little fender bender in three years," Chris argued in her own defense.

"Mom, it cost eight hundred dollars to get the car fixed. That's not a fender bender."

"Of course," Tiffany interrupted, "if you think the weather is really that bad I could stay here tonight."

She looked at Keith's bent head adoringly. Chris couldn't be sure, but she thought Tiffany might actually be flirting with her son.

"I can sleep on the couch in the family room, and if there isn't any school tomorrow you and Chris can teach me how to play cribbage."

Keith looked up, surveying the calculating little girl through narrowed eyes. "You've got this all planned out, don't you, squirt?"

"I'm only trying to be helpful," Tiffany replied innocently.

Too innocently, Chris decided. She turned and busied herself at the sink to hide her smile. Tiffany *was* flirting with Keith. It was obvious her case of hero worship for Chris's son was as strong as ever.

"Okay," Keith said in a strangled tone, "you've convinced me you're better off at home. Mom, forget the pizza. I'll eat it later." He took Tiffany by the shoulders, spun her around and gave her a push toward the hall closet. "Get your coat and hat, squirt. Mom and I are taking you home. Now."

ETHAN LET the lace curtain that covered the bay window in the front room fall back against the cold glass. He glanced at his watch. It was only a little after eight.

Tiffany wasn't due home from her visit with Chris for nearly an hour. Even though the weather was getting steadily worse, he knew she was safe with her Big Sister, but still he couldn't shake the uneasiness that kept him pacing restlessly from room to room. Maybe he was coming down with the flu? That would explain the nagging pain in his neck and shoulders, the tightness in his chest when he took a deep breath.

He doubted it was the flu. He hadn't been sick a day in fifteen years. It was more likely the long string of sleepless nights he'd been experiencing since the first of the year were catching up to him. Maybe all he needed was to take some antacid and a couple of aspirin. It wasn't Mrs. Baden's fault his hours were so irregular that more often than not he ate her excellent dinners warmed over, at his desk, while he wrestled with the next day's complement of retooling problems.

He walked into the foyer and flicked on the porch light, seeing the reflection of wet, dark concrete shining through patches of half-frozen snow on the sidewalk. Another miserable night was in store for the area if the weatherman was correct. Then he headed back to his desk, determined to finish the work he'd brought home from the plant at a reasonable hour for a change.

He paused at the bottom of the stairs. Above him he could hear Jeff's laughter and Ashley's and Brandon's happy squeals as his son roughhoused with the younger children. They, at least, seemed happy with their lives. The tensions and uncertainties in the relationships surrounding them, which seemed to affect Tiffany so strongly, went mostly unnoticed by the little ones. Ethan was grateful for that small mercy.

Jeff's casual attitude toward his parental duties hadn't changed much over the months. He was available to his children when it suited him, and tuned them out of his life when it didn't. Nothing Ethan said or did made any difference. After four months together under the same roof they were polite, reserved, scarcely more than the strangers they'd been when Jeff had arrived in Bonaparte.

It seemed to Ethan his own life was in stalemate. It was frustrating for a man of his temperament. He enjoyed a challenge; he couldn't deny that aspect of his personality. But he didn't like feeling helpless to move events in his life forward toward a goal of his own choosing. His courtship of Christine Baldwin seemed almost as mired in uncertainty as his relationship with his son.

A car door opened and shut outside, followed closely by another. He heard footsteps on the porch, a rhythmic tattoo as snow was stamped from two pairs of boots. The door opened and Tiffany bounced into the foyer, filling the house with warmth and light like a small sun coming into the room. Ethan smiled despite the darkness of his thoughts.

"Hi, Grandpa, I'm home," she announced, unzipping her coat. "Chris and Keith brought me back early. The streets are getting very slippery. We skidded twice just coming over here!" She tugged off her coat and dropped it on the old church pew sitting along the wall—the foyer's only furniture. "Keith stayed in the car, but Chris came with me to see my birthday presents."

"If you hurry and bring them down," Chris reminded her, then looked up with a smile of greeting for Ethan, a special smile that belied the everyday tone of her voice. "I can only stay a few minutes. Tiffany's correct. The streets are very slippery."

"There's a blizzard coming," Tiffany said over her shoulder excitedly as she scampered up the stairs. "Didn't you listen to the weather report on the news, either?"

"I'm afraid I worked straight through dinner," Ethan answered with a shrug, lifting his hand to the back of his head in another attempt to ease the painful tightness in his neck and shoulders.

"Grandpa, you should eat regular meals," Tiffany scolded as she leaned over the railing halfway up the flight. "I've told you that and told you that."

"Problems with the refitting at the plant?" Chris asked.

"Nothing that we didn't anticipate. But it's a big job. Any problems or holdups in one section create problems and holdups in other sections. I'm no engineer. I have to do my homework or I can't keep up with those guys." He held out his hand to help her off with her coat.

Chris hesitated, then slid her arms out of the sleeves. "I told Tiffany the truth. I can't stay. The streets are almost impassable and Keith hasn't had his dinner yet."

"As a matter of fact neither have I. Why don't we invite him in? Mrs. Baden left pot roast and vegetables, mashed potatoes and gravy, the whole nine yards warming in the oven. There's three times more than I can eat."

"That should be almost enough to satisfy him." She looked through the beveled glass oval in the door and laughed. "Why not? I don't think a few more minutes will make that much difference in the weather.

The brunt of the storm isn't supposed to arrive until after midnight. I don't think Keith will turn down Mrs. Baden's roast beef. Especially when the alternative at home is leftover pepperoni-and-mushroom pizza.''

"Good. Then it's settled." It was another of those nondates he seemed destined to pursue with this woman. They rarely spent time alone together. They never even shared a meal alone together. Always it was some spur-of-the-moment gathering such as this. It was as if they both knew there was only one place they would end up in if they had the luxury of privacy—a bedroom. Ethan wanted Christine with a fierce passion belonging to a man twenty years younger, the kind of passion he'd assumed would never be a part of his life again. It was exhilarating and damnably frustrating. Some nights, lying awake thinking of her, wanting her with a fierce, aching need that wouldn't go away, he thought it just might be the death of him.

Their hands met, brushed over each other, as he took her coat to hang on the halltree beside the door, and he heard her quick sharp intake of breath. Her face flushed with a pale pink blush of excitement and confusion, and Ethan settled for the dubious pleasure of knowing she wanted him as much as he wanted her and was just as powerless to do anything about it.

"WE REALLY SHOULDN'T stay any longer," Chris said worriedly as another blast of wind-driven snow rattled against Ethan's kitchen window. "The wind's blowing harder all the time. And it's snowing harder, too," she added as she handed him the big blue roaster she'd just finished washing.

Ethan dried the heavy utensil and sat it on the counter. "You're probably right. That sounds more like sleet hitting the windowpane than snow."

Chris nodded. "The streets were terrible coming over. They'll be even more treacherous now." She opened the drain in the sink and watched the sudsy dishwater swirl away. "This is definitely not a night to be out paying visits."

"But it's the only time we've had alone in sixteen days," Ethan said, taking a last swipe at the roaster lid with his towel.

Chris took it from him and dried her hands. *He's been counting the days, too?* She smiled to herself as he stepped into the pantry near the back door to put the roaster away. She was glad he was no longer close enough to reach out and touch. It was harder and harder to keep her hands to herself. She wanted to be in his arms, to feel his weight resting on her in bed, to have him fill her with heat and joy. Chris shook her head, marveling at the erotic direction of her thoughts. She'd assumed this part of her, this completely feminine, desiring part of her nature, was behind her, had died when Jack had died; but she was wrong. She wanted Ethan Connor with a hunger that surprised no one as much as herself.

"I'm afraid I have to agree with you about the weather," Ethan said, coming out of the pantry. "I just stepped out the back door. The storm's getting worse." As though to emphasize his words, the kitchen lights flickered and dimmed before returning to full power. Tiffany's and Ashley's squeals and Brandon's high piping laughter could be heard from the living room, where Keith was watching television with the children. Jeff, after a minute or two of stilted conversation with Ethan and Chris around the kitchen table, had gone back upstairs to his room to read. The teenager grumbled a warning to be silent and the adoring children did just that.

"He's good with the kids," Ethan said.

To Chris, the strain and worry of his situation was plain to see in the darkness shadowing his hazel eyes. "He likes your grandchildren a great deal," she said. "We all do." She lifted her hand and touched his cheek for just a moment. She hadn't seen the two younger children in more than a week and it surprised her how much she missed them. It was just another sign of how very close she was to losing all objectivity in her match with Tiffany. Chris turned away from Ethan. "We really must be going," she said.

Ethan frowned, rubbing his left arm and shoulder as he spoke. "I think you're right."

"Is something wrong, Ethan?" Chris asked, coming close once more. He looked pale and even more tired in the harsh overhead light. She shivered, not entirely from the chill drafts still skating across the linoleum floor from when Ethan had opened the back door. "Are you ill?"

"No," Ethan said quickly. "I'm fine."

He'd answered too abruptly for Chris not to be concerned.

"I probably ate too quickly." He grinned ruefully. "Or ate too much. It's hard to turn down seconds on Mrs. Baden's pot roast, even warmed over."

"I know." Chris smiled, too, forcing her uneasiness to the back of her mind. He was a grown man, under a lot of pressure, but he wasn't foolish. If he was ill, he'd tell her so. "Is everything all right, Ethan?"

"Absolutely. As long as the weather cooperates." He glanced up at the ceiling fixture as the lights dimmed once again. "Right on cue. Come on, let's round up Keith and get you two back home. I won't be a bit surprised if the electricity goes out."

"Oh, dear, that means the furnace won't run. I'd better have Keith bring in another armload or two of wood for the fireplace when we get home, just in case."

"Good idea." Ethan put his arm around her waist and guided her out of the kitchen. Chris leaned her head against his shoulder for one long, delicious second, felt his lips brush lightly across her hair, then stepped away as the sound of footsteps pounding down the hallway reached their ears.

"KEITH SAYS the lights are going to go out," Tiffany said, flying into the kitchen. "We need to get the candles out of the drawer and find the matches. Keith's going out to start your car and says to hurry and get your coat on." She scampered to the kitchen drawer where Mrs. Baden kept emergency candles and matches. "Isn't this exciting, Grandpa? My first real blizzard."

Jeff had come down from his room. He followed his daughter into the kitchen in a more sedate manner. "For once I think Miss Gloom-and-Doom is right, Dad. Have you looked outside lately?"

"Yes."

Ethan's tone was clipped. Chris glanced up into his face to find his expression obscured by the frown that pulled his brows close together.

"Will you get Chris's coat from the closet for her, please?"

"Sure."

If Jeff noticed Ethan's unusually abrupt behavior he made no comment about it. Or perhaps it wasn't unusual behavior between the two men, Chris concluded with a sigh. Ethan had said little about his relationship with his son in the stolen moments they had found to spend alone together. For her part she hadn't questioned him on the subject, either, preferring his kisses and caresses to talking about family matters, no matter how important.

"You haven't seen the rest of my birthday presents," Tiffany moaned, turning from the drawer with her hands full of half-burned, stubby white candles. "I've been showing them to Keith, but you've only seen the ones I had downstairs."

"Some other time," Ethan said so harshly that even Keith looked surprised and puzzled as he walked into the kitchen in time to hear the last exchange. "We want Chris to get home safely, don't we?" he added in a softer tone.

"Yeah," Tiffany said grudgingly. "You'll come back to see them all, won't you, Chris?"

"As soon as I can," Chris promised, anxious to go, yet reluctant to leave. Something was wrong. She wasn't certain what, but Ethan wasn't himself and she longed for the time, the privacy and the intimacy to find out what it was.

"Okay. Here's your coat," Tiffany added unnecessarily as they all walked toward the front door.

Jeff held the garment for Chris to slip into.

"Drive carefully," Tiffany said.

She sounded so grown-up that Chris couldn't help but smile. "We'll be very careful," she promised.

"No *problemo,* squirt. Remember, I'm driving. Goodbye, Mr. Connor, Jeff," Keith said with a wave.

Outside, the wind hit Chris with enough force to almost knock her off her feet, and she gasped behind her scarf as she nearly lost her footing on her way down the porch steps. The sleet had turned to snow in the past few minutes, but it wasn't falling so much as being driven before the howling wind, like tiny chips of glass that stung her face and took her breath away.

Keith sprinted around the idling car. Chris turned to wave goodbye to Tiffany and saw Ethan standing in the doorway behind her. Her heart squeezed painfully in her chest. She didn't want to leave him or the child. She wanted to be with them both. An impossible dream but a very precious one, she knew, as another blast of wind sent her sliding across a hidden patch of ice. She held on to the car door with both hands to keep from falling into the street.

"Hurry, Mom, it's gotten a whole lot worse since we got here," Keith urged from inside the car.

"Let's go," Chris said, tugging hard to shut the door against the angry strength of the wind.

Inside the car it was cold but sheltered from the storm. Keith shifted into gear and attempted to pull away from the curb. The back tires skidded sideways, caught and spun. He shifted into reverse and tried again to move off the patch of ice that had formed under the wheels. They went only a foot or two and were stuck again. Keith shifted the car back and forth, trying to rock the vehicle out of the icy ruts. It didn't work. The tires spun uselessly. The car was stuck.

Keith opened the car door and prepared to get out and push. "You'll have to steer, Mom," he instructed.

Chris was already halfway out of the car. She tucked the ends of her scarf into the collar of her coat to keep it from blowing in her face and surveyed the two back wheels, buried in a drift of frozen snow, beneath the faint eerie glow of the streetlight.

"Get her rockin' good and I'll push her out," her son yelled over the increasing fury of the storm.

Chris bit her lip. She really didn't like the maneuver. What if Keith slipped and fell under the car?

"Mom," he hollered, exasperated. "Do what I say."

Chris nodded, then looked up. Ethan had appeared beside Keith. Because of the blowing snow she hadn't seen him walk the few yards from his front porch, but evidently he had noticed their predicament—or, more likely, had heard the sounds of the spinning tires even over the howling of the storm.

"You get on that side. I'll push from here," he ordered, motioning Keith to move to the far side of the car.

"Ethan, you aren't dressed to be out in this weather," Chris said in immediate, automatic protest.

He was wearing a heavy pea jacket but no gloves or hat. The wind pulled and tugged at his hair. His breath streamed out behind him in a frosty trail of icy vapor.

He turned up the collar of his coat and leaned against the back bumper of the car. "I realize I'm not dressed for this kind of work, but if you'd kindly quit pointing out the obvious and help us get you moving I'd be able to get back into my warm, cozy house without suffering permanent frostbite."

He grinned, but the shadows thrown by the uncertain overhead light turned the smile into a grimace.

"Ethan, are you sure you're feeling all right?" Chris asked, preparing to climb into the driver's seat.

"It's indigestion, that's all," Ethan said, waving off her concern. "I'll take something for it as soon as you're gone, okay?"

"Okay," Chris said, wishing she had time to make certain he'd do as he'd said he would.

"Ready?" she heard him yell above the storm.

"Ready." She shifted the car into reverse, then into drive, and stepped on the gas. She could feel the combined strength of both men as the car lurched forward, but the vehicle didn't quite clear the drift. Hurriedly she set the car into a rocking motion again. This time the tires lifted over the icy rim of the drift and she skidded out into the middle of the street. She threw the car into park and opened the door to step out and call out her thanks to Ethan for his help. The sight that met her eyes made her blood run cold and would haunt her dreams for weeks to come.

Ethan was on his knees in the snow, with Keith bending over him in concern. For one heart-stopping, irrational second she was afraid he'd slipped and fallen under the car, but she dismissed the thought as quickly as it came. It was impossible. She would have known if she'd run over him. Something else was wrong. Perhaps he'd twisted his ankle or hurt his back. She hurried toward them as quickly as she could.

"What's wrong?" she gasped, dropping to her knees beside Ethan.

"I don't know, Mom," Keith said, his face almost as pale as the man's beside him. "We pushed you out, then he grabbed his chest and dropped down in the snow."

"Ethan, what's wrong?" Chris asked, her voice sharp and high with worry and fear.

He didn't answer, couldn't answer.

It was Keith who spoke. "Mom, we'd better get him to the hospital. I think he's having a heart attack!"

CHAPTER ELEVEN

A STEADY BEEPING SOUND came from somewhere above his head and to the right. It was soft, but annoying, audible even above the relentless howling of the storm wind outside the window. Ethan tried to lift his arm to shut off the sound. His right hand hit a metal rail with a clang. The contact hurt and he grunted in surprise. That was strange. His alarm clock should be on the table by his bed, where he could reach it and turn it off with only a flick of his wrist. Except that this morning it seemed to have been moved. And he was just too tired to get up and search for it to turn it off. He tried to go back to sleep. The irritating beep continued.

He had to get up. He couldn't lie there all morning. He had to get moving, or he'd be late for work and Tiffany and Ashley would be late for school. There were a million things he had to do this morning.

Morning? Was it morning? It didn't feel like morning. It felt like the middle of the night. He twisted his head to look out the window beside his bed. It wasn't there—only a wall of glass with shadowy figures moving behind gauzy curtains.

Where was he? What was this place? He wasn't dreaming—he was sure of that. So what had happened to him?

Ethan frowned, trying to remember, coming up with bits and pieces of memories, images of cold and snow. Crushing pain. Heart-stopping pain? His memory refused to function properly. His body was weighed down with fatigue and the ache of battle wounds, but his brain registered the connection between that word and what had happened to him. He'd had a heart attack. He had almost died. Maybe he would still die. He didn't want that to happen. He was too young. There were still too many things he had to do in his life, too many people he loved who depended on him, too many questions left unanswered and problems unsolved.

He attempted to sit up in bed but couldn't manage it. He lifted his hand, or tried to. It was strapped to a long board with strips of white tape. An IV line ran into the back of his hand. He became aware of a slight hissing sound and lifted his right arm tentatively to his face. Plastic tubing, lying across his face, was feeding oxygen into his nose. That, at least, explained the hissing noise he hadn't been able to attribute to the storm. His restless movements had alerted someone sitting in a chair in a darkened corner of the small room he occupied.

"Ethan?"

It was Chris's voice, soft, sweet. He turned his head, blinking to bring her into focus. His head felt like a block of wood; each thought he formed took an effort that left him reeling with fatigue. Still, he wanted to talk to her, needed to know what was happening.

"Chris, is that you?" The words came out all cracked and ragged. He swallowed, but his throat was as dry as cotton and his tongue refused to obey his commands.

"Yes, it's me. How do you feel?"

"I feel like hell," he said, still sounding like someone else, whose voice was as gravelly as a dusty country road. "And I'm thirsty."

Chris laughed, but it was all shivery around the edges as though she'd been crying or badly frightened.

"You have a right to feel lousy. You've had a rough five or six hours." She leaned toward him, holding a plastic glass of water and a straw. "Take it slow," she said, lifting his head slightly. "Just a few sips at first."

The effort of holding up his head and swallowing the water exhausted him. He lay quietly while she replaced the glass on the bedside table and brushed his hair back off his forehead.

"I had a heart attack, didn't I."

"Yes." Her voice broke. "Oh, Ethan, I was afraid you might die."

He closed his eyes, nodded once. He didn't want to talk about it out loud, not yet. He was too tired and too weak and too scared. "I know what happened. Or at least I think I remember.... How bad is it?" He couldn't deal with dying just yet, but he didn't think he could deal with being an invalid the rest of his life, either.

"The doctor was just here. Perhaps that's what woke you," Chris said, stroking his hair with the tip of her finger. "The first set of tests look good. He thinks there's not going to be any permanent damage to your heart...if you take care of yourself from now on. He's going to run more tests just as soon as the storm is over and the electricity comes back on."

"I don't recall hearing anyone come in," Ethan said, frowning that he should have missed so important a conversation.

"They gave you something to make you sleep."

"Maybe that's why I can't remember. You..." he said suddenly as scattered bits and pieces of memory fell into place. "Your car was stuck in the snow. We pushed it out." He stopped speaking abruptly and was still. "You...and Jeff brought me here, to the hospital, in your car." The effort to form coherent sentences was almost too much. He closed his eyes.

She took his right hand, the one that was free of tubes and needles, and held it tight. "Yes, Keith stayed with the children, do you remember? And Jeff rode with us. We thought it would take too long to get you help if we waited for the emergency squad...because of the storm...and everything...." Her voice caught on a little sob.

"It was a wild ride," he recalled. "You drive like A. J. Foyt."

"It was a miracle I didn't land us in a snowbank. The power went out all over town. There were no streetlights, no traffic lights. I just kept praying we didn't run off the road or end up wrapped around a light pole. Thank God the hospital's got its own generator. They were able to take care of you the moment we arrived."

She sounded as if she might be crying. Ethan opened his eyes. He moved his hand, enfolding her fingers in his own. "Don't cry, Chris," he said. "We made it just fine."

"I'm not crying," she insisted with a sniff, but crystal tears glittered on her eyelashes, making a lie of the brave words.

The room was dimly lit, but he could see her features very clearly. Her nose was red, her hair mussed. She was still the most beautiful woman he'd ever seen. He wanted to tell her so, but it took so much effort to speak he couldn't spare the words.

"And you're going to be fine, truly you are. I've known Dr. Betts for years. He never lies. Never."

She squeezed his hand so tightly he winced.

"Oh, Ethan, I was so frightened for you. I felt so helpless. I don't know CPR. I've never learned. I always meant to... but I never did. If you had stopped breath—ing—" her voice caught and broke on a ragged sob "—I wouldn't have been able to help you."

"Shhh, don't think about it." He found the strength somewhere to go on talking, to comfort her as best he could.

"I'm going down to the Red Cross office the very first thing tomorrow—today, I mean—and sign up for a course."

"Okay. Me, too," he said, echoing Brandon's favorite phrase. "Only it's going to be the second thing I do when I get out of here."

"What's the first thing?" Chris whispered, brushing at her tears with the back of her hand.

"Marry you," he said before something else happened to prevent him from saying the words aloud.

"Marry me?"

Chris sounded confused. Perhaps the words hadn't come out the way he'd wanted them to. He wasn't as clearheaded as he'd like to be, but he thought he'd been making sense so far.

"I love you," he said, speaking as clearly as he could manage. God, if he just wasn't so damnably tired and shot full of drugs. He tried hard to focus on her face, gauge her reaction. It took all the concentration he could muster. "Didn't I say that right?"

"Yes," she replied very softly, "you said it exactly right."

His eyelids felt like lead weights. He could barely keep them open. "You didn't answer me," he complained, dismayed to hear the words come out even more wobbly and slurred than previously.

"I love you," she admitted, sidestepping the more important question of marrying him. "Go to sleep." She leaned over and kissed him very lightly on the cheek.

He'd have to leave the question of whether she'd marry him unanswered for the time being, he realized. He was just too tired, too bone-achingly tired to marshal his arguments right now. He turned his head to brush her lips with his. He wanted to kiss her, really kiss her, more than anything else on earth, but he couldn't manage the feat just then.

"Go to sleep," Chris said, still very softly, still with a little catch in her voice. "We'll talk about everything tomorrow when you're stronger. The doctor said I could only stay five minutes and my time is up."

"Don't go," he pleaded, feeling weak as a kitten. Weak and sore and aching, but the bone-crushing, breath-stealing pain in his chest was gone, and that in itself seemed like a miracle.

"I have to." The nurse is signaling me through the window. They're very strict about these things here, you know."

She smiled and he tried to smile, too. He must have succeeded well enough for the expression to be recognized, because she bent closer and kissed him again.

"I love you, Ethan Connor. Now I have to go. Jeff wants a moment with you and I'm stealing his time."

"You'll be back." He squeezed her hand harder, but it seemed not to inconvenience her in the least. She slipped her fingers out of his grasp with no trouble at all.

"Yes. As soon as they will let me." She turned away and beckoned to a figure standing in the doorway. "Jeff, he's awake."

Ethan heard their whispered conversation at the foot of his bed but paid little attention. He was so sleepy he could barely stay awake, but he had to ask Jeff how the children were getting along. Even over the sounds of the various instruments connected to his bed and to his body, he could hear the storm wind howling outside the window and he wanted to make sure they were safe and warm.

He drifted closer to sleep but heard Jeff say Tiffany's name. Tiffany. He struggled to stay awake. The poor child would be terrified. She wouldn't understand what had happened to him. They had to tell her he was all right. What had Chris said about the storm? The power was out. The hospital was running on emergency generators. Did that mean there was no phone service, either? He'd ask Jeff. He'd have to rely on his son to help him, and to help Tiffany.

But when Jeff stepped up to his bed he was followed by a nurse. Ethan barely had a chance to mumble a response to his son's anxious questions about how he felt before she slipped a needle into the IV tubing in his arm and sent a rush of potent, numbing medication pushing through his veins.

"Tiffany," he said, and Jeff had to lean close to hear him speak. "Tell Tiffany I'm okay." He was asleep almost before the last word left his mouth.

TIFFANY COULDN'T SEE even a couple of inches past the window of Mr. Leonard's Jeep it was snowing so hard. She leaned forward against her seat belt, trying to look past Keith, see out his window, but it didn't help.

"We're almost there, Tiffany," Mrs. Leonard said from the front seat with a smile and a shake of her head. "You'll just have to be patient. The streets are very slippery. Walt is driving as fast as he can."

"We have to *hurry*, Mr. Leonard. My grandpa needs me," she said, making fists of her hands on the cold, hard seat of the Jeep.

"I know, Tiffany, honey," Mr. Leonard echoed his wife. "We just can't go any faster, or we'll miss our turn and go right past the hospital."

"We couldn't be out in this weather at all if we didn't have four-wheel drive," Mrs. Leonard added, peering anxiously into the almost-solid white wall of wind-driven snow, which the windshield wipers could barely keep away.

"It seems like it's taken hours to get this far."

"It's only been twenty-five minutes since we left your house," Keith said, pushing up the sleeve of his parka to check his watch.

"That means it's way after midnight," Tiffany said wonderingly. "I've never been up this late before, not even on New Year's Eve."

"Yep, it's way past your bedtime, squirt," Keith pointed out.

Tiffany wanted to say something sharp and witty to make him talk nicer to her, but just then the Jeep skidded on an icy patch of pavement and Tiffany had to hang on for dear life. She was glad all of them were wearing their seat belts. She was quiet for a little while, then thought of something else. "There won't be any school tomorrow, will there," she said, wiping a spot clear of mist on the window to look outside again.

"Probably not for two or three days," Walt Leonard replied with what sounded like a chuckle.

"Good," Tiffany said. "That means I can stay with my grandpa all the time and make sure he's getting taken care of properly."

"Better slow down, Walt. I can't see the street signs at all anymore," Miriam Leonard cautioned, and she sounded worried.

"Not too slow."

"Tiffany," Keith said, shaking his head.

She was thankful to Mr. and Mrs. Leonard for their help, but didn't they understand she *had* to get to her grandfather as quickly as possible? Maybe if she explained it to them one more time... She jiggled her leg and searched for the best words.

"I'm really glad you brought Mrs. Baden to our house to watch the little kids while they sleep," she began. "But—"

Keith reached over and squeezed her leg so she would stop talking. "Your dad and my mom both talked to you before the telephone went dead," he reminded her. "They both said your grandpa was resting comfortably. You have to trust them."

Tiffany wanted to cry. Trust them. That was one of the problems; couldn't Keith tell that? Tiffany felt an awful lump of just plain fear lurch up from her stom-

ach and stick in her throat. People said nice things like
that all the time to make you feel better, even if they
weren't true. She had to see her grandfather for herself so that she knew for certain he really was going to
be all right. Her dad had kept saying hopeful things
about her momma getting better over and over, even
when Tiffany had known she wasn't going to get well
ever again. She could remember the words right now:
"There's nothing to worry about, sweetheart," he
would say, looking so sad Tiffany would start crying
then and there. "Momma's resting comfortably. She'll
be all better soon."

Only, her mother hadn't gotten better. She'd gotten
sicker and sicker, and then she'd died and her father
had left her alone with strangers. She didn't want that
to happen ever again. Never. Ever.

"Chris said they gave him a shot of something so
that he could sleep," she finally managed, wanting
more than anything for Keith to tell her everything was
truly going to be all right. She trusted Keith. He was
her friend. And she trusted Chris. Chris had never lied
to her. Not once. Ever.

"They might not let you see your grandfather right
away," Mrs. Leonard cautioned, turning around in
her seat once again. "They have very strict rules about
children in the cardiac unit." She was frowning as she
spoke.

Tiffany frowned, too. "I have to see him," she repeated loudly and stubbornly. She'd gotten this far,
and no doctor or mean nurse who went around poking needles into her grandfather was going to stop her
now.

"Tom Betts will understand, Miriam," Walt said bracingly. "He'll let the child see Ethan. I'll speak to him myself if need be, Tiffany."

"Thank you, Mr. Leonard," she said, letting her fists uncurl.

"C'mon, squirt," Keith said, holding out his hand. "Don't worry. We'll get you in to see your grandfather. Dr. Betts has been taking care of me since I was littler than you. He can break any rule they have at Hobart Memorial. You'll see." He flashed her a smile that she could see even though it was almost pitch-black inside the Jeep.

Tiffany smiled, too, or tried to. She put her hand in his and felt his big fingers close tightly over hers in a comforting squeeze. "Okay, Keith," she whispered, feeling just a little bit better than she had since the awful moment her grandpa had gotten sick. The big, scary lump in her throat got smaller. It was easier to breathe and she didn't think she was going to cry again. "Will you come with me to my grandpa's room?" she asked hopefully.

"I'll be right beside you all the way, squirt," Keith replied, his voice almost husky, as though he was getting a cold.

"Don't call me squirt," she retorted almost happily, and settled back against the seat to wait.

CHRIS COULDN'T SIT STILL a moment longer. She'd paced the length and breadth of the hospital and always kept ending up back in front of Ethan's cubicle in the combined Intensive Care/Cardiac Care Unit. He was sleeping, peacefully, comfortably, normally, the nurse told her patiently time and time again, but she had to keep checking for herself to make certain it was true. She'd thought she was over Jack's death; now she wasn't so sure. She'd dealt with the reality of his loss but not, obviously, with the trauma of his dying. She'd pushed those last awful days and weeks out of her mind, and tonight the horror of them had come rushing back. She couldn't bear to lose Ethan that way, too.

She loved him. There was no longer any use in denying it to herself. She'd never been so frightened in her life as when she'd knelt beside him in the snow, seen the awful pallor of his skin, watched him struggle to take each breath. She knew then she couldn't bear to lose him, still couldn't bear to think about it. Chris crossed her arms beneath her breasts and hugged herself tightly to blot out the terror of the hours just past. He wasn't going to die. He was going to live a long, happy life.

And she could live that life with him, by his side each and every day. He had asked her to be his wife. But was she ready to marry him? She couldn't take his garbled proposal at face value, of course. The man was drugged, nearly senseless, had come close to death. He probably wouldn't even remember asking her to marry him and all this soul searching would be needless. But she knew now that the subject was on his mind, and sooner or later it would come up again. Was she ready for a formal commitment? Was she ready to be Ethan Connor's wife?

In her heart and in her dreams and in her need for him she was. But in reality, in the harsh light of day, it wasn't that easy. Her children would need time to adjust to the idea of her falling in love and getting married again. She didn't know how much Keith had guessed about her feelings for Ethan, but she'd bet her last nickel that Erika had no idea at all her mother was involved, however innocently, with a man. Perhaps she and Ethan had been too discreet about their relationship these past months?

Chris leaned her head on the door frame of Ethan's cubicle and closed her eyes to ease the sting of tired, anxious tears. What was best for everyone involved, including Tiffany and her brother and sister—and Jeff? She'd come so close to losing Ethan that night that it had taken all the willpower she possessed not to give him the answer he had wanted then and there. Dr. Betts had assured her, more than once in the past few hours, that all the preliminary tests looked good, that if Ethan took proper care of himself, he could expect to live to be a hundred. *If he took proper care of himself.* With all the pressures he faced in his life, would the additional strain of adjusting to a new marriage, of consummating it in a way that promised to be something very special and exciting, be too much to ask?

She couldn't be sure. And as long as she wasn't sure, she couldn't marry him. She'd never forgive herself if he had another heart attack. If they couldn't go on the way they had been, lovers in spirit if not in the flesh, then she'd have to break off the relationship, for Ethan's sake, if not her own.

She stood silently a few moments longer, watching him sleep, her eyes flicking briefly over the myriad monitors that stood sentinel beside his bed. Their readings made no sense to her, but the nurses all nodded approvingly when they entered the room. "Dear Lord," she prayed softly, aloud, so that He would be sure to hear her petition, "Tiffany and I love him so. Please let him get well."

"Christine, I thought I told you to get some rest," Tom Betts said from somewhere close behind her.

She whirled around, blinking tears from her eyes. "I'm not tired, Tom, really."

"It's two-thirty in the morning. Anyone in their right mind is tired at this hour."

"All right, I'm tired," she admitted with a rueful grin, "but I'm not sleepy."

"They're setting up cots in the main lobby for refugees from the storm, as well as our own people who are stuck here for the duration." He smiled down at her, his weather-beaten face a mass of wrinkles that seemed to make his smile even broader than it was. "Why don't you go claim one for an hour or two?"

"I'm fine—" She broke off as Keith came striding through the swinging doors that blocked the unit off from the main hallway. "Keith!"

"Mom, I'm glad I found you," he said, pulling off his gloves and pushing them into the pockets of his parka.

"How did you get here?" she asked, before spotting Walt Leonard coming through the doors only three steps behind her son.

"Walt brought us in his Jeep. Mom, the nurse out front won't let Tiffany come back here. Mrs. Leonard's with her now, but Tiffany's fit to be tied."

"The child wants to see her grandfather, Tom, and she's not about to take no for an answer," Walt added, brushing snowflakes from the top of his nearly bald head.

"Tiffany's here?" Jeff had heard their voices, and now rose from the couch in the small private waiting room adjacent to Ethan's cubicle.

"Tiffany is only nine, Tom," Chris said, laying her hand on the doctor's arm in her need to convey her urgency. "She lost her mother last year. She's very close to Ethan."

"The poor little kid's half-scared to death," Keith said, looking fierce.

Dr. Betts frowned, rubbing his chin with the tips of his fingers. "You two brought her out here in this weather?"

"She's terrified that Ethan's dying," Walt said more quietly. "Besides, Miriam insisted on coming. You know she's one of the hospital's senior volunteers. She figured you'd need her sooner or later. How is Ethan, Tom?" he asked, returning to the subject uppermost in all their thoughts.

"He's damn lucky. Ought to make a full recovery if you can keep him from working himself to death out at the plant."

"Don't worry. I'll follow him around like a hen with only one chick. But what about the little girl? Can't she see him, just for a minute or two?"

"He's asleep—" Dr. Betts began, but was interrupted.

"I'm awake."

Ethan's voice sounded surprisingly strong coming from the cubicle behind her. Chris turned, a smile lighting her face, giving away her feelings for anyone who cared to see. Three of the four men in the corridor did choose to see. Jeff Connor was already striding to his father's room. Chris was only a step behind him.

"Walt Leonard and Chris's son brought Tiffany out here," he said. "Doc's deciding if you can see her."

"Chris—" Ethan lifted his arm in a pleading gesture that underscored his weakness and his urgent need to reassure his granddaughter. "Chris, make them let her come in, please."

"Just for a minute," Tom Betts said, strolling into the cubicle, making the small, crowded area seem even smaller. "Just long enough for her to see you're among the living and then it's back to sleep. If you don't do it on your own, we can keep filling you full of sedatives until you do."

"I'll sleep," Ethan promised, setting his jaw. "Just let me see her."

"It's a deal. I'll go get her. Otherwise Enid Slater out at the front desk will never let her back here. Damn, I wish the electricity would come back on. Never knew how much I missed the paging system until it conked out on us." He turned and hurried out of the room, motioning Jeff to follow him and still mumbling to himself.

Ethan lifted his hand once more, beckoning Chris closer. "Go tell her...not to worry about how I look," he said, closing his eyes with the effort of making himself understood.

"I will." She squeezed his hand once, hard and strong, and left the room.

The corridor was empty. Moments later Tiffany came through the swinging doors holding her father's hand. Keith and Tom Betts trailed behind with Walt and Miriam bringing up the rear.

"It's a damn parade," Dr. Betts muttered, moving on past the assemblage gathered outside Ethan's room. "Walt and Miriam will just have to wait till morning to do more than stick their heads in the door.

Is that understood." It wasn't a question; it was an order.

"Understood." Everyone nodded in unison.

"Then let the child see her grandfather." He smiled down at Tiffany, looking very much like a tall, wind-bent oak. "You can stay two minutes young lady," he said, and disappeared into another cubicle.

"Chris." Tiffany's whisper was jubilant. "He said I can stay two minutes." Her eyes filled with tears and she was trembling so hard her teeth chattered, but she managed a smile. "Where is he? Where's my grandpa? I have to see if he's really truly going to be all right."

"He's very tired," Chris cautioned, taking the little girl into her arms, holding her close, knowing she loved her as deeply as she loved her own children. It didn't matter if it was right or wrong; it didn't matter if she'd gone beyond the guidelines of being Tiffany's Big Sister. None of those considerations made any difference at all to her heart. "Remember, there are all kinds of tubes and wires and monitors attached to the bed. You mustn't be scared."

"I'm not scared," Tiffany said staunchly. "I just have to see him, that's all. What if they aren't taking good care of him here?"

"They are, sweetie," Chris assured her, giving her Little Sister another big reassuring hug. "They are."

"Tiffany?"

Ethan's voice carried out into the hall, once again sounding strong and sure. Chris understood the effort it took to mount that small, comforting deception and she fell just a little more deeply in love with the wonderful, caring man in the room behind her.

"Is that you, Tiff?"

"It's me, Grandpa!" Tiffany pulled at Chris's hand. "Come with me," she whispered, smiling through her tears. "He'll want to see you, too."

"IS SHE SLEEPING?" Jeff stood in the shadows, beyond the small pool of light cast by the emergency lamp. Tiffany was curled up at one end of the waiting-room sofa; Keith was slouched at the other, his long legs propped up on a chair he'd pulled close.

"They both are," Chris answered in a whisper. She turned away from the window to find him holding two cups of steaming coffee. "Where did you find that?" she asked gratefully, accepting the cup he handed her. "I assumed they would have shut the vending machines down when they went to emergency power."

"They did. This came from the cafeteria. Walt and Miriam Leonard are manning a huge urn of the stuff and about six big trays of sandwiches. I could go back and get you one if you're hungry."

"No, thanks. The coffee's enough." She wrapped her hands around the cup, but little of the warmth from the scalding liquid was transferred to her cold fingers. "I think the storm's starting to die down," she said, and saw his gaze go to the windy darkness beyond the window. She was glad Erika was safe with Michael and his parents and not home alone. It was one less thing to worry about.

"That's what the weather bulletins say. They have a battery-powered radio out at the nurses' desk," he explained. "The local station's managed to stay on the air all night. They're broadcasting emergency information, tips on keeping warm, what to do about frostbite, stuff like that." He was talking very quietly so as not to disturb the sleepers, but his nervousness was apparent beneath the surface of his words.

"I was just about to check on your father," Chris said, taking a sip of her coffee. "Would you like to come with me?"

Jeff nodded. He walked over to where Tiffany lay on the couch, covered by Keith's thick down parka, and touched her tousled hair lightly, almost tentatively. "She's exhausted, poor little kid."

"She'll be fine now that she knows Ethan will recover."

"God, what a hard couple of years she's had." Keith stirred restlessly as the sound of their voices disturbed his rest, but Tiffany slept on, unaware of the conversation around her. "I guess most of it was my fault." Jeff turned away from his daughter and followed Chris down the hall toward Ethan's room.

"Blaming yourself at this late date doesn't do anyone any good," Chris said, still in a whisper. The hallway was lit at both ends by emergency spotlights. Other smaller lights illuminated the nurses' desk and individual cubicles.

"You're right." Jeff took a hefty swallow of his coffee, draining the cup. He crushed it between his hands and tossed it in a nearby wastebasket. "My dad's done a hell of a job with my kids. Of course, that's his specialty, you know," he said with a mirthless, almost angry grin. "Producing miracles through good old-fashioned hard work and attention to details. He only failed at two things in his life. His marriage to my mom and trying to make something out of me. I've spent a lot of years trying to be as different from him as I could be. I've succeeded pretty well, don't you think?"

"Your father loves your children." Chris stopped herself before she said anything else. She couldn't tell Jeff Connor she agreed, at the moment, with his father's assessment that he would never grow up. Maybe if she listened, if she helped talk him through his problems, some good would come of it. She hoped so; she devoutly hoped so.

"More than I do?" One of his straight, dark eyebrows, so like Ethan's, quirked upward. "Are those the words you're too polite to say out loud?"

"I don't know what you mean," Chris said truthfully. Her temper flared despite her good intentions. "I'm tired. It's been a long, terrifying night. I'm Tiffany's Big Sister. I care for her a great deal and I'll fight for her happiness. I want to see her confident and fulfilled, sure of herself, ready to meet the challenges of growing up in such an uncertain world—not the subject of an emotional tug-of-war between you and your father."

"I want to see her happy, too," Jeff said, balling his hand into a fist, leaning against the door frame of an unoccupied cubicle. "I *don't* want to have to be in competition with my father to do it."

"Have you told him how you feel?" Chris stared down at her half-empty cup of coffee. The sight of the dark, oily liquid suddenly turned her stomach. She wasn't up to such an emotionally charged confrontation with this angry, frightened young man. Her loyalties were torn. How could she be expected to help Tiffany choose between her father and her grandfather, when she loved one so desperately and felt such pity for the other's loneliness and alienation?

"Maybe you haven't noticed," Jeff said with a snort. "My father and I aren't on the best of terms.

We haven't been since I was fifteen years old...maybe for longer than that, when I think about it." He leaned slightly forward from the waist, bringing his face closer to hers so that he didn't have to raise his voice. "He's a pretty tough act to follow."

"I understand. My husband had many of those same qualities your father possesses—strength, integrity, determination, plus a lot of drive and ambition, perhaps too much." She looked back into the past and wondered what problems might eventually have surfaced between Keith and Jack if he had lived.

"My father hates weakness of any kind. He's never forgiven me for deserting my children when their mother died. I was crazy that night. I loved my wife, Chris. I never told her enough times, showed her in enough ways. I wouldn't believe I was losing her, and then she was gone, and I just took off. I still can't believe I just walked out on my own kids. I can't forgive myself and he won't forgive me. Stalemate."

"You didn't run out on us tonight."

"He didn't die, thank God."

"You love him," Chris said.

"He's my father," Jeff replied simply. "Of course I love him."

Chris felt trapped. She loved Ethan. She wanted to see him reconciled with his son, but if she offered Jeff her help and friendship, would she be betraying Ethan's trust? If he lost custody of Tiffany and her brother and sister, would he blame her? It was all so complicated and so sad. "Have you told him how you feel?"

Jeff gave a snort of derisive laughter. "Hell, no. He's been so damn busy at the plant there hasn't been time in his life for anything else. He's cut a pretty wide swath through life. When the corporate powers that be at Castleton find out their star troubleshooter's had a heart attack, they'll be jetting in here before the runways in Toledo are plowed. He's being groomed for a vice presidency, did he tell you that?''

"We never discussed it."

"At least you didn't try to tell me it's none of your business." He straightened to his full height and shoved his hands into the back pockets of his jeans. "You might have most of the people in this town fooled, but not me. I've seen the way my dad usually acts around women on the make—" He broke off before Chris could open her mouth to protest. "Hell, I'm sorry," he said with that sexy, charming grin that must have melted harder hearts than hers. "I didn't mean that the way it sounded. What I mean to say is, I don't think my dad's allowed himself to become interested in any woman until he met you. His work was always too damned important. He's got his sights set on a corner office at corporate headquarters, chauffeured limousine, the works. Turning Bonaparte's plant around will be a real feather in his cap if he lives to see the job done."

"He's going to be just fine. He'll make a complete recovery," Chris insisted, not wanting to hear any more. Her head was spinning not only from the hours of tension and fatigue, but from the intensity of their conversation. She didn't want to deal with all these matters now. She wanted to concentrate all her energy on Ethan's well-being. She didn't want to counsel his wayward son. And she didn't want to hear what he said about Bonaparte being only a temporary stopover in Ethan's life.

"Sure he is." Jeff reached out and touched her arm awkwardly. "He'll come out of this thing with flying colors. Hell, he never even lost consciousness, remember. Never gave up control till they filled him full of enough drugs to stop a bull elephant in its tracks. Don't worry, Chris." He patted her arm again. "I can guarantee he'll be up and around in record time."

"I pray you're right," she whispered, unable to keep the demons at bay a moment longer. She felt tears push against the back of her eyelids and she blinked hard to hold them back.

"Come on, we'll sneak in and check on him ourselves. Or are you chicken to try to make it past the old dragon at the desk?"

He was smiling again, Ethan's smile, and she couldn't help but smile back. She wanted to like Ethan's son for his own sake, and hoped that someday they could be friends. "I'm not chicken," she whispered, looking over her shoulder as she pitched her unfinished coffee into the wastebasket. "But you go first."

"Okay." He held out his hand and she took it.

"Jeff," she said, holding back for a moment, "promise me something."

"What?" he asked, wary again.

"Talk to him when he's stronger. Get some of this out into the open. Work it out for both your sakes."

"That's a pretty tall order," he said, frowning.

Chris was determined to have the last word. "Then do it for the children, if not for yourselves. Do it for Tiffany."

CHAPTER TWELVE

"HURRY UP, Grandpa. If you don't put this sweater on, we'll never get out of here," Tiffany urged, pointing to the gray cardigan in the small suitcase Jeff had packed with clothes for Ethan to wear home from the hospital.

"I think I might be too warm riding in a heated car in a flannel shirt and a sweater and my overcoat," Ethan said as he finished taking his shaving things off the bathroom shelf. He was trying very hard to keep the amusement out of his voice. Tiffany looked so grown-up, so concerned as she watched him pack. "It's really a very nice day outside. March is coming in like a lamb."

Tiffany wasn't in the mood for observations about the weather. "Dr. Betts said you were to be very careful and stay out of drafts for the rest of the winter, remember. I heard him." She slid off the high unoccupied second bed in his semiprivate room and handed him the sweater herself. "We don't want you to catch cold, now do we."

"Tiffany, you've spent entirely too much time around the nurses these past three weeks. You're even beginning to talk like them. Chris—" he turned to the woman sitting in the high-backed armchair by the window to support his argument "—you're her Big Sister. Tell her to give me a break, will you?" He liked being the center of attention as well as the next man, but the women in his life were definitely overdoing it these days. "I feel fine, Tiffany," he assured his skeptical granddaughter for the tenth time that afternoon when Chris only shrugged and smiled in reply.

"Put it on," Tiffany insisted. "You have to learn these things so you can take better care of yourself."

"But it's too warm," he said, caught between laughter and exasperation.

"No buts," Tiffany ordered.

"Chris..." He threw out his hands in a pleading gesture.

"Dr. Betts put Tiffany in charge of your convalescence," she reminded him. "I'm only her assistant."

"You are going to pay for this," he said, catching her brown eyes and holding her gaze captive with his own. "It's mutiny."

"It's love," she said very softly. She looked away, as shaken as he by the silent exchange of emotion between them.

Ethan reached out and took the sweater from his granddaughter's hand. "Tiffany, why don't you go on down to the nurse's station and tell them I'm ready to leave. All of the paperwork is taken care of, but they won't let me walk out under my own steam. Someone will have to bring a wheelchair and ride me out of here in style."

"Okay," she said, missing the undercurrent of tension in the room. "I'll go look for Miss Fackler. She's the nicest nurse on this wing. We'll find the best wheelchair they have and I'll push you all the way to the car myself."

"It's a deal," Ethan said. The shadows of fear and anxiety he'd seen in his granddaughter's eyes that first night were gone, replaced by a stubborn determination to watch over his every move, keep him safe. He knew it was going to take time to allay her fears for his health. If for no other reason than Tiffany's peace of mind, he intended to take damn good care of himself in the future.

"You look real nice in your sweater, Grandpa," Tiffany observed on her way out the door. "Don't forget to button it up." She smiled at him over her shoulder, pleased with her success in keeping him safe from an errant March draft.

"What am I going to do with that child?" he asked, only half joking as he struggled to adjust the sleeves of his charcoal gray flannel shirt beneath the sweater.

"Humor her. She's working out her fears the only way she knows how," Chris said as she rose from her chair.

"I look like an old man in this thing," he complained, straightening his collar.

"Not an old man." Chris smiled up at him as she smoothed the wool sweater across his shoulders. "More like one of those guys they use to model riding and hunting clothes in the sporting magazines. You know," she said, fixing her gaze somewhere just past his left ear. "Those mature, well-preserved gentlemen sitting in front of a stone fireplace with a couple of hunting dogs. The ones who look good in tweed coats and flannel shirts... and gray cardigans. Why don't you let me button this for you," she added innocently, attempting to do just that.

He was too quick for her. He grabbed her hands and held them captive against his chest. "Don't tease me, Chris." He couldn't keep the low, intense note out of his voice. He didn't want to. She'd been keeping him at arm's length ever since he'd regained his senses the morning after the attack. He was tired of it. He wanted her back in his arms, back in his life, not hovering watchfully on the fringes of it.

"I . . . I'm sorry," she whispered. "I thought you liked me teasing you now and then."

"Not today. Not now." She was looking at him now, directly into his eyes, with a mixture of alarm and anticipation, and he felt his pulse kick into overdrive without a twitch of discomfort from his healing heart. "No more of Tiffany's mother-hen attitude from you."

"I've been so worried about you," she said.

The catch in her voice made him regret for a moment the harshness of his words. But only for a moment. His need for her, his desire to feel her in his arms again was too great to deny. "Don't worry anymore. And I'm not going to play your good little invalid any longer. Get used to it." He pulled her into his arms, hard against his chest. Before she could step out of his grasp and caution him about his recovery yet again, he kissed her, quick and hard, then more slowly, softly, as he felt her respond. "God," he whispered with real reverence, "it's been so long, so damned long since I've had you to myself for even a minute. Don't fight me, Chris. Just kiss me back."

"Ethan, we shouldn't be doing this," she said breathlessly. Her words were somewhat mumbled because he wouldn't stop kissing her while she spoke.

"Yes, we should be doing this. It's what I want. It's what you want, too," he said gruffly. He slid his hands up to cradle her face, silencing her in the most delightful and effective way he knew.

"What if someone walks in on us?" she asked, twining her arms around his waist, pressing herself closer.

"I don't give a damn who walks in here." Ethan skimmed his hands down her back to mold her hips against his.

Chris gasped, unable to deny the evidence of his desire for her. Ethan saw her face flood scarlet. She looked dismayed and apprehensive and completely desirable all at the same time.

"Ethan, you shouldn't allow yourself to become so..." She stopped talking, forcing her hands between them to hold him slightly at bay.

"Is *aroused* the word you're having so much trouble with?" he asked, teasing her just a little in return.

"Yes," she said. "Is it safe? I mean...I've always heard..." She broke off in confusion once more.

"I have discussed all aspects of my recovery with Tom Betts," Ethan said solemnly, watching her intently. It was the first time he'd seen her blush and he relished the experience. Small things, he'd realized during the weeks of his recovery, meant so much more than they had in the past. Or was it only that for the first time in his life he'd slowed his headlong pace enough to enjoy them? "The good doctor said there is every reason to believe that I can enjoy a normal, healthy sex life. The only problem is that I don't have a sex life...at the present time. I didn't point that out to the gentleman because I intend to remedy that situation as soon as possible. Does that, by any chance, answer your question?"

Chris swallowed hard, the delicate muscles in her throat working beneath the skin, making him want to string a line of kisses along the slender column of her neck.

"But it's so soon. . . ." she stammered. "I mean . . . shouldn't we take it more slowly . . . work up to it a little bit at a time?"

"I assume that means you are interested in making love with me sometime in the not too distant future?"

"Yes." The word was a mere whisper of sound. "But your heart . . . the strain . . ."

"Is this misguided thinking the reason I've been treated to pats on the head and quick pecks on the cheek for the past three weeks?" he asked, feigning surprise.

"Yes," she said, still looking embarrassed, although the blush had faded from her cheeks. "I thought . . ."

"Woman, how can you have reached the advanced age of forty-two years and still be so woefully ignorant of the recuperative powers of the human body?" He pressed her close yet again.

"I don't know," she said.

She smiled this time with such brilliance that it almost took his breath away. But still he saw the shadow of something troubling her in the depths of her warm brown eyes. Had he been taking her feelings for granted? Were the words they'd exchanged the night of his heart attack only a memory of a dream? He'd had to concentrate all of his energy and willpower on regaining his health these past weeks. Now that he was well on the way to full recovery he intended to focus on wooing and winning Christine.

"I love you, Chris." Ethan watched her closely. He hadn't said the words aloud since that first night.

"I love you, Ethan," Chris answered, but warily, as if she didn't want to admit to the strength of her feelings for him.

"I want to marry you." He was rushing things, he knew, but he had only a minute or two before Tiffany returned. He had no doubt whatsoever that once he arrived home Mrs. Baden and Tiffany would refuse to let him out of their sight, even to release him into Chris's custody for an afternoon. Conducting a courtship in front of an all-too-interested audience of friends and relatives was a complication he hoped to minimize, if not avoid altogether.

"Ethan, I don't know..." she began.

She was still smiling, but still looking troubled beneath the smile. Her face was so expressive, her thoughts so easy to read once you knew the depth of the emotions beneath the surface calm.

"Is it because of the children?"

"Yes," Chris replied, biting her lip, "and no." She smiled a little shakily. "It's myself I'm not sure of."

"This isn't the first time I've asked you," he said, smoothing the palm of his hand across her thick, shining hair, imagining it spread over the pillow, imagining himself burying his face in its softness, inhaling its scent.

"No, it isn't," she agreed, her fingers twisting the buttons of his sweater as she refused for a moment to meet his gaze.

"I've been thinking about that first night a lot the past couple of days—those first few hours in the hospital when I was hooked up to all those tubes and monitors, listening to the storm and wondering if I'd make it through to morning. I almost convinced myself I must have dreamed that I asked you to marry

me. Then I remembered that you never answered me,
and I knew it wasn't a dream, because even as sick as
I was, in my dreams I'd never have let you say anything but yes." He tipped her chin up with his knuckle
and smiled at her, but uncertainty tightened the muscles of his neck and shoulders, made him want to hold
her closer, hold her so tightly she'd never get away.

"I was terrified we would lose you that night,
Ethan," she replied, sidestepping his proposal yet
again.

The pain that seared through his chest had nothing
to do with his damaged heart, and everything to do
with his bruised emotions. "Are you turning me down
again?"

"I'm asking you for some time," she said, dropping her head against his chest, hugging him so tightly
he grunted. "We have time now and I need just a little to prepare my kids, my family...." She lifted her
head and looked up at him with tears sparkling on her
lashes. "I've been so worried about you I've put
everything else on hold. Erika's wedding plans are at
a standstill. I have mounds of paperwork on my desk,
including two reports that should have gone off to
national headquarters last week. I'm—"

"You're not sure you want to be my wife." He was
feeling the strain of his first full day out of bed. He
was tired and weak. He wanted to take a nap, for
God's sake. He wasn't thinking as clearly as he'd like.

"Ethan..." She moved out of his arms, turning to
fuss with one of the several elaborate floral arrangements that had come from corporate headquarters
while he was ill.

"I don't want to lose you." He didn't want any
more delays; he'd come too close to death to feel

comfortable waiting patiently to win what he wanted
most in the world.

"You won't lose me, but I need some time." She let
her fingers trail over the spiky petals of a bird of par-
adise plant. Ethan still hadn't figured out how Bonaparte Florists had managed to come up with a full
half-dozen of the exotic blooms. He hoped they'd
charged Castleton Soups plenty for trucking them
down from Toledo.

"I may not have time," he growled, angry with
himself for being weak enough to give voice to that
persistent and bedeviling fear.

Chris shook her head but didn't turn around. She
sounded on the verge of tears. "You don't believe
that, and thank God, neither do I. I'm not going to let
you browbeat me into marrying you before I'm ready,
Ethan Connor. I love you."

She turned around then and if he had any doubts of
her true feelings for him, they died in the glory of seeing her love reflected in the depths of her warm brown
eyes.

"That doesn't change the fact that I need time," she
went on. "I owe it to my children, my parents, Jack's
parents, to give them a chance to adjust to my loving
you." She took a deep breath and folded her hands in
front of her. "You owe it to Jeff and the children to do
the same thing. Please, Ethan, all I'm asking is a few
more weeks, until after Erika's wedding, when I can
relax and enjoy being the future Mrs. Ethan Connor.
Please." She closed the small distance between them,
reaching up to brush her lips over his. "Give me just
a little more time."

"I don't seem to have much choice." He didn't like
being thwarted in his plans. He didn't like the idea of

waiting months and months to make her his wife, to
have her in his arms and in his bed, but he didn't have
a choice. Wasn't that what Tom Betts had told him
would be the hardest thing for him to do? Learn to
wait, learn to be patient, learn to accept the things he
couldn't change, instead of wading in feetfirst and
trying to reshape the world to his design? He released
Chris when they both heard the sound of Tiffany's
voice in the hall outside. He'd try to follow Tom's advice, but he wasn't looking forward to the exercise in
self-denial. "But believe me, the day after Erika's
wedding, if you don't agree to set a date for ours,
I'll..."

"You'll what?" Chris demanded, smiling as she
detected the smile lurking behind his scowl.

"I don't know," he admitted, letting the smile turn
up one corner of his mouth. He slammed the lid on his
suitcase with more force than absolutely necessary,
and felt better. "But I'll think of something."

"I don't doubt that for a moment," Chris said, and
turned to greet Tiffany and Nurse Fackler as they
wheeled Ethan's chair into the room.

FOR THE FIRST TIME in the weeks since they had fallen
into the habit of an evening walk together, Chris
wasn't happy to see Ethan and Tiffany on her front
doorstep.

"Come in," she said, forcing a smile to her lips that
she was certain Ethan, at least, would detect was false.

He did. Immediately. He knew her so well. Or perhaps it was the sound of Erika's sobs, subdued but still
audible, from the family room.

"Problems?" he asked.

"Domestic crisis." She tried to make her smile more genuine. It wasn't all that hard. Just looking at him, healthy and fit, made her feel better. "Erika and Michael just had a terrible argument about the cost and questionable taste of the groomsmen's gifts."

"But the wedding is next week," Tiffany blurted out, appalled by the news. "What happened? Should I go talk to her? Where's Keith?"

"It's nothing, really," Chris said, and hoped she was telling the truth. "Just bride's nerves."

"And groom's nerves, too, I'll bet." Ethan chuckled, ruffling Tiffany's short dark hair.

"Grandpa, why are you laughing? It's terrible that Erika and Michael are fighting, isn't it? They're supposed to be in love," she reminded him, shifting anxiously from one foot to the other. "People who are in love don't fight. Do they?" She cocked her head and looked at Ethan for enlightenment.

"People who are in love do quarrel," Chris said, taking a lightweight green jacket from the hall closet and slipping it over her shoulders before Ethan could answer Tiffany's questions or offer to help with the jacket.

"Then they get divorced," Tiffany said knowingly.

"No, they don't," Ethan responded, managing to help settle the jacket on Chris's shoulders despite her ploy.

Chris felt the warmth of his fingers through the light fabric and the soft cotton of her blouse. It was growing harder and harder to maintain a polite distance from Ethan. She wanted him; she wanted to be with him, to be his, and it simply wasn't possible until she met the immediate obligations of her life. But it was very hard to wait. She'd realized early in their relationship that their lovemaking would be all or nothing. With Ethan's return to full health, she had every expectation of the "all" being as marvelous as the "nothing" was frustrating.

"Even people who love each other very much quarrel now and then, Tiffany," Ethan said, shutting the front door behind him. "It doesn't mean they're getting divorced. It doesn't even mean they're going to stay angry at each other for a long time."

"They aren't going to stop loving each other," Chris said, feeling her own anxiety over her daughter's future happiness begin to slip away.

"Michael will drive around in his car for a while and play the stereo loud and let off steam," Ethan predicted as they walked.

"And Erika will lock herself in her bedroom and have a good cry." Chris smiled up at him, letting him enfold her hand in his.

"And then they'll kiss and make up. That's good," Tiffany said, skipping ahead a little as they turned onto the sidewalk that fronted Chris's house. "I'd hate for them to get so mad at each other they called off the wedding and I didn't get to wear my dress and pass out little bags of birdseed." She dashed ahead, leaving Ethan and Chris alone.

"She is something else," he said, watching her jog to the corner and turn to wait for them, still running in place.

"She certainly is." Chris stopped walking a moment to examine the red-and-yellow emperor tulips that edged her neighbor's front lawn.

"You've done wonders for her this winter. She's more self-confident. She's not so afraid of the unknown. She's not quite so..." He hesitated over his choice of words.

"Managing?" Chris asked, wrapping her hand around his arm so that they could walk more closely together.

"Yes," he said.

Then he laughed, and Chris couldn't help but respond to that sexy, charming laugh that suited him so well.

"I wasn't certain she was going to give me permission to go back to the plant full-time last week, even though Tom Betts assured her it was okay, but she never said a word. That isn't to say she's not watching me like a hawk. I'd hate to think what she'd do if I tried to smuggle work home from the office."

"Someone has to make you toe the line." Chris giggled, taking a deep breath of moist, cool, spring-scented air. April was a month for love and lovers, and she felt like a giddy teenager in the midst of it all. "You shouldn't be doing work at home," she said, trying to get her heartbeat and her imagination under control. "I thought that's why Castleton's sent that hotshot young assistant out from headquarters. To keep you from overtaxing yourself."

Ethan grunted. "He's hell-bent on making a reputation for himself in my plant."

"Wouldn't you be doing the same thing if your positions were reversed?" Chris asked innocently, too innocently.

Ethan gave her a dark, knowing look, then grinned with wry amusement. "Of course I would. That's the trouble with him. He's too much like me." He stopped walking for a moment and looked down at her. "Or the way I used to be."

Chris tilted her head and studied his face in the fading light of the April evening. A dog barked somewhere nearby, startling the birds nesting in the big maples that lined the street. "How have you changed, Ethan?" she asked, holding her breath, not certain she wanted to hear what he had to say. She was aware of the deference paid to him by the Castleton executives who had visited Bonaparte during his convalescence. She knew how valuable an asset they considered his experience and expertise. Had they made him an offer he couldn't refuse?

"I don't know exactly how I've changed. I just know I have. My priorities are different, maybe even my goals." He shrugged, his broad shoulders straining the fabric of his gray sweatshirt jacket. "It's hard to explain. The trouble is it didn't happen all at once like some big blast of cosmic light that gave me no choice about what path to follow. It just keeps coming to me in bits and pieces. Things that used to mean the world to me..." He ran his hand through his hair, exasperated, as he searched for the words he needed to express his thoughts.

"You nearly died of a heart attack," Chris said softly, touching his cheek, unconcerned if the whole population of Bonaparte was watching them. "It's bound to change your perspective on everything in your life. Give it time." What was he trying to say? Did he want to leave Bonaparte, get on with his life and his career? Would he ask her to go with him? Or would he be content to stay here, where her life and her family and her roots would always be, and sacrifice the brilliant future they had planned for him at Castleton Soups?

Did he love her enough to stay if she asked him?

Did she love him enough to follow him if he chose to go?

"Chris?" He bent his head toward her.

She closed her eyes, pushing her difficult, unanswerable questions to the back of her mind, and waited for his kiss. A car rounded the corner a block away and headed toward them.

"Keith! Keith!" Tiffany hollered, jumping up and down at curbside, her thumb outstretched in the hitchhiker's classic pose. "Give me a ride, please!" she squealed. "I want to ride in your new car."

"Curses," Ethan growled, frustrated and showing it. "Foiled again. I suppose this is the fantastic new sports car Keith is buying for his graduation present to himself?" he inquired with exaggerated patience as Chris took a deep breath and forced herself to move forward again, act normally, speak intelligently.

"The one and only. One owner. Mint condition. Twenty-eight thousand highway miles. It's a steal at twice the price," she said, quoting Keith's enthusiastic argument for securing her signature as cosigner of his bank loan.

"Let's take a look." Ethan ran his hand through his hair and grinned. "Checking out a hot little number like that beats standing in the middle of the sidewalk feeling sorry for myself."

Tiffany was already squirming into the bucket seat on the passenger side of the almost-new red Firebird. "Isn't this a great car, Grandpa? I just love it," she gushed. "Keith's going to take me right down Main Street so everyone can see me in it."

"Just one circuit, okay, Mr. Connor? If I know this brat at all, she's got homework to do yet this evening."

"Do not," Tiffany insisted with a scowl, her hands folded across her chest.

"Do, too," Ethan said, shaking his head at his granddaughter's bold-faced fib. "But if you promise to do your spelling and arithmetic as soon as you get home, you can go cruising with Keith." He glanced at his watch. "For half an hour. Deal?"

"Deal!" Tiffany beamed, her good humor restored. "Let's go, Keith. I'll tell you all about the fight Erika and Michael had," she promised with a wicked grin.

"Are those two at it again, Mom?" the teenager asked as he gunned the motor for Tiffany's benefit.

"I'm afraid so."

"Would you mind dropping Tiffany off at my house?" Ethan asked without even looking at Chris for confirmation. "I don't think your mother's in the mood for a long walk tonight."

"I think I should be getting back to spend some time with your sister. She really is very upset."

"She's a nut case about this wedding," Keith said with a younger brother's total lack of sympathy. "And so's Mike. Those two deserve to spend the rest of their lives together."

"Careful what you say, young man. I can always call the bank and tell them I withdraw my consent to the loan," Chris warned, trying her best to hide a smile at the shocked look on Keith's face.

"I'll come straight home after I drop off the brat here and let Erika cry on my shoulder all she wants."

"You are a prince among little brothers," Chris said with a laugh.

"Ain't I, though!" He gunned the motor again and the sound echoed through the quiet residential neighborhood like spring thunder. A look of supreme contentment crossed Keith's face.

"Let's go!" Tiffany insisted once again. "'Bye, Chris. 'Bye, Grandpa. See you later." They drove away with just a tiny spurt of gravel from under the back wheels.

"I am sorry, but I really should get back to Erika."

"Give me credit for knowing you well enough to figure that out," Ethan said, still sounding out of sorts.

They started walking back to Chris's house. She glanced at Ethan from the corner of her eye. His straight dark eyebrows were pulled together in a frown.

"There just doesn't seem to be enough hours in the day anymore for everything I have to do... and everyone I want to be with," she began.

"Don't apologize," he said, his expression lightening. He tucked her hand beneath his elbow. "I can wait. Until Erika and Michael have tied the knot, at any rate." He turned his head so that she could see the smile in his eyes. "After that I'm not making any promises."

"THIS CAR IS simply elegant," Tiffany said, running her hand over the silver-gray upholstery on the bucket seat. It was soft and furry and felt smooth as silk beneath her fingers. She stretched out her legs and watched Keith drive, one hand on the wheel, one hand on the gearshift. "Someday I'm going to have a car just like this."

"By the time you can afford a car like this I'll be ready to sell it to you."

"Okay," she said happily, "you've got yourself a deal."

"You seem real full of yourself today, squirt. What kind of Machiavellian plans are running through that fevered little brain of yours now?"

"Machi what?" she asked, instantly on guard. She couldn't get away with too much where Keith was concerned. He had an uncanny knack of being able to read her mind.

"Machiavellian," Keith repeated patiently. "He was this real twisted Italian dude. He was always thinking up ways to get what he wanted, no matter what. You'll probably have to study about him in history someday."

"In high school," Tiffany said, nodding wisely. "I do like to make plans, but I'm not real twisted and I don't have a fever," she pointed out.

"I guess you got me there." Keith settled back in the low-slung seat.

Tiffany tried to do the same, but when she did, she couldn't see a thing, so she sat up straight again.

"Want to tell me what you're planning, though?" Keith said.

"No!" Tiffany almost yelled. The last thing she wanted was for Keith to know what she was thinking.

Because, as usual these days, she was thinking about her grandfather marrying Keith's mother, and she wasn't sure how he would like that. Even though she had a hundred good reasons why they should get married. And she'd bet he couldn't think of one why they should not.

"Okay, okay," he said with a laugh that was halfway between a grunt and a snort. "Don't get all bent out of shape. Go ahead and plot all you want. Sit back and enjoy the ride. You're the first girl who's set foot inside this car. It's an honor, so act suitably impressed.''

"Okay," Tiffany said. She was only half listening to him, and the remark sailed right past her, which was unusual enough in itself.

Maybe it was because spring was finally here and the winter was over. Her grandpa wasn't sick anymore and her father seemed to like living in Bonaparte, so she didn't think he was going to decide to move far away again, at least not right away. He didn't seem to be very happy, it was true, but if he stayed around long enough this time, maybe she and Ashley and Brandon could make him feel better. She hoped so. That would make everything easier.

It was kind of complicated. Should she call Chris "Grandma" or still call her "Chris" if she got married to her grandfather? Chris didn't look like a grandmother, so Tiffany would probably just go on calling her "Chris." And the worst thing of all was that Chris and her grandfather might not know they were in love. She'd only seen them kiss once and that was a long time ago. She wondered how she should go about trying to help them figure it out.

Maybe she wouldn't have to.

Her grandpa was a great dancer and he was going to be at Erika's wedding. She knew dancing for old people was a very romantic thing. If he danced with Chris, maybe they would realize they were in love, the way people did in the movies and on TV, and decide to get married on their own. Then everything would be great and she wouldn't even have to come up with a better plan.

Tiffany folded her hands in her lap and grinned. Everything would work out just fine. And if it didn't—if Chris and her grandfather didn't figure out they were in love—she'd just have to tell Keith about it and get him to help. She glanced at his profile and felt a squiggle of happiness deep inside her. He was her special friend, the most handsome boy in the senior class, and she was riding in his car. Suddenly something Keith had said popped back into her mind. She scooted around in her seat.

"Keith?"

"What, squirt?"

"Am I *really* the very first girl you've taken for a ride in your new car?"

CHAPTER THIRTEEN

"Dad, do you have some time to spare?"

"I've got a minute or two, unless Tiffany needs some last-minute help getting dressed for Erika's wedding." Ethan recalled the dozen minor emergencies they'd encountered already that balmy Saturday afternoon and wondered how many more there would be to deal with before they left for the church. He grinned at himself in the bedroom mirror. He was almost as excited about today's celebration as Tiffany was, but for different reasons. The only possible obstacle he could see standing in the way of Chris's accepting his proposal of marriage was Keith's graduation from high school, and after everything else they'd been through, that was only a bump in the road.

"I need to talk to you," Jeff said from the doorway.

Something in his tone of voice put Ethan on guard. He glanced over at his son, standing with one hand in the pocket of his jeans and the other resting on the door frame just above eye level. "What's on your mind?" he asked, working to straighten the knot in his tie.

"It's about the kids," Jeff said, advancing into the room. He sat down on the walnut blanket chest at the foot of Ethan's bed and stared down at the carpet between his spread knees.

"I'm listening." His gut instinct told him Jeff didn't just want to discuss Tiffany's *D* on a spelling test or the fact that Ashley had thrown a crayon at one of her kindergarten classmates in a fit of temper the previous day. Ethan picked up the hairbrush and ran it through his hair before turning away from Jeff's reflection in the dresser mirror to face his son in the flesh. "Go ahead."

"I've been living here with you for over six months," Jeff began.

It seemed to Ethan that Jeff was choosing his words with great deliberation. "God knows there's plenty of room in this big old house for the five of us," he replied encouragingly, straightening his cuffs. He'd known this conversation was coming. He'd seen the restlessness growing in Jeff's eyes for the past several weeks. He wondered what corner of the country or the globe his son would head for this time? But why did he have to choose today of all days to make the announcement that he was going? Ethan wanted to be able to tell Jeff of his own plans for the future, and the future happiness of Tiffany and her brother and sister. "We can always remodel the attic over the garage, if you're feeling cramped."

"That's not the point, Dad." Jeff's eyebrows drew together in a frown.

"Then why don't you tell me what the point of this conversation is?" Ethan prompted. He brushed a speck of lint from the lapel of his dark gray suit jacket with fingers that trembled ever so slightly.

"I want my children back."

"What?" Ethan wanted to believe his ears were playing tricks on him, but his hearing was perfect. So was his eyesight, he knew when he looked at Jeff. His son's expression was dead serious.

"It's time I took responsibility for their welfare," Jeff said, his blue eyes locked with Ethan's.

"Just how do you intend to do that?" Ethan felt his gut tighten with apprehension and anger. "You haven't even found enough work to support yourself this past winter."

"Bonaparte isn't exactly Colonial Williamsburg," Jeff said with equal anger. "There just isn't all that much custom work to be had in this town."

"All right, I'll agree with you there." Ethan took a deep, steadying breath. Nothing would be gained by their trading insults in voices loud enough for the children to overhear and become upset. "What plans do you have in mind?"

"I'll probably head back out to California."

"Why California?" Ethan put his foot on the corner of the blanket chest opposite where Jeff was sitting and swiped at a smudge on his shoe with the T-shirt he'd discarded before showering.

"I made some friends out there. I can make good money restoring antiques and crafting reproductions on my own. Besides, I like it out there. I might settle in somewhere close to Mom," he added.

Jeff's dismissive shrug made Ethan's hands itch to curl into fists. "You *might* settle somewhere close to your mother? You *might* find work? You *might* come up with a decent place for your children to live and go to school?" Ethan stood up straight. "Is that the best plan you've come up with so far?"

"I want my kids back," Jeff said belligerently.

He was talking just the way he had when he was four or fourteen, and determined to have his own way, Ethan realized. "I'm not ready to give them up." He would never be ready to give them up, but he couldn't say that out loud to his son, not now, not yet. He couldn't be certain that his insistence on retaining custody of Tiffany and the younger children wouldn't merely solidify Jeff's determination to win them back, regardless of the emotional upheaval it would cause in their lives.

"Dad, why are you fighting me on this?"

Jeff looked genuinely puzzled, hurt and defiant, and Ethan didn't answer for a moment. Why was he fighting his son? Was it because he truly believed that Jeff didn't understand his own feelings, had over-estimated his commitment to his children's welfare, his capacity to love on an ongoing basis? Or was it because he didn't want to acknowledge that his son had changed, matured, was capable of being a good father, not just when it suited him, but for the rest of his life? Was he trying to ignore the fact that the children should be with Jeff and not with him...and Chris?

"I'm not fighting you, Jeff," he said at last, suddenly as drained of energy as he had been after his heart attack. "I need time to think about this. So do you. Having full-time custody of three children isn't the same as giving them their baths and tucking them in at night. Even while I was in the hospital you had Mrs. Baden here, and Chris and Miriam Leonard to fall back on in an emergency."

"We got along fine," Jeff said stubbornly.

"You were playing house," Ethan said between his teeth. He took a deep breath, then let it out slowly. "I want what's best for the children, nothing else."

"Then why won't you let me take them with me?"

"Because I don't trust you," Ethan growled, goaded beyond discretion by his own emotional pain. "How can I be sure the next time you want to pull up stakes and head off into the sunset you won't just leave them behind the way you did when Katherine died." He should have never spoken the words aloud in anger and he knew it, but it was too late to take them back.

"Damn it," Jeff yelled, jumping up off the blanket chest. "Why the hell did you have to bring that up again? Don't you understand I didn't know what I was doing that night?"

He ran his hands through his hair in a gesture that Ethan recognized as one of his own nervous habits.

"I . . . I think I was crazy with grief for a while after Katie died."

"And your children ended up in a shelter, separated, frightened, alone." Ethan shrugged into his jacket, determined not to let go of the fraying edges of his temper again. If it took all the willpower he possessed he would not let unchecked anger sever the last strands of communication, of caring, between him and his son.

"You're going to keep throwing that in my face for the rest of my life, aren't you?" Jeff said between clenched teeth. "I didn't just walk out on the kids. They were with a baby-sitter. She didn't have to turn them over to the juvenile authorities."

"You didn't contact her for eighteen hours after Katie died."

"I . . . I didn't know what I was doing, right or wrong. I wish it had all been different."

Ethan looked him straight in the eye. He could see so much of his ex-wife in the boy, his ability to focus only on his own dreams and desires, his constant need for reassurance and attention. Yet there was much of himself in Jeff as well, his stubbornness and determination to achieve his goals. "I would never mention what happened that night anymore if I was certain it wouldn't happen again."

The color drained out of Jeff's face. His jaw tightened and he narrowed his eyes. "Okay," he said through clenched teeth. "At least I know where I stand with you."

"Grandpa! Dad! I can't find my good shoes."

Tiffany's urgent shout from her bedroom halted what more he might have said.

"I'll bet that whiny little brat Brandon hid them again. Someone come and help me look for them!" The last sentence was not a request. It was a command.

Ethan grinned at her imperious tone in spite of himself. "You'd better go," he said to Jeff with a nod.

But Jeff ignored his suggestion. "Did it ever occur to you that I might be thinking of your best interests, as well as my own, if I take the kids away with me?"

"How the hell do you figure that?" Ethan picked up his wallet, pocket comb and small change from the dresser tray and put them in his pocket. The action was sheer force of habit. His thoughts were entirely on the matter at hand.

"I'm not blind," Jeff responded. "I can see that what you've got going with Chris Baldwin is no casual, roll-in-the-hay kind of affair."

"It isn't an affair at all," Ethan said with a thread of steel in his voice.

Jeff nodded, acknowledging the warning in his father's tone. "Maybe the lady of your choice isn't interested in a ready-made new family. Maybe she wants you all to herself. Have you asked her how she feels about being a mother again?"

"Not in so many words." There was ice in Ethan's voice this time. He didn't want to discuss the matter when he didn't know the answers to Jeff's questions himself.

"Then I suggest you think about your own plans for the future, as well as mine."

"Where is everybody? Grandpa! Dad! I can't find my shoes!" Tiffany's shouts had risen a notch or two in volume and intensity. "Is anybody in this house listening to me?" She appeared in the doorway wearing her special lilac-colored dress, her face flushed, her feet in white lacey anklets planted well apart in a belligerent stance. "I'm going to give that bratty brother of mine a real beating if I find out he hid my shoes," she warned.

"I think Mrs. Baden took them downstairs to polish before she left yesterday afternoon. Why don't you look for them on the dining-room table?" Ethan suggested.

"Oh, okay." She glanced over at him a little sheepishly. "You're sure that's where they are?"

"Yes," Ethan said firmly.

"I'd better go get them or we'll be late." She sounded disappointed that Brandon was going to escape retribution, then clapped her hands and smiled from ear to ear. "Grandpa, you look great. Real handsome, doesn't he, Daddy?"

"A credit to us all," Jeff agreed, his voice even, his tone natural, though his eyes smoldered with hostility and unresolved conflict.

"Are you ready to go?" she asked, skipping backward out of the doorway, vanishing as quickly as she'd appeared.

"I'll be down in a minute," Ethan assured her, his attention fixed once again on Jeff.

"Hurry," Tiffany urged, already halfway down the stairs, "I don't want to miss any of the wedding."

"You'd better not keep her waiting," Jeff said, refusing to meet his eye.

"We'll talk about this later, son," Ethan said, making no attempt to reach out and touch the angry, confused young man standing before him. They had never been close that way.

"I'm not going to change my mind. They're my kids. I want them back."

"You want them back today, but what about tomorrow?" This time it was Ethan who paused in the doorway, who looked back at his son, silhouetted by the bright afternoon sunlight pouring through the big double-hung windows that looked out over the river.

"Don't fight me on this, Dad," Jeff said, meeting Ethan's gaze head-on. "I'll get a lawyer if I have to, but I'm going to win in the end. And we both know it."

"WEDDINGS ARE WONDERFUL," Tiffany announced as she settled back against the car seat with a dreamy sigh. "I have never seen anything so beautiful in my life. Didn't Erika and Michael look just like a prince and princess out of a fairy tale?"

"Exactly," her grandfather said as he steered the car out of the Lutheran church parking lot.

"The guys looked great in their black tuxedos. Especially Keith," she added loyally. "And the bridesmaids. Their dresses floated around them just like they were spring flowers swaying in a breeze."

"Did you think up that description yourself?" Ethan asked, eyeing her. She wanted to say she had, but she never lied to her grandfather. He caught her at it every time. "No, I heard Mrs. Leonard say it. But it's what I think, too."

"The bridesmaids did look very pretty. And you look just as pretty in that dress."

"It is a very nice dress," Tiffany agreed contentedly as she smoothed her hand over the soft folds of her skirt. "What's next?"

"The reception at the Veterans of Foreign Wars hall, as you very well know," Ethan reminded her.

"I want to drive along Main Street with the other cars that are following Erika and Michael and honk the horn and everything," she said, making one last attempt to change her grandfather's mind. "It's just like a parade. The limousine Erika and Michael rented is as big as a school bus." She turned around in her seat to try to catch one last glimpse of the astonishingly long white car that the bride and groom had hired to convey them to the reception as a gift to themselves.

"Did you have any bags of birdseed left?" Ethan asked, changing the subject adroitly as he turned in the opposite direction of the parade of cars following the wedding party.

"Three," Tiffany proclaimed, eyeing the lacy bags still nestled in the bottom of her white wicker basket.

"It looked like it was raining birdseed when Erika and Michael ran down the church steps. I made sure *everyone* had a bag of it to throw at them."

"I'm sure no one will say you shirked your duty in that respect."

"Grandpa, are you making fun of me?" Tiffany asked suspiciously. "'Shirked' sounds like a word you use to make fun of someone."

"Well, it isn't," her grandfather replied, and he didn't look as if he was trying to hide a smile. "It means you did your job very well."

"I did," she said, pleased with the compliment. "How much farther is it to the VFW hall?"

"Just another couple of blocks."

"I can't wait for you to see what the place looks like. Yesterday it was just a big ugly room with lots of flags standing around and pictures of old dead soldiers on the walls. Chris is just great at that kind of stuff. She started telling all of us where to put the crepe-paper streamers and the great big heart made all out of balloons and those funny little paper bells that look so flat and pop up into whole round, waffley ones...."

Her grandfather laughed at her confusing description of the tissue-paper decorations and so did she.

"Oh, you know what I mean," she said, and giggled because she was having such a good time. Maybe it wasn't so bad being a girl if you could have a dress like this one and go to weddings with your favorite grandfather who looked just elegant himself in a dazzling white shirt, gray-striped tie and dark suit. "But let's do hurry. I didn't get to see the table decorations because they're made out of real flowers and they

would wilt if we put them out yesterday. And the cake.
Erika says the cake is simply elegant."

"Then, by all means, we'll hurry. I can't wait myself to see such a beautiful cake."

"It has real crystal swans on top instead of a bride
and groom. And a fountain in the middle. I picked
that out from a book," she added proudly. "It has
pink water bubbling up in it."

"I'm impressed."

"Chris said I have a real knack for decorating."
When you were wearing a dress like hers you could
toot your own horn a little, Tiffany decided. "I bet
she's already at the VFW hall. That's why I want to get
there quick. So we can check to make sure everything
is just right. Planning this wedding has been fun. I
never thought I'd like doing girl things so much, but
this was different." She sighed and shook her head.
"It just went by so fast."

"Happy times have a way of doing that. But soon
you'll see the photographs and you'll remember the
fun all over again."

Tiffany smiled. Her grandfather always knew just
the right things to say. "I didn't get a chance to tell
Chris how pretty she looked," she said, frowning a
little as she recalled how quickly the people behind her
had pushed her past her Big Sister in the receiving line
after the ceremony. "Did you, Grandpa?"

Ethan kept his eyes on the traffic ahead, but his
voice sounded a little bit funny when he answered.
"No, I didn't have a chance to tell her how very lovely
she looked," he admitted.

"That's all right," Tiffany said, satisfied that he'd
taken the hint. It was time to get him and Chris together for real, as a couple, get them married. Yes,

married. Weddings were fun. It would be nice to have another one. "You'll have plenty of chances to tell her at the reception. And if you forget, I'll remind you to tell her when you ask her to dance."

"HERE YOU GO, Sis. Have a glass of champagne. I hid this bottle from Michael's groomsmen for just this occasion." Chris's younger brother Dale handed her a plastic glass of bubbly wine and pulled over a metal folding chair for her to sit on. "Sit down. Rest your feet. It's been a great party."

"It was very nice," Chris said, tired, but contentedly so. "Thanks for all your help." She unpinned the white orchid corsage from the beaded jacket of her dress and dropped it beside her handbag on the table behind them.

"Hey, what are handsome younger brothers for?" he joked.

Since he looked exactly like their father, just an inch or so above middle height, stocky and broad shouldered, with thinning hair and an infectious grin, Chris pretended not to hear the lighthearted remark.

"It meant everything to Erika and Michael that you were all here to share their special day." Dale was Erika's favorite uncle and she had asked him to give her away in her dead father's place.

"They're great kids. And you are going to make a great mother-in-law," he said, lifting his glass in a salute, his blue-gray eyes sparkling with deviltry.

"Don't call me that!" Chris said in mock horror. "I'm just not ready for it."

"Mother-in-law. Mother-in-law," he teased, just as he had teased her mercilessly when they were children more than thirty years before.

"Dale! I'm going to tell Mom," she shot back, laughing.

"Can't. The folks took Mr. and Mrs. Schroeder back to the Shady Rest Motel about half an hour ago. Will and his wife left with the baby about the same time." Will was Chris's second brother, two years younger than Dale, six years younger than Chris. "Didn't you notice they were all gone?"

"No," she said truthfully, looking around. "I've been too busy saying goodbye to the guests." So many special friends had come to share the day. Most of her Bigs and Littles had been in attendance either at the wedding or the reception, as well as her co-workers, friends of Jack's from school and work, friends of her own.

"Hey, Mom, Uncle Dale, glad I caught up with you. I need the keys to your van," Keith announced, coming up behind them. "Time to get the loot loaded up and hauled off for safekeeping."

"Shhh, not so loud, people will hear," Chris cautioned with a giggle. The wine was going straight to her head. She must be more tired than she'd thought.

Dale patted his pockets. "Go see your aunt Marvel. She has the keys to the van in her purse. She said filling my pockets full of junk spoiled the line of my tux." He patted the beginning of a spare tire protruding from beneath his cummerbund.

"Okay." Keith shoved his hands in the pockets of his pants.

If Dale noticed there wasn't an ounce of excess fat on his nephew's slim, athletic frame, he didn't show it.

"The band's getting ready to start the last set," Keith continued. "I'll make sure the wedding party sticks around to help clean this place so we can all get out of here before midnight.''

"Got a hot date?" Dale asked with a wink for Chris.

"Yeah, a date with my pillow. This wedding business is downright exhausting. And these shoes are killing me." He stuck out a long leg and eyed the black leather dress shoe on his foot with disgust.''

"That's my line," Chris said, lifting one nylon-clad shoeless foot. "I can't believe I let Erika talk me into those spiked monsters. They're not only uncomfortable, they're dangerous to walk in."

"You were almost as pretty as the bride, in that slinky gray dress, Sis," Dale said.

His expression made Chris blink in surprise. He wasn't teasing. She couldn't think of a thing to say except, "Thank you."

"Oh, no," Keith moaned as the band broke into a favorite novelty song. "Who talked those guys into playing the chicken song? They're supposed to play slow dances this late at night."

"Not when the groom requests the number," Chris said, watching a very tipsy Michael pull his protesting bride onto the dance floor, urging her to flap her arms like a chicken and bounce up and down within a circle of laughing young people.

"How embarrassing," Keith said, groaning again. "Good thing they aren't leaving on their honeymoon until tomorrow night. We're going to have to haul my new brother-in-law home in a wheelbarrow as it is."

"Shh. No one is supposed to know they're spending tonight at their apartment. I'm sure Michael's fraternity brothers would like nothing better than to know where they've gone so they could pay them a visit.''

"Erika would have kittens if that bunch showed up at the apartment unannounced. My lips are sealed."

Keith was looking across the dance floor. Chris followed the direction of his gaze, expecting to find him watching one of the bridesmaids or one or another of the pretty senior girls he'd been dating the past few months. She was surprised to find his attention focused on Tiffany and Dale's three young children as they went about denuding the hall of the balloons and ribbon streamers that were easiest to reach.

"I think I'll give the squirt the thrill of her life and ask her to dance the chicken with me," he said, and walked off before Chris could comment on his plan.

"Well, I'll be," she said, half under her breath.

"Your Little is a cute kid," Dale remarked, unaware of the significance of the exchange he'd just witnessed.

He tipped his folding chair back on two legs at such a precarious angle that Chris was afraid he might topple over.

"I can't imagine not having her in my life," she answered truthfully. "She's made me remember all the good things about having a small child around the house."

"I should be so lucky," Dale said fondly and facetiously, watching his own lively brood as they joined the laughing circle of young people and a few adventurous elders on the dance floor. "Those three are giving me gray hair."

"Enjoy them," Chris said with a wistful smile, her tongue loosened by the champagne. She smiled as Keith executed some creditable chicken moves for

Tiffany's benefit and her Little Sister burst into delighted laughter. Chris wondered briefly if Ethan was watching their antics but resisted the temptation to search him out in the thinning crowd of wedding guests. "They'll be going off to live lives of their own soon enough."

"That's true," Dale said, setting his chair back down on all four legs. "But I'll still have Marvel when they're gone and we'll start a new life of our own together, traveling a little, making love with the bedroom door unlocked, not tripping over bicycles and roller skates on the sidewalk in the dark." He grinned down into his glass of wine, but when he lifted his head his expression was grave. "You're too young to dwindle off into being a doting aunt to my kids and Will's. And you're way too young to sit around and wait to become a grandmother," Dale continued, the wine and the occasion making him more talkative than usual.

"You're not the first person to make that observation," Chris said, wiggling her aching feet back into her shoes, counting on the pain to help clear her fuzzy brain. "Only the latest in a long string that includes Will and his wife, Mom and Dad, Walt and Miriam Leonard and . . . I don't know who else." Even Keith, not one to beat around the bush when stating his opinions, had told her he had no objections to Ethan Connor as a stepfather. And neither would Erika, he advised, when she got over being married long enough to notice her mother was in love.

"Good Lord, Sis, are you blushing?" Dale asked, narrowing his eyes to get a better look at her in the dim light.

"Of course not," she answered much too quickly. "It's the wine."

"There is someone in your life, isn't there?"

Dale and his wife and children lived in Toledo. They spoke on the phone often but didn't see each other in person all that much. There was no way he could know she was hopelessly in love with Ethan Connor unless she told him. But she didn't want to tell him until...she and Ethan had made a commitment to each other.

"There might be," she acknowledged, and realized her lover's smile gave her away. "But please don't say anything until I know for sure."

"Know what? That you're in love?" Dale chortled. "Heck, I can tell that from the way you're smiling right now."

"No, I want you to wait until I ask him to marry me," Chris said, standing up.

Dale whistled. "He must be one special dude if my very prim-and-proper sister is thinking of proposing to him instead of waiting to be asked."

"Oh, he's special, all right," Chris agreed with a very feminine, very satisfied smile. "And he asked me once. I told him I needed more time. I figure turnabout is fair play."

"Have I met him?" Dale probed, rising also.

"Earlier this evening." Chris didn't elaborate. Let Dale figure it out for himself. She studied the remaining guests, looking for Ethan as the chicken dance ended and the band launched into something slow and romantic.

She spotted him at last as she moved around the edge of the hardwood dance floor. He was kneeling in front of a flushed and smiling Tiffany, tying the long

ribbon streamer of a helium-filled balloon around her
wrist so that it couldn't float away and be lost.

Chris had been aware of him, at the edges of her
consciousness all evening, although their paths had
crossed only briefly now and again. He always seemed
to be the center of a group of admiring people, and for
the first time Chris realized just how respected and
well liked he'd become in her home town.

She loved him. They could work out the problems
between them, his children and hers, his career and
hers. Nothing could keep them apart any longer if they
truly were meant to be together. Tonight was the night.

"Chris," Tiffany called when she saw her coming
toward them. "Come here! Did you see me dance the
chicken with Keith?"

"Yes, I did."

Ethan rose from his knees. He looked lean and fit
and almost unbearably handsome in his dark gray suit
and tie.

"It was a blast." She looked sharply at her grandfather as she spoke, obviously trying to convey a great
deal of meaning with her expression. "Chris likes to
dance, Grandpa," she reminded him politely.

"I know that."

"Well, then ask her," Tiffany prompted, disgusted.

"Perhaps she's too tired."

Chris couldn't be sure if Ethan was teasing or serious. He looked at her, and she remembered the first
time he'd held her in his arms at RiverFest. She remembered the first time he kissed her later that night,
and she ached to be held in his arms again. If she was
going to take matters into her own hands tonight, she
might as well start with asking him to dance.

"Would you like to dance with me, Ethan?"

"Of course," Tiffany answered for her grand-father.

"Of course," Ethan echoed, his voice strangely harsh, and held out his hand.

"I'll be at the punch bowl," Tiffany told them, beaming with satisfaction as she skipped away.

"She's a shameless matchmaker now that the idea of marrying us off to each other has crossed her mind."

"Oh, dear." Chris steepled her fingers before her lips. "I had hoped..."

"What did you hope, Chris?" Ethan asked gruffly, pulling her into his arms.

He slipped his hand inside the filmy, sparkling jacket of her gown so that his palm was splayed across the gray silk of her dress just above the curve of her waist, and she could feel the heat of him through the thin layer of fabric. "That she hadn't noticed we were in love... quite yet. I... I wanted to prepare every-one...."

"Chris," he said, and her name was almost a groan as he pulled her closer still, "shut up. You talk too much."

"I know." She sighed and laid her head on his shoulder.

"I've wanted to hold you in my arms like this all night," he murmured against her hair.

"I want you, too," she said boldly, tucking her hand, snuggled inside his, close to his heart as she lifted her head to meet his dark, guarded gaze.

"Chris," he began, then stopped himself. "I love you."

"I love you." Chris licked her lips. Her throat was suddenly very dry. She'd never proposed to a man before. She'd thought about it long and hard. She didn't see any other way to accomplish her objective, becoming Mrs. Ethan Connor, because so many long, lonely weeks had passed since he'd asked her the first time that day in the hospital.

"If you don't quit looking at me like that I'm going to kiss you here and now in front of whoever's watching," he warned.

He swung her into a turn that left her dizzy. "Promise," she managed to whisper, despite being breathless with desire and light-headed from champagne and the strength of her longing to be with him, alone and undisturbed.

"Promise." The passion in his voice, in his touch, made her feel bold and reckless, aggressively feminine. She would do it. She'd ask him to marry her. Then and there. And if there was any justice in the world, by this time next week they would be man and wife. They had waited long enough, been prudent and practical and concerned for others long enough. This night, from this moment on, would be for them.

"Ethan," she said, closing her eyes, unable at the last moment to hold his gaze, "will you marry me?" She held her breath waiting for his answer, marveling at her own courage in asking, so very certain he would accept.

"Oh, God, Chris," he said. "I'd hoped you wouldn't ask me that question tonight." He kept on dancing, but Chris stumbled, missing a step.

"I . . . I don't understand. I . . . thought you wanted to marry me," she said, feeling bewildered and hurt.

"I do," he said, and there was no mistaking the sincerity in his voice.

"Then why not say yes?" Maybe it was the champagne making her so bold. Or maybe it was desperation as she fought to hold on to her dreams of a future with Ethan.

"Because now I'm the one who needs time."

"I don't understand." The band stopped playing. They were still standing on the edge of the dance floor. If the other guests were watching, Chris didn't care. "Tell me what's wrong. Please."

"It's Jeff. He wants the children back. I'm sorry, Chris. I can't marry you until my son and I have settled what's between us."

"I'll wait," Chris said. "And I'll help."

"I love you, Chris Baldwin," he said very softly. "But I can't ask you to wait when I don't know what's going to happen next myself."

"That's not good enough." Chris attempted a smile and succeeded well enough to coax one from him. "C'mon. Let's get Tiffany and blow this pop stand. You can make me a cup of coffee and tell me exactly what happened between you and Jeff. Then we'll decide whether there's any hope of ever getting this marriage off the ground."

CHAPTER FOURTEEN

"Is TIFFANY all tucked in?" Chris asked as she finished pouring water into the coffeemaker.

"Yes. She's exhausted, poor little kid, but she never stopped talking about the wedding. She fell asleep in midsentence."

Ethan shrugged out of his suit jacket and hung it over the back of a chair. Chris watched his reflection in the dark mirror of the kitchen window. He stood quietly a moment, his hands on the chair, his head bent in thought, before he straightened his shoulders and moved behind her to slip his arms around her waist. She felt his breath warm her cheek and the heavy aching pain inside her retreated just a bit.

"Thanks for coming home with us," he said very quietly, his lips against her hair. "I doubt I could have gotten Tiffany to leave the reception without you."

"I should be getting back." Chris watched as the coffee began to filter through into the pot. She was uncertain what to say next, what to do next. She didn't really want to leave. Ethan hadn't yet explained to her exactly what had transpired between him and Jeff.

"Don't go," Ethan said, turning her to face him, pulling her hard against him. "Your brother said he'd make sure everything was taken care of. Miriam and Walt will get the leftover food and cake safely back to your place. Stay with me. For a little longer, please."

"I'll stay as long as you want me," she promised, responding to the desperation she heard threading its way through his words. She reached up on tiptoe to kiss him quickly, gently. "Most women who have just had their proposal of marriage turned down by the man they love wouldn't be so accommodating," she couldn't resist pointing out with a laugh that was shaky around the edges.

"Oh, God, Chris, I'm so sorry. You looked so beautiful tonight and I love you so much."

He kissed her then, hard and desperate, and she could do nothing more than cling to him and ride out the storm of his need.

"Ethan, tell me about Jeff and the children," she begged when the kiss ended, leaving her breathless and wanting more. Her hands were trapped between his and she felt the driving beat of his heart beneath her fingers.

"Jeff came to me this afternoon." His voice was harsh, the words rough. "He's decided to pull up stakes and head out West to California. He wants the children to go with him."

"California. Oh, no." Chris felt as if a great weight had settled on her all of a sudden. It was happening just as she had dreaded it might, a final confrontation between Ethan and Jeff, with the children's future happiness hanging in the balance between them. "When is he planning to leave? Certainly he isn't going to take Tiffany and Ashley out of school so close to the end of the term?"

"I doubt if that even occurred to him," Ethan said, shaking his head.

The anguish in his eyes made her ache for his pain. "But surely he wouldn't act so rashly, disrupt their lives—'' She stopped talking when she saw his expression harden into steel.

"He's never considered anyone's feelings but his own in his whole life."

"Ethan, you know that's not true." She didn't think she could make him see Jeff's side of the argument, but she had to try, for the children's sake, if not for father and son.

"I'll fight him through every court in the land if I have to," Ethan said, interrupting her attempt to present Jeff's actions in a better light. "I won't give up those kids. I love them. I want to keep them with me, watch them grow up. I won't let Jeff hurt them again."

He held her by the shoulders, made her listen to him, though she didn't think she wanted to hear what he was going to say next.

"I won't let anything or anyone stand in my way. Even you, Chris. God, if it comes to a court fight I don't want Jeff's lawyers using our marriage against me."

"What do you mean?" Chris asked, confused and angry. His grip was tight enough to cause her pain. "Let me go, please." He didn't but his touch turned gentle.

"Don't you see? It will look as if I married you just to find a suitable mother for the children. I don't want anyone saying I married you because it was convenient, because as a married man I'd have a better chance of retaining custody of the children."

"I don't see it that way at all," Chris began, but she was so tired and so emotionally drained by everything, good and bad, that had happened in the past eighteen hours that she couldn't form a coherent argument.

"I can't take that chance. I need time now, Chris," he said with a harsh laugh that held no amusement at all. "Just as you did last winter. I need time to talk to a lawyer. I need to find out where I stand with regard to Ohio's custody laws."

"Ethan." Chris caught his face between her hands. The muscles of his jaw were rock hard. "You need to sit down and discuss this as calmly and rationally as possible with Jeff. Perhaps he'll change his mind."

"He won't change his mind," Ethan insisted.

She felt him relax slightly so she kept on talking. "Don't do something you'll both regret for the rest of your lives until you talk to him. Please, say you'll do that for my sake, for the children's sake."

"Am I wrong to fight to keep the children?" he asked, his gaze searching her brown eyes for a sincere answer.

"I don't know," she replied truthfully, from her heart, knowing he would feel betrayed by her response. "I just don't know."

ETHAN LOOKED UP from his desk at the plant and stared sightlessly at the activity on the factory floor below him. The new machinery was on-line and performing well. Engineering and production crews were fine-tuning the new lines, ironing out the glitches and gearing up for full production starting with the first shift Monday morning.

"Ethan, I need to talk to you about some of these closing figures," Walt Leonard said, sticking his bald head in the door as he waved a sheaf of computer printouts in Ethan's general direction.

"Come on in, Walt." Not only were they at the end of a week but the month, as well. When weekly and monthly payroll reports coincided with the end of a regular pay period, Walt could be pretty hard to live with. "What can I do for you?"

"Just thought you might like to see these payroll projections for the third and fourth quarters. We'll be at full capacity by the middle of summer. Plant output should show improvement of over twenty percent, as you already know," he said, sinking gratefully into a comfortable swivel chair in front of Ethan's desk, "and we'll be running twenty-four hours a day, seven days a week for approximately four months. That works out to about one hundred part-time jobs and close to one hundred hours of overtime for our regular full-time employees. Thought you might want those figures up front so you can incorporate them into your next report to the big bosses in Chicago."

"Thanks, Walt," Ethan said, accepting the sheaf of papers. "I'll look over them this weekend."

"Did you get young Gilson on the plane okay this morning?" Walt asked, lighting up a cigarette, one of the three a day he allowed himself since he'd decided to quit smoking again, two weeks earlier.

"He should be safely back in the fold at corporate by now," Ethan said. He got up from his desk and walked to the big soundproof window overlooking the factory floor. He pulled the cord and closed off his view of men and machinery and row upon row of cans of chicken noodle soup bearing the familiar red-and-white Castleton label as they rolled off the assembly line. "The kid has what it takes. He'll go far. I'm just glad he's out of my plant and out of my hair." Now that Ethan's superiors had recalled his erstwhile and ambitious temporary assistant, he felt in control of his life. At least this part of his life.

His health was restored, his career was back on track—and his personal life was a total disaster.

Ethan glanced at his watch. "I think I'll cut out a little early today. Tiffany's spending some time with Chris at her office after school. She's learning to file, or so she says. I think it's just an excuse to drink sodas and run up and down the staircase at the courthouse."

Walt chuckled and bent his head to savor the last drag on his cigarette before stubbing it out in the pristine ashtray on Ethan's desk. Ethan didn't smoke; he never had, one big factor in his rapid recovery.

"She's quite a handful, that kid," Walt noted.

"Quite a handful. And if I don't get moving, she'll bite my head off for making her stand outside the courthouse in the rain."

What he didn't tell Walt was that before he picked up Tiffany he had an appointment with his lawyer, the second that week, to discuss his options in regard to retaining custody of his grandchildren. In reality he knew he might as well save himself the trip. Jason Meyer, his attorney, was going to recommend the same course of action he'd laid out earlier in the week. He'd advised Ethan to work out some agreement with Jeff, up to and including letting Jeff take the children away with him for a trial time together. If Ethan didn't agree, Jeff could very well win custody of his children back through the courts, or simply disappear with them. It happened all the time and it was almost always difficult and expensive to get the abducted children back.

And there was his relationship with his son to consider. He could lose any chance of earning Jeff's allegiance and trust by initiating a battle over the children. And if he didn't fight to keep them, he would lose Ashley and Brandon and Tiffany. And possibly Chris. It was a no-win situation.

An hour later Ethan left the lawyer's office with exactly the advice he didn't want to hear: "Work it out between you for everybody's sake," Jason Meyer had told him. "Or everyone will suffer."

Ethan drove toward the courthouse through a steady spring rain falling from a leaden sky that exactly matched his mood. He'd made arrangements to meet Tiffany outside the Main Street entrance to the building so that he wouldn't have to see Chris. She was angry and hurt at his behavior this past week and he couldn't blame her. He also couldn't seem to help himself. He needed to work through his feelings alone, the way he always had. He needed to make certain of the children's future before he attempted to gain Chris's forgiveness.

And because of his stubborn insistence on facing this crisis alone, he ran the risk of losing her forever. She loved him. He loved her. But sometimes love wasn't enough. Sometimes other obligations, being responsible for others, took precedence over your own happiness. If she loved him enough she would wait until he was free to offer himself without reservations.

And if she couldn't wait, if she didn't love him enough, he would forever mourn her loss. And he would have no one to blame but himself.

"THESE LAST THREE FOLDERS go in the *M* to *Z* drawer, Tiffany," Chris said, handing the child the thin manila folders. "Remember to check the vowels first when you're alphabetizing the names."

"I know," Tiffany said, sounding a little miffed at being reminded again. "Martinez slides in just behind Maples, right?"

"Correct. This one is Sunderman and it follows..."

"Stinson," Tiffany crowed, flipping through the Ss.

"And the last one is Warnimont."

"It goes just *before* Wensink," she said, hoping to catch Chris with a curve ball.

"You're right," Chris said, hesitating just long enough to let Tiffany know she had to think about it a moment. "We're done." It didn't matter a great deal if Tiffany had made a mistake or two in her filing lesson. Chris had just been sifting through the inactive file for her own edification, and since the agency was fairly new, there weren't all that many terminated matches to begin with. The two bottom drawers of the file cabinet nearest the window were barely half-full.

Tiffany slammed the door shut with the toe of her shoe and turned to look out the window. "It's raining harder than ever," she observed. "I'm glad I wore my raincoat to school this morning. The sun was shining then, but look how dark and dreary it is now."

"'April showers bring May flowers,'" Chris quoted as she tidied her desk.

"It's May already," Tiffany pointed out. "What do May showers bring?" she asked, still looking out the window.

Watching for Ethan, Chris realized with a painful clutching of her heart. She wanted to move to Tiffany's side and watch for him, also, but she made herself stay busy at her desk. If he didn't love her enough to confide in her, to let her help him through this difficult time, she would have to accept that and go on with her life. Somehow.

"June...bugs?" she asked with a giggle she forced out of a throat clogged tight with emotion.

"No, mosquitoes," Tiffany declared, and giggled, too.

"And roses. And it helps the crops grow," Chris said, giving up the fiction that she was busy. She stared at Tiffany's stubbornly straight back and longed to pull her into her arms and rock away her own fears.

"Grandpa's here," Tiffany said, pointing out the window.

Chris walked over and put her hands on Tiffany's shoulders. "You've been a big help to me today. Thank you. Now you'd better run along. You don't want to keep your grandfather waiting."

"It was fun," Tiffany said, making no effort to move away from the window. "Chris? Are you mad at my grandpa?"

"No," Chris said, bending forward to brush her lips over the top of Tiffany's dark head. "We've had a difference of opinion, that's all."

"Like when Erika and Michael were arguing before they got married?" she asked, resting both palms on the windowsill, craning her neck as if looking for something or someone else in the street below.

"Yes." Chris hoped she wouldn't have to go into more detail. She wanted, with all her heart, for their differences to be settled as quickly as possible. She just didn't think she would be so lucky.

"Is it because of me?"

Tiffany didn't turn around, but Chris felt increased tension in the slim shoulders beneath her fingers. "Why do you think that, sweetheart?"

"Because my dad wants to take us away to live with him. I heard them arguing about it the other night. Did my grandpa argue with you about us, too?"

"He's very worried that he will lose you and your brother and sister."

"I don't want to go. California is too far away." She swallowed a sob. "But my daddy needs us, too."

"We'll work something out," Chris promised, but she didn't have the faintest idea what that solution would be, or whose heart it might break.

"I love my dad," Tiffany said. "I love my grandpa. Why can't we all just stay here?"

"Because life isn't always that easy and uncomplicated." Chris knelt down and turned Tiffany to face her. Tears glistened in the child's dark eyes, but none of them were allowed to fall.

"It's not fair," Tiffany said miserably. "It's not fair."

"Your grandfather and your father both love you. They'll work something out that will be right for all of you. Just give them some time, okay?"

"I don't think we have any time." Tiffany looked over her shoulder into the street again. "My dad wants to take us away now. For a long weekend because of spring break and me and Ashley not having to be back at school until Tuesday. It's supposed to be a surprise."

"Where does he want to go?" Chris asked, being careful not to show how anxious she was to know.

"To a state park someplace. He said it would be fun. There're ponies to ride and canoes and stuff like that. It's a secret from grandpa until it's time to leave so he can't think up some reasons for us to stay home."

Chris was angry at Jeff all over again for putting the burden of keeping such a secret on a child Tiffany's age. Ethan was right in that respect: his son was thoughtless and uncaring about so many things.

"That does sound like fun," Chris said as her mind groped frantically for the best course of action to follow. Should she tell Ethan? Should she try to contact Jeff and talk him out of this clandestine jaunt? Should she stand back and let Ethan and his son destroy their relationship and the children's happiness without trying to prevent the disaster if she could?

"Keith told me the weatherman said it's going to rain all weekend," Tiffany informed Chris with a sniff.

"When does your father plan to leave on your camping trip?"

"He's going to load the van and get the little kids at home, then come here to pick me up. I ... I didn't tell him Grandpa said he would pick me up, too. I didn't know what to do."

"Is your father down there now?" Chris asked, rising to look out the window as Tiffany was doing.

"Yes, he just drove up in his van. I don't want them to fight." One crystal tear escaped to roll down her cheek. "I don't like it when they fight."

"There won't be a fight," Chris said, handing Tiffany her raincoat from a hook behind the door. "Not if I can help it."

RAINDROPS PELTED his head and shoulders as Ethan got out of the car and approached Jeff's beat-up VW van. He hadn't bothered with his suit jacket and it didn't take more than a few seconds for his shirt to be soaked through. Ethan tugged at the knot of his tie, pulled it free and stuffed it in his pocket as he walked.

"Didn't Mrs. Baden tell you I made arrangements to pick Tiffany up this afternoon?" he called, giving Ashley a smile and a wave. Brandon was strapped into the seat beside his father and his sister peered out the window from the bench seat behind him.

Jeff had rolled down the window, but he made no move to get out of the van. "Dad," he began, then stopped as he saw the angry look on Ethan's face.

"Where the hell do you think you're sneaking off to with those kids?" Ethan demanded, glancing into the cargo section of the van to find it packed full of suitcases and camping gear.

"I booked a cabin at Salt Lick State Park."

"That's a hundred and fifty miles from here."

"I know that. I want to have the kids to myself for a few days so we can talk things over, maybe get to know one another a little better."

"They're not psych majors or members of one of your mother's encounter groups. You can talk to them here," Ethan said between clenched teeth. A drop of rain splashed into his eyes and he brushed it angrily away.

"I can't make any progress with them here. Not with you looking over my shoulder every minute, second-guessing every move I make."

"The weather's supposed to be rotten all weekend," Ethan said, taking a different tack, aware of the apprehension on Ashley's round little face peering through the window. "What do you intend to do to keep them entertained?"

"I'll think of something."

"We're going to ride ponies," Ashley announced, bouncing up and down in her seat. "Daddy promised."

"Ponies. Me, too," Brandon hollered.

"We'll go riding if it stops raining," Jeff qualified.

Ethan narrowed his eyes against the rain and fixed his gaze on Jeff's face. "You know you can't take them anywhere without my permission."

"I don't give a damn about any court orders," Jeff said. "They're my kids. I'll take them with me if I want to. We'd be gone by now if I hadn't gotten held up by a train on the Elm Street crossing."

"Damn it, Jeff, if you drive off with those children in the van I'll call the cops, so help me God."

"No, you won't, Ethan."

He spun around at the sound of quiet finality in Chris's voice. He'd been so caught up in his confrontation with Jeff he hadn't heard her approach. Tiffany was standing by her side, staring at him from beneath the sheltering hood of her purple raincoat. Chris held a bright yellow-and-red striped umbrella above their heads.

"Don't start telling me what to do, Chris," he warned, because he could tell by the set look on her face that she was going to take Jeff's side in the argument. "This is none of your business."

Her chin went up and pain deepened her brown eyes to black. They stood there at the edge of the busy street staring at each other and Ethan knew he'd hurt her dreadfully with his cutting words, but it was too late to take them back.

"You're wrong, Ethan. You're bullheaded and foolish and you're dead wrong. I love you. I love Tiffany and Ashley and Brandon. I won't stand idly by and watch them being used as pawns in a power struggle between two grown men." Her eyes, only moments ago so bleak and shuttered, now flashed with righteous fire. "What exactly *is* going on here?"

"Jeff is planning to take the children away without my permission."

"Where are you going? How long do you plan to be away?" she demanded, rounding on an astonished Jeff.

"Salt Lick State Park. We'll be back Monday evening," he stammered, catching Ethan's eye, as if to find a clue for dealing with Chris's behavior from his father. "I think it will be good for us to spend some time alone together."

"What do you think about all this, Tiffany?" Chris asked more gently as she rested her hand on her Little Sister's shoulder.

"I...I don't know."

Tiffany looked at Ethan hesitantly, apologetically, and he felt like a jackass. He was acting like a fool, scaring her, making her feel guilty for wanting to spend time with her father.

He knelt in front of her, not even noticing when Chris shifted her umbrella to shield him from the rain. "Do you want to go camping with your dad this weekend?" he asked her, pushing his anger to a far corner of his mind. He'd deal with it later when he was alone, but not now. Not in front of the children. He glanced up at Chris, but her head was bent protectively toward his granddaughter and she couldn't see the apology, or the longing in his eyes.

"It might be fun," Tiffany admitted, scuffing the toe of her shoe through a rivulet of rainwater meandering across the sidewalk toward the curb.

"I want to go," Ashley clamored from inside the van as she bounced up and down on the seat.

"Me, too," Brandon hollered through the open window. "Me, too."

"But Grandpa, will you be all right all by yourself if I go?" Tiffany asked, hesitating as Ethan opened the van door for her to climb inside.

"I'll be just fine." Nothing was more important than his grandchildren's happiness, even if it meant returning them to their father. He recognized that with his brain, but he couldn't reconcile it with his heart.

"Sure you will," Tiffany said, giving him a big hug from the seat of the van. "Because you won't be alone. Chris will be here to take care of you."

CHAPTER FIFTEEN

"WILL I HAVE YOU to take care of me?" Ethan asked, still standing in the rain as he watched the van pull away and head south out of town on Main Street.

"At least long enough to see that you get dry clothes and something hot to eat. I did promise Tiffany to do that," Chris said, shaking her head as she looked at his soaked shirt and wet hair.

"Do you have plans for the evening?" he asked, making no move to get into his car and out of the rain.

Even though it was May, the air was chilly. Chris shivered, glad she was wearing a sweater along with her cotton skirt and blouse.

"No. Keith has rehearsal for the senior class play until ten. And Erika—" she laughed and felt a little sheepish "—Erika has a home of her own."

She wanted to be with Ethan tonight, and it wasn't because her house was empty. Ethan needed her whether he wanted to admit it or not. And if she didn't let her anger and hurt get in the way of her feelings, she knew she needed him, too. She loved him. She wanted to be with him for the rest of their lives. If she couldn't see past her pain to help him, she didn't deserve to have such a love.

"Then will you come home with me?"

"Why, Ethan?" So much depended on his answer.

"We need to talk." He ran his hand across his jaw, wiping raindrops off his face. "And we need to be alone. Do you realize we've never spent an evening alone together, just you and me, in all the months we've known each other?"

"Is this a date?" she asked, trying not to let her nervousness show in her smile.

He looked surprised at the question, then grinned. "Yeah, I guess it is a date. If you don't mind just sitting at home in front of the fire, sharing a glass of wine, listening to music and—" He broke off abruptly, as if suddenly remembering where they were.

"Grilling a steak?" Chris finished the sentence for him.

"That's not what I meant to say," Ethan replied.

The look on his face made her forget she was standing in the rain with wet feet.

"But it's not a bad idea, either," he added.

"I think we'd better get out of the rain before this conversation goes any further," she suggested as a car sped by and splashed water onto the sidewalk where they were standing. The wind was blowing harder than it had been when they had started talking. New green leaves stripped from the maples on the courthouse lawn blew by, sticking to whatever obstacle blocked their flight path.

"I'll follow you home so that you can drop off your car," he suggested.

"Okay." She nodded, not having anything else to say. This weekend could be the beginning of all their tomorrows. Or it could be the end. If Jeff didn't return with the children, Ethan could rightfully place some of the blame on her shoulders for arguing that he should be allowed to take them away. Still, she didn't know how she could have acted any differently. Jeff, no matter what his faults, deserved his chance to build a relationship with his children. She understood and accepted that. And so must Ethan, if his family was going to survive intact.

"I WANT BLANKEY," Brandon yowled for the twenty-seventh time since they'd turned off the highway onto the country road that her dad said would take them right to the park lodge gates.

"You can't have Blankey," Jeff repeated.

Also for the twenty-seventh time, Tiffany noted. She had counted each and every one of them. "I'm sorry Mrs. Baden forgot to pack his blanket," she said, pulling her knees up to her chin and wrapping her arms around her legs to keep them warm. The heater in the van didn't work very well. She hoped Mrs. Baden hadn't forgotten to pack their coats, as well. She probably hadn't. It was just that Brandon was always dragging Blankey off and hiding it in all these weird places so no one could try and take it away from him. "He'll whine and carry on like this all night if he doesn't have it to sleep with," she reminded her father.

"I know," Jeff said, looking at Tiffany in the rearview mirror. The lights from the dashboard gave his face a spooky red-and-green kind of glow. "I should have thought of it myself. I was just so excited getting everything packed without letting your grandpa know we were going...." He laughed and shrugged when he saw that Tiffany didn't think it was a very funny thing to sneak out on her grandfather that way. "I forgot all about it," he finished lamely.

"It'll be okay," she said, but she wasn't so sure. She glanced over at Ashley, who rolled her eyes.

"Remember the night Mrs. Baden washed his Blankey and the dryer was broken and he couldn't have it to sleep with because it was still wet?" Ashley whispered across the seat.

Tiffany nodded glumly. "Grandpa had to go out in the snow to the Laundromat at ten o'clock so that the rest of us could get some sleep."

"What are my two girls discussing so seriously back there?" Jeff wanted to know. "Don't worry, I didn't forget any of your favorite breakfast cereals or the milk and sugar."

"Good," Ashley said.

"Yeah, good," Tiffany seconded. "We're not talking about anything important. It's okay about Blankey, too. Brandon's so tired from the long drive, he'll probably go right to sleep without it."

"Sure you will, won't you, buddy," Jeff said too loudly and too heartily as he reached over and patted the little boy on his knee. "You're a big fellow now, aren't ya. You don't need Blankey to go to sleep."

"Blankey," Brandon wailed yet again, then began squirming around in his seat. "Peepee, Daddy," he said, sniffing. "I peepee. Now!"

"This is going to be a *long* weekend," Ashley predicted, looking at Tiffany, her eyes two dark circles in the white oval of her face.

Tiffany had had no idea the woods would be so dark. She could barely see her hand in front of her face. She could hardly even see her sister sitting two feet away at all. She began to wonder what kind of animals would be lurking around outside their cabin when they got there, but didn't ask her dad about them. Ashley was such a sissy about stuff like that.

"You can say that again," Tiffany whispered back, and looked out the window into the dark, rain-swept night.

"THIS IS a lovely room," Chris said, leaning back into his arms. The wicker couch on which they were seated creaked a muted protest. Ethan bunched a pillow behind his back and settled her more comfortably against him.

"I don't get to spend nearly enough time in here." He looked around the softly lit, plant-filled greenhouse room as though seeing it for the first time.

"Was it expensive to restore?" she asked.

It pleased him that she felt comfortable enough with him to ask such a question. "Not as much as you think. The foundation was in good shape. I had the old glass panes replaced with insulated glass, and new heating ducts put in the walls. I thought about a tile floor but opted for the tile-patterned vinyl flooring instead of the real thing because it's warmer and safer for the kids when they're playing out here."

"Do they like to play out here?" she asked.

He crossed his arms beneath her breasts and was rewarded by feeling her heartbeat quicken beneath his hand. "On cold or rainy days, yes. Especially Brandon. He thinks it's like being outside without having to wear a coat or hat. I wonder how the little guy is going to get along tonight without his Blankey?"

He'd asked the question more of himself than of Chris, but she answered anyway. "Brandon will survive the loss. And Jeff will learn an essential lesson about traveling with children. Pack for them first and never, never forget something as important as Blankey." She steered the subject back to the room around them gently but firmly. "I feel like I'm living a Victorian fantasy here," she murmured, resting her head against his chest. "Wicker and ferns and a fountain in the corner. It's like being in another century. Especially tonight with the rain and the mist swirling beyond the glass."

"You'll like it even better in the daylight," Ethan assured her. "The view out over the river is fabulous. And I swear that this summer I'll get the flower beds up to the neighborhood standards."

"If you don't, the garden club is liable to run you out of town on a rail." She tilted her head and smiled up at him.

"God forbid," he said, and kissed her, lightly at first, then more thoroughly as he shifted her in his arms until her breasts were pressed against him and her mouth met his.

"I'll help you with the flowers," she promised when he released her from the kiss. "I like gardening. I don't have enough room in my yard to really indulge myself."

"My flower beds are your flower beds," he said, and he was only half teasing. He wasn't certain he should bring up the subject of marriage again. It was too soon; things were still too uncertain between them.

"We'll have to discuss what you want planted in them," Chris agreed, her half serious, half teasing tone matching his. "But not tonight." She kissed him again, demandingly, hungrily. "Not tonight."

A long time later she lay back in his arms and watched the raindrops chase one another down the glass panes of the greenhouse room. "It's late," she reminded him. "I should be getting home."

"Don't go," Ethan said before he could stop himself. "Not yet. Stay for a little while longer."

"Yes," she said, sliding her arms around his waist and kissing his cheek as they lay side by side on the wicker sofa. "I'll stay for a little while."

"It's very quiet in the house tonight," he observed, surprised that it should bother him so much. He'd lived alone for years between his divorce and getting the children. The children. Of course it wasn't the silence alone that bothered him. It was the children's absence that made the house feel so cold and empty.

"It's always quiet in a house when the children who live there are away," Chris said quietly, musingly, so that he knew her thoughts were the same as his.

"We don't have to talk about marriage tonight," he said softly, folding his hand around her long delicate fingers and lifting them to rest above his heart. "But can I ask you to be a mother to my grandchildren someday soon?"

"Yes," she said simply, serenely and without hesitation. "I made that commitment to myself weeks ago."

He kissed the tips of her fingers.

"Can I ask you if you will stay here in Bonaparte no matter what Castleton's has planned for your future?"

"I want to, Chris," he said, knowing he had to be honest with her, no matter how painful it was to tell her the truth. "But I just don't know. I'm not a rich man. If the children do stay with me, I need to think of their future, their education, getting them started in life." He put his arm behind his head and stared up at the dark, swaying tree branches visible through the room's glass ceiling. "I'd like nothing more than to stay here and tell corporate to be damned, but I can't. Not yet, anyway. Does it make a difference in the way you feel?"

She was quiet for a long time. He continued to look out into the night. He felt the tension growing in her and cursed himself for bringing up the subject. Yet if they were going to have a future together, these issues must be dealt with.

"I don't want it to make a difference in the way I feel. But I'm not sure. I've been avoiding thinking about it." She lifted her hand, ran her fingertips along the line of his jaw, up along his cheek, urging his head down so that she could look directly into his eyes. "I'd like to go on avoiding it. At least for tonight, for this weekend."

She traced the outline of his lips with the tip of her fingernail and Ethan groaned at the subtle eroticism of her touch. "You're right," he said gruffly. "Let's put the questions on hold for now. All of them. God knows they'll still be there tomorrow or Monday or next week." He'd be rational and logical; she'd be composed and practical—later. Maybe by then some of the questions unanswered between them would find their own answers. Maybe they wouldn't, but by then they would be strong enough in their love to face them together.

"Yes," Chris whispered, lifting herself on one arm so that she could lean her weight on his chest as she kissed him.

The kiss was long and sweet and powerful, her breath warm on his lips. As always when they were together, he knew they could overcome every obstacle between them.

"That's what I want, too," she said. "Not to think. Not to plan. Just to be together, to be alone and to love."

"I DON'T THINK Ashley likes wearing a garbage bag with holes cut in it for a raincoat," Tiffany pointed out to her father Sunday morning as they sloshed along the trail from their cabin to the stable where the ponies were housed. It hadn't stopped raining since they'd left Bonaparte and the weather was getting pretty boring. Their cabin was pretty boring, too. Real little and no television. And the bathroom was outside. They hadn't even been able to go out in a rowboat on the small lake at the bottom of the hill beyond their cabin to go fishing. All in all, it was turning out to be a bummer of a weekend.

"I thought it was a pretty ingenious solution to the problem myself," Jeff answered without slowing his pace. "Isn't it better than staying in the cabin all day again today, Ashley?"

Brandon looked over his father's shoulder and grinned from beneath the hood of his winter parka. It was heavy enough to keep out the rain. And it was cold enough that he needed to wear it, anyway. Tiffany could see her breath when they talked.

"She can't hear you, Dad," Tiffany announced. "She's back there, hiding behind a tree." Her dad hadn't seemed to notice Ashley was no longer one of the group.

"Damn it." He stopped and turned around. "Ashley, come on, honey. I'm sorry you forgot your raincoat at the restaurant. But you should have told me before we were fifty miles on down the road."

"I look stupid," Ashley grumbled as she obeyed her father's summons. "Look at me. This is a garbage sack."

Tiffany agreed that her sister looked silly with her blond head and arms poking out of the green plastic bag, but she didn't say so. "It's keeping you dry, isn't it?" she demanded, holding out her hand for Ashley to take hold of. "We're outside, aren't we? Anyway, you should have told Dad about your raincoat right away."

"I didn't want to get yelled at," Ashley sniffed, threatening to burst into tears again.

"He wouldn't have yelled at you. Much," Tiffany added, qualifying her answer. She wasn't sure how mad her dad would get if they lived with him all the time. It was one of those questions that was hard to figure out. Her grandpa got mad and yelled a lot sometimes, but it was usually when they were driving him crazy, yelling and fighting around the house. Their dad just went upstairs and shut himself in his room with a book. Actually, he didn't bother to correct them much at all. Tiffany wondered how that would change if they went to live with him all the time.

"I can't go on a pony ride in this thing." Ashley continued to sniffle and moan as they walked.

"Oh, shut up," Tiffany commanded, giving her sister's arm a jerk. She didn't want to have to think about going to live in California. She wished she could think up some plan so that they could all stay in Bonaparte together. That would be the best of the best that could happen.

"I look stupid," Ashley insisted defiantly, but quietly so that Tiffany couldn't jerk her hand again to shut her up.

"Here we are!"

Her dad was talking too loud, trying too hard to make it seem as though they were having fun. "Wow! Real horses," Tiffany said loudly, too, so that Ashley and Brandon would be fooled into thinking she was having fun just like her dad. He threw her a grateful look over his shoulder and she felt good for trying. "Can I pet one of them?"

"I guess that would be all right," he said, checking around for one of the park rangers in charge of the stables, but no one was in sight. "They look gentle enough."

"They're so big," Ashley said, hanging back as Tiffany clambered up on the corral fence where three placid-looking ponies stood patiently in the light rain.

"They're not anywhere near as big as a real horse," Tiffany informed her sister knowledgeably.

Ashley walked closer to the fence as one of the ponies ambled forward to see if Tiffany was bringing a snack. He poked his head through the bars and nuzzled Ashley's fingers with soft velvety lips, just as he had done to Tiffany. Ashley screamed as though she'd had her hand chopped off at the wrist. Rangers came from all directions. Her dad put Brandon down so fast he stumbled and fell in the mud. Ashley continued to scream at the top of her lungs and Tiffany was so embarrassed she thought she would die.

"He bit me! That horse bit me! My hand. My hand," Ashley hollered over and over again, hiding her hand so that no one could see if she was hurt.

"Come here, honey. Let me see. Let me see," Jeff said.

Tiffany thought his face was kind of white and pasty looking. "The pony didn't bite her," she tried to explain, but no one could hear her over Ashley's bellowing. "He just felt her fingers with his lips."

Jeff finally got Ashley to show him her hand while one of the park rangers went for a first-aid kit. "I don't see any bite marks," he said, relieved and embarrassed at the same time as one of the rangers squatted in the mud beside Ashley.

"He tried to bite me. He felt me with his lips," Ashley sobbed, beginning to sound sheepish. "I...I guess he just scared me."

"I'm terribly sorry," Jeff said, gathering Ashley into his arms.

"That's all right," the ranger, who was a lady, said with a smile. "Things like this happen all the time."

She took a bandage and put it on the back of Ashley's hand just to shut her up, Tiffany suspected.

"Do they?" Jeff asked, and he didn't smile at all.

"Would you still like to ride one of the ponies?" the lady ranger questioned Ashley. "He's really very gentle."

"No." Ashley shook her head vehemently. "He's too big and he had bad breath."

"I think we'd better head back to the cabin," Jeff said. "Thank you for your help."

"I don't want to stay here anymore. I don't like this place. I don't like going to the bathroom outside."

"I'm sorry, Dad," Tiffany said, picking Brandon up out of the mud and settling him on her hip. "I guess we'll be easier to take care of when we grow up some more."

"It's not your fault, Tiffany." He used his handkerchief to wipe Ashley's tears away, then handed it to Tiffany to wipe the mud off Brandon's fingers before he smeared it all over her purple raincoat. "Maybe I'll be better at taking care of you when I grow up some more."

"Don't be silly," Tiffany said, not really understanding what he meant. "You're already grown-up, Dad."

"Yeah. At least that's what everyone tells me. Hey. I've got a great idea. Let's go somewhere warm and dry and where we can swim all day long."

"Swim. It's too cold to swim," Tiffany pointed out.

"I know a place," Jeff said with a wink. "Want to come?"

"Maybe we should call Grandpa first and let him know where we'll be." She didn't want to come right out and ask if her dad meant he wanted to go to California right now or someplace else. Tiffany didn't know any place close by where you could swim and play outside on a day like this. "I don't want him to worry about us."

"Okay. We'll call from the pay phone at the lodge gate. Do you think you can walk?" he asked Ashley, setting her down on the path.

"Yes."

"Good. I'll carry Brandon. The faster we get back to the cabin, the faster we can pick up and hit the road."

"Okay," Tiffany said, but she wished she knew where they were going. She didn't think she could take too many more of her dad's surprises. She wished he would figure out she liked to be told about things ahead of time.

"YOU HAVE WALKED ME off my feet," Chris said, dropping onto the unforgiving wooden seat of the antique church pew just inside the front door of Ethan's house. "I'm pooped."

"We only walked three miles." Ethan hung his jacket on the halltree and pulled her to her feet. "You told me you could do that easily! And I thought you wanted to get back before it started raining again." He began unzipping the pink hooded sweatshirt she was wearing over her sweat suit.

"It wasn't the distance," she said, panting a little. "It was the pace you set."

"That's the pace they recommended at the cardiac rehabilitation classes and you know it."

"I know it. I didn't say I could keep up with it." She flopped back down on the pew again as Ethan put her sweatshirt alongside his jacket.

"C'mon, wimp, I'll make you breakfast," he promised.

He pulled her to her feet again, this time not so gently, so that she ended up against his chest, wrapped in his arms, which was exactly where she wanted to be. "I like that idea," she said after a long and very satisfying kiss.

"I'll even serve milady in the greenhouse room if you help grill the bacon."

"Bacon? That doesn't sound very 'heart smart.'"

"One strip. Let me have my little vices," Ethan said, taking her hand to lead the way into the kitchen. "We're having scrambled egg substitute and fresh fruit, both of which are very 'heart smart.'"

"Okay. I'll let you have your one strip of bacon."

"Thank you."

"But only because it's such a glorious morning and I want to eat in the greenhouse room."

"You are a conniving and manipulating female," Ethan said, making a grab for her.

But she slipped past him. "The light on your answering machine is blinking," she pointed out as he twined his arms around her waist and pressed a kiss to the back of her neck.

"Let it blink. It's probably something wrong at the plant and I don't want to think about work on such a lovely spring morning."

"What if it isn't?" Chris asked, her maternal instincts taking over, even though she wished she could keep them at bay another day or so. "What if it's Jeff and the kids?"

Ethan reached around her and pushed the message retrieval button without saying another word.

"Hi, Grandpa. It's Tiffany."

It was a good machine, Chris noticed. As she listened it sounded as if her Little Sister were right there in the room with them.

"I told Dad maybe you went to church and we'd miss you, but he said to call, anyway."

To Chris she sounded smugly pleased with herself for being right about not finding anyone at home. "We should have gone to church. We would have been back in time to take the call," Chris said to Ethan.

"We're leaving this place," Tiffany's recorded voice continued. "We're going somewhere warm and dry where we can play and swim. It's a surprise, but I don't think it's California, though."

Tiffany didn't sound convinced to Chris's perceptive ears, or to Ethan's either, for Chris could feel him grow tense where their bodies touched.

"Deposit thirty cents, please," an operator's voice interrupted.

"What the hell's Jeff up to now?" Ethan growled close to Chris's ear.

Chris began to feel her own stomach tighten with apprehension. What was Jeff planning to do?

"C'mon, Tiff. This call's too expensive to talk to a machine," Jeff could be heard saying as he came on the line. "Don't worry about us, Dad. We're doing fine. Talk to you later."

"'Bye, Grandpa." Tiffany sounded as if she were shouting into the receiver. "Say hello to Chris and Keith for me."

The connection was broken. And so was the tenuous peace of Chris's weekend with Ethan.

He stood stiffly beside the telephone table for a long minute, then straightened slowly. "They're gone. I have no idea where he's taken them," he said, his voice hollow and filled with raw pain. "If he decides not to bring them back I may never see them again."

"Ethan, you have to learn to trust your son," Chris said, although her own heart beat heavy and slow with dread.

He swung around to face her. "I should never have listened to you, to any of you, and let him take them in the first place."

The heedless words hurt, but Chris knew how much he feared losing the children and she ignored the pain. "You can blame me for this if you want, but in your heart you know you had no other choice but to let them go. Jeff is their father," she said, stressing the word ever so slightly. "You're only their grandfather. Even if it breaks our hearts to lose them, he has to be given his chance."

CHAPTER SIXTEEN

CHRIS LEANED her head against the back of her chair and let her gaze wander to the pattern of plaster swirls on the ceiling of her office. The county had run out of money to renovate the building before they got to the third floor and she was glad. Perhaps the first-floor offices were less drafty and more energy efficient, but they lacked the charm of this long narrow room. She liked the high ceiling and dark wood floor, the oak paneling on the wall behind her desk and the tall double-hung window in which her brand-new air-conditioning unit purred contentedly. Overnight the weekend's cold rain had given way to the muggy heat of an Ohio spring and this sunny Monday afternoon her office would have been a sauna without it.

The clock on the courthouse tower chimed five. It had been ten minutes fast as long as Chris could remember, but she liked that, too. She wondered if Ethan had heard from Jeff and the children. She wondered if he was on his way back to Bonaparte, or if he had taken them and disappeared, the way she'd read so many other disgruntled parents had.

Would Ethan ever forgive her if so?

Chris sat up straight and planted her feet firmly on the floor. She'd promised herself not to let such self-defeating thoughts overwhelm her. Most of the day she'd been able to accomplish just that. As long as she kept busy. She picked up a stack of manila folders and walked to the filing cabinets along the far wall. She and Ethan would deal with whatever the future held in store. Together.

Six of her Big/Little matches were nearing the end of their year together. Two of them were coming to a natural conclusion: both girls were graduating from high school and one of them, through her Big Sister's help and encouragement, had been accepted into nursing school beginning with the fall term.

Three other matches seemed to be progressing well and all parties concerned had indicated a willingness to continue for another year. The last match was not working out. The child was a difficult one. Chris hoped she could match the youngster with another Big Brother, but as usual her list of applicants was far smaller than the list of children needing to be matched. Thankfully, the boy's Big Brother was interested in remaining in the program despite the disappointment, so at least one other youngster would receive the benefit of his time.

In the past this failed match would have made Chris doubt her own suitability to hold this position. Now she recognized it for what it was: a personality conflict no one could have foreseen. It was a setback, but not the end of the world. She'd keep trying until she found just the right match for Timmy Grayson. She wasn't about to give up on him or let him give up on the program.

"I'm leaving now," Lena said, coming into the room after a quick knock on the door jamb.

The knock was a courtesy; Chris had left the door to her office wide open so that her secretary could benefit from the air conditioner, as well.

"I'm almost ready to leave, also. I just want to put these files away," Chris said, remembering, despite her good intentions, that Tiffany might never return to the office for another filing lesson.

"Have you come up with a new match for the Grayson boy?" Lena asked, recognizing the file with its distinctive red flag, which was Chris's personal notation of a match in trouble.

"The new Methodist minister, Mr. Lehman, was okayed by the board at the meeting last week. He's agreed to meet with Tim. And I think Pedro Ochoa might be a good match for Scott Burkeman, Tim's current Big Brother."

"I'm glad they both decided to give the program another chance. I really hate to see it when a match doesn't work out."

"So do I."

"Of course you don't have that problem with your match, do you? Tiffany adores you."

"She's a great kid," Chris said, and turned back to her work before Lena could begin asking questions that would be too painful to answer.

"They're all great kids," Lena said. "See you Wednesday morning."

"Goodbye, Lena." Chris finished filing the match reports and locked the file drawer.

She would not be renewing her match with Tiffany when their year together ended in the fall. Not for the same reasons Tim Grayson and Scott Burkeman's match hadn't worked, but because she hoped with all her heart that by the end of their year together Tiffany would no longer need to be in the program. She wanted to be Tiffany's mother. Or grandmother? Or more correctly stepgrandmother? Chris smiled to herself as she switched off the air conditioner. Was there even such a term as *stepgrandmother?* It didn't matter. She just wanted to be there for Tiffany, to love her and take care of her and her brother and sister for the rest of her life. And she knew now that she had more than enough love left over for another girl, another Little Sister, no matter what age.

Chris had learned that much about herself this long eventful winter. She had a lot of love to share. She hadn't realized until she'd fallen in love with Ethan Connor that she'd been holding so much of her ability to care, to give to others, at bay within herself because she didn't want to lose someone she loved, as she had lost her husband, ever again.

But she'd also learned that you can't live in a vacuum or your heart will shrivel up and die. And if Jeff didn't return with the children tonight, or if he and Ethan couldn't work out some compromise over their custody, she would do her best to help Ethan see that truth, also. *But, dear Lord,* she prayed silently, *don't let that happen. Please don't let that happen.*

Ethan's car was parked beside hers in the employee parking lot when she walked out of the courthouse. He was standing alongside it, leaning against the driver's side door. He'd taken off his tie and unbuttoned the collar of his gray-and-white striped shirt. He'd rolled back the cuffs of his sleeves and Chris felt a little flutter of excitement at the memory of his touch, the strength of his hands, the gentleness of his caresses.

"Hi," she said, fishing her sunglasses out of her handbag. "Is...is everything all right?" She hadn't called him during the day, preferring to believe that no news was good news.

"I didn't expect them home before this evening," he said, his dark, straight eyebrows drawn together in a frown. "I thought you might not feel like cooking on such a warm day. I thought we could eat out."

"Make the time go faster?" Chris said, laying her hand on his arm, feeling his tenseness in the rock hardness of the muscles beneath his skin.

"That's partially why I asked. The other reason is that I want to be with you. I also think it's time we started to be seen in public in this town," he said with a smile that just failed to reach his eyes.

"In any case, whether for propriety's sake or the pleasure of my company, I accept." She smiled, too, and was rewarded with a flash of golden humor deep within his hazel eyes.

"I don't know what I'd have done without you these past few days, Chris," he said.

The deep tone of his voice made her heart beat hard and high in her throat, and she couldn't think of an answer to his declaration. But she didn't have to. Keith's sporty Firebird pulled into the lot and roared to a halt behind them. He was wearing his Panther baseball uniform and looked very handsome to his mother's not unbiased eye.

"Hey, Mom, glad I caught you. The game with McComb High was called off because their field got flooded by the rain yesterday. How about taking your favorite son out to dinner?''

"Oh, dear," Chris said, turning to Ethan with a rueful grin. "What shall I tell him?"

Keith leaned his chin on his arm and stuck his head out the window as he surveyed Chris and Ethan with a teenager's knowing eye. "Don't worry. I know when two's company and three's a crowd."

"Don't be absurd," Ethan said with an answering grin, guiding Chris to the passenger side of Keith's car with his hand under her elbow. "I've been itching for a chance to take a ride in this baby. Do you suppose there's room enough for your mother in the back seat?"

"It'll be a tight fit," Keith said, looking over his shoulder at the tiny back seat of the Firebird. "You know she's gained five pounds since Erika's wedding."

"Two pounds," Chris said indignantly, climbing into the car, undecided whether she was piqued or relieved to have her first public meal with Ethan turn into a family affair. And then she laughed softly and quietly. Why not? Family, after all, was what mattered most.

"IT'S ALMOST DARK," Tiffany said, watching the lights come on in the garage across the highway from the fast-food restaurant where they were eating. "I don't think they're going to be able to fix the van tonight."

Her dad looked up from his hamburger and stared across the busy street at the van. They hadn't even taken it inside the building to see what was wrong with it yet. "They're open until nine o'clock, the tow-truck driver said. They should have plenty of time to check it out."

"What time is it?" Ashley asked, tearing her chicken nuggets into tiny pieces.

Tiffany hated it when she did that.

"It's seven-thirty, honey," Jeff informed her, looking at his watch.

"I'm tired," Ashley complained. "And I want to go home."

"Mo' pop," Brandon hollered.

Tiffany poured a little of her cola into his paper glass. He promptly dumped it onto the tray of his high chair. "Mo'," he hollered again, so loud that Tiffany noticed three or four people turned around and stared at him with the silly smiles grown-ups got watching a real little kid do something that anybody else would get slapped for.

"Drink it nice," she said, giving him about ten drops this time.

He eyed the small amount of liquid in the bottom of his glass suspiciously, but drank it without complaint, then started playing with his French fries.

"Tomorrow's show-and-tell," Ashley continued, ignoring the fuss her brother was making. "I want to show everyone where the horse bit me." She held up her hand where the bandage covered her nonexistent wound.

"That poor little pony never bit you," Tiffany said scornfully, still embarrassed by the fuss her dad and the park ranger had made over Ashley's encounter with the horse the previous day.

"Did, too," Ashley insisted, puckering up her face the way she always did before she started bellowing and blubbering.

"Kids," Jeff said, lifting his hands in a gesture to cease and desist, "what if we stayed here tonight and headed on home tomorrow?"

"No," Tiffany said. "I have a spelling test tomorrow."

"No," Ashley wailed.

"Yuck," Brandon said, missing his mouth and sticking a French fry up his nose.

Tiffany grabbed it and threw it in the sack with the other junk they were throwing away. "I studied hard on my spelling words," she explained when she saw the surprised and kind of mad look her dad had on his face. "I want to get a good grade."

"Show-and-tell," Ashley said, nodding very hard. "I want to be there."

"There's a nice motel right down the road," he went on.

He was talking evenly and slowly, the way grown-ups did when they wanted to make you think they were going to really listen to what you had to say. "I thought we could stay there tonight. Start home tomorrow after we get the van out of hock." Seeing the puzzled look on Tiffany's face, he quickly added, "I mean, when the mechanic finishes fixing the van's engine, we can drive home tomorrow when everyone's not so tired."

"I'm not tired now," Tiffany said, wiping Brandon's hands and face clean after she took the ketchup away from him. He started to whine, but not too loudly. "Why don't you call Grandpa to come and get us?"

"Honey, we're only a few miles north of Dayton. That's over a two-hour drive from Bonaparte."

"He'll come," Tiffany said stubbornly.

"No. We'll stay here at the motel. It doesn't have an indoor pool like the motel we stayed at last night, but I'm sure it's a nice one."

They had had a good time yesterday and this morning. The motel they'd gone to after leaving the cabin in the park had an indoor swimming pool with a waterfall made of fake rocks that had a slide built in. Her dad had taken them to a mall and bought them all bathing suits so they could go swimming. They had eaten in the motel restaurant, which had had nice white tablecloths on the tables and heavy knives and forks that looked like real silver and waiters who kept coming around and filling up your water glass almost every time you took a swallow. This morning they had eaten breakfast in their room. Dad had ordered it over the telephone. "Room service," he'd called it. It was fun, but Brandon had spilled his orange juice on the rug, and even though her dad had said not to worry about it, Tiffany did. It spoiled her enjoyment in taking one last swim in the pool before they'd left. But it didn't spoil the pretty, warm spring day. She was having fun with her dad and her brother and sister, but now she was tired and she wanted to go home.

"If we call Grandpa he'll come and get us," she insisted. "We want to go home."

Jeff looked across the street at the garage. The mechanic had driven the van inside and put it on the hoist. "The old credit card is pretty well maxed out," he said half to himself, half to Tiffany. "Do you really think your grandfather will drive all this way tonight to bring us home?"

"Of course," Tiffany said without a doubt in the world. "He's your dad. Don't you know that he would?"

"ARE THEY ASLEEP?" Chris asked as she set the cruise control and checked her side mirrors.

"Sleeping like little angels," Keith said, settling into a comfortable slouch in the passenger seat, Brandon cradled in his arms, his feet propped up on the dash. "Too bad the three of them are such little monsters when they are awake."

"Actually," Chris said, trying hard to keep the laughter out of her voice, "they remind me a lot of you and your sister at those ages."

"Hey! You don't have to insult me after I volunteered to make this mercy run with you and Ethan."

"I know. And I do appreciate your company."

Keith had returned to Ethan's home with them after dinner to see if there had been any message from Jeff and the children, and he had stayed on, ostensibly because he'd had nothing better to do. But Chris guessed her extremely mellow and laid-back son was as worried about the outcome of Jeff's trip as she and Ethan were. And after he'd insisted on accompanying them to Dayton when Jeff's call came through a little after eight o'clock, she was sure of it. His friendship with Tiffany was something special, she realized, something that went beyond the tolerance of a caring and giving young man for a lonely little girl.

"I am a prize among progeny," Keith said, preening just a little. "If you get tired, Mom, I'll drive," he added with no trace of mockery or teasing in his voice.

Keith sounded very grown-up all of a sudden, very much like his father, and Chris's throat tightened with feelings of love and pride. She swallowed them away. "Thanks. I might take you up on that offer. It's been a long day."

"I doubt if Jeff and Ethan will get home before dawn, even if that garage mechanic agreed to work on the van's engine tonight."

"I'm afraid you're right about that. Do you think the girls are warm enough back there? I hate to turn on the heater. The cool air's helping to keep me awake."

"They're sleeping like babies, Mom." He shifted the sleeping toddler to a more comfortable position and was silent for a long while.

Mile after mile of fertile farmland rolled by on either side of the interstate. The wheat fields Chris glimpsed as she drove by were faintly green beneath the light of a bright spring moon, while other newly plowed fields, waiting to be planted with corn and soybeans, stretched out alongside them, dark and glistening with moisture.

"Tiffany has quite a game plan worked out for everybody," Keith said quietly after a while.

They hadn't been able to agree on a station at the beginning of the journey so they'd turned the radio off. Now only the hum of the tires on the pavement and the wind rushing by outside the car disturbed their solitude.

"Game plan?" Chris asked, intrigued as always by the chance to hear one of Tiffany's creative flights of fancy.

"She says there's no reason that all of us can't live in that big house together when you and Ethan get married."

"Oh, dear," Chris said. Most of the time she could believe that happy-ever-after for her and Ethan was in the future. Sometimes she could not, so she'd avoided talking about the subject at all when she could.

"What's the 'oh, dear' supposed to mean? You love the guy, don't you?" Keith asked.

"Yes," she answered just as truthfully. "But I'm not sure it's going to work out between us."

"Why not?" Keith inquired bluntly.

"Things," Chris said helplessly. "This is real life. It isn't a television show where a half-dozen zany but lovable crazies live happily under one roof, solving their problems every week in a half-hour span of time."

"Why not?" Keith asked again.

Chris felt her exasperation grow as well as a tight knot of pain just beneath her heart. "Life just doesn't work that way. Jeff and Ethan may not be able to come to an agreement over the children's future."

"People work out custody arrangements about their kids every day. Besides, I don't think Jeff Connor's going to take these kids anywhere," Keith said, lowering his voice a little more in case Tiffany or one of the other children should come awake and overhear. "I just don't think he's got it in him to be a full-time dad."

"He loves them," Chris said, feeling bound to defend the young man, as she often did, and still not sure why.

"I didn't say that. I just said I don't think he's got what it takes to raise them. A lot of guys are that way. And some women, too," he added fairly.

"He may not be able to accept that about himself."

"I think he will. Eventually." Keith was quiet for a moment or two. "Anyway, I can't see Tiffany letting him cart them off to California without putting up a real battle. Can you? That kid knows what she wants and she goes after it. She wants you to marry her grandfather and I think you'd both better give up and do what she wants."

"How do you feel about my marrying Ethan?" Chris asked.

"I think I already told you that. Erika and Mike and I discussed it after they got home from their honeymoon. They're all for it, too."

"They are?"

"Yeah. And don't think it'll upset us a lot if you sell the house," he added.

"I thought you liked our house." Chris felt a small twinge of sadness for the dreams she and Jack had dreamed together for that house."

"It's a good house," Keith agreed. "But Dad's been gone a long time. And when I go to college this fall, it's going to be a lot of work for you to take care of it. Besides," he added with his usual devastating candor, "it can't hold a candle to Ethan Connor's house."

"It's not selling our house or even whether or not I have my children's blessing that's holding me back," Chris heard herself say. "There are a lot of things be-

tween us that Ethan and I need to work out. What if
his company transfers him back to Chicago? I'm not
sure I want to quit my job and go with him. But most
important of all is what Jeff and Ethan decide about
the children's future.''

"Jeez," Keith said, swiveling around in the seat so
that he could look directly at her and make his point.
"What happened to just being in love with someone
and getting married?"

"I don't know," Chris said truthfully. "I've always believed if you loved someone enough nothing
could or should keep you apart. Now—" she lifted her
hands from the wheel for a moment in a gesture of
confusion and uncertainty "—now I just don't know
if that is enough."

"It is if you love someone with all your heart and
soul," said Keith.

"I want to believe that's true," Chris said, amazed
at the conversation of her practical and obviously romantic son, amazed to be seeking guidance and reassurance from her own child. "I just can't be sure
Ethan shares my beliefs. Or if he loves me as much as
I love him."

If SHE WERE QUIET and kept her eyes closed, Chris and
Keith wouldn't know she was awake and maybe they
would go on talking. Tiffany didn't understand some
of what they were saying, but she could tell that Chris
was worried her grandfather didn't want to marry her.
Tiffany didn't think that was very likely. Maybe she
was only nine, but she saw the way her grandfather
looked at Chris. She knew how much she and her

grandfather talked about her Big Sister when she wasn't around.

Ashley was snoring and Tiffany wished she would be quiet. It made it hard to hear what they were saying in the front seat of Chris's car. She shifted around a little, poking Ashley real softly with her elbow. Her sister grunted and slid around on the seat until she was lying down. Keith turned his head and looked back over the seat—Tiffany could see him through tiny slits in her eyes.

"Those two are crashed," he said, and went back to talking to Chris. "Did you know she has a plan for all of us?" he said after a while.

Tiffany wondered if she'd fallen asleep for a little bit. It didn't seem as if they had been talking about her plan just a moment ago. She held her breath, turning her head slightly to watch the moon follow alongside them high in the sky. She didn't know how the moon always seemed to be following their car, but it did. Someday she'd have to ask her grandfather...or Keith why that was.

Chris and Keith were talking real quietly now. It was hard to hear them over the noise of the tires on the road. She overheard her dad's name, and her grandfather's. And then Keith said he wouldn't mind living in her house! Tiffany almost sat up straight and whooped with glee. Keith wouldn't say what he thought of her plan when she'd told him about it the other day. Now she knew. He liked it, too. That would help. She settled back in her seat and folded her arms in front of her. If Keith liked her plan for all of them to live together in Grandpa's big house, then Chris would like it, too.

There was room for everybody in that house. All of them, including her dad, if he wanted to stay. She closed her eyes and felt the nice, heavy feeling of sleep come over her. She didn't fight it this time. Everything was going to work out. Everyone would be happy if she could make it happen, even her dad.

"I APPRECIATE your coming down here after us," Jeff said in a rush, as though the words were hard for him to speak and he had to say them quickly or not at all.

"That's what family's for," Ethan said, sliding down on the base of his spine, trying to find a comfortable position on the hard seat of the van. It had been a long night spent sitting in a truck stop café two doors down from the garage where they were working on Jeff's van. They'd passed the hours in near silence. Sunrise was gilding the eastern sky with pink and gold before they had gotten back on the road and Ethan was tired, but he wasn't about to lose the opportunity to open a dialogue with his son.

"So you keep telling me," Jeff said, but there was no malice in his voice. He curled and uncurled his fingers around the steering wheel as if searching for a place to begin, a crack in the wall of animosity between them. "This weekend's been a real education for me. I had no idea how upset the kids would be by the van breaking down until I tried to suggest finding a motel for the night." He shrugged, a rueful smile lifting the corner of his mouth. "It nearly blew their minds. Tiffany, especially."

"Children are great creatures of habit," Ethan reminded him. He rested one arm along the back of the seat and turned slightly to face his son. "Routines represent security. And Tiffany does not like surprises," he added with a chuckle.

"Tell me about it," Jeff said. "Katie always used to tell me what to do with them. I was never alone with my kids for so long a time. And they were babies then—they did pretty much what you told them to do. Now they've got personalities of their own."

"And opinions," Ethan added.

And Jeff laughed, short and rough around the edges, but a laugh filled with genuine amusement. "They're incredible kids, aren't they? You're doing a great job with them. Thanks, Dad."

"I love them," Ethan replied. That was all. That was enough.

"I could have pulled up stakes and taken them all the way to California this weekend," Jeff said after the noise of an eighteen-wheeler coming alongside them in the passing lane died away.

Ethan watched the rear end of the big truck pull ahead of them. "I know that."

"I just couldn't do it," Jeff continued. "I tried to picture the four of us together, living together, a family. I just couldn't do it." He lifted his right hand from the steering wheel and raked it through his hair. "Is there something wrong with me, Dad?"

"No," Ethan said. "I think it means you realize in your heart you're not ready to take responsibility for them on a permanent basis, that's all."

Jeff nodded. "When I got to California I'd planned on crashing at Mom's commune. Somehow, sitting in that fast-food joint last night, watching the three of them wolf down chicken nuggets and burgers and fries, I couldn't see them thanking me for setting a meal of brown rice and herbal tea in front of them.''

"They'd adjust," Ethan said with a grin, determined to let Jeff see he was willing to discuss the children's future rationally and calmly. So much depended on this conversation. He couldn't force the issue. He had to wait, let Jeff make up his own mind about his place in his children's lives. The choice had to be Jeff's alone—Chris was right about that—but all their happiness rested on his decision.

"Yeah, I guess they would adjust. And it would do them good in the long run, I suppose. Maybe that's where Mom was wrong and you were right. She never made me do anything for my own good. It's taken me a hell of a long time to learn you've got to earn your own way in this world.''

"Brown rice and herbal tea might have done them some good.''

"I don't think I'd have lived long enough to see the results,'' Jeff said with a laugh that sounded less strained, more natural.

"They are pretty strong-willed kids,'' Ethan said.

"C'mon, Dad, say it. They're bullheaded as hell and we both know it.''

"Just like you and me.''

"I can't do it, Dad,'' Jeff said, and his voice broke. "I can't take care of them alone. I'm not ready to be a full-time father. Maybe that's why I didn't head west with the kids when I had a chance.''

"Leave them with me, son. We'll all be here waiting for you when you get back.''

Jeff took his eyes off the road for a moment to meet Ethan's steady gaze. "You mean that, don't you?"

"Yes I do."

"Thanks, Dad. That makes it easier for me to go." Ethan felt his heart contract with regret that he and Jeff hadn't been close enough to talk this way for so many years. Perhaps it wasn't too late for him to make amends to his son, as well as for Jeff to find his rightful place in life. Admitting he wasn't ready to be a full-time father was taking a big step in the right direction. Jeff was learning some hard lessons and he was making hard choices without flinching or running away.

"I've got a plan worked out for making some money. Real money, a steady income. Want to hear it?"

"Sure," Ethan said, settling back to enjoy the ride and the conversation with his son.

"If I can get established out on the West Coast in the custom furniture business, I might be able to work it up into a real nice mail-order market."

"Mail order?" Ethan asked, less surprised than he might have been even a few hours earlier that Jeff had given any thought at all to securing his future income.

"With UPS and Federal Express and toll-free phone numbers I could do business all over the country. There's a hell of a market out there for good reproductions of period furniture. Yuppie couples furnishing their first house, Baby Boomers on the way up who can't afford real antiques but who want the quality of hand craftsmanship and are willing to pay for it."

"Once you make a name for yourself, establish your reputation..." Ethan said thoughtfully.

"I can run my business from anyplace in the country," Jeff finished triumphantly.

"It just might work." Ethan shifted in his seat, running his hand through his hair. "I know a couple of kids who started a market research firm out there. They're about your age, bright, innovative."

"And cheap," Jeff inserted irreverently.

"Reasonable," Ethan corrected with a grin. "I'll give you their name and phone number when we get back to Bonaparte...if you want it."

Jeff smiled, but his expression was serious. "I'd be a fool to turn down expert advice, but I am going to make a go of this on my own. That's why I need to be in California. It's the best place right now to make a name for myself."

"Then I agree, you'd better go."

"And I agree the kids should stay here with you." Jeff took his right hand off the steering wheel and held it out to his father. They clasped hands. "I know right now they belong with you. And Chris."

Ethan covered Jeff's hand with both of his for a long second, then released his son. He remained silent. There was no more to be said and they both knew it.

"I'll be leaving Bonaparte before too much longer," Jeff said, taking a deep breath, as though he'd just cleared a great hurdle, crossed a barrier that had been blocking his progress for a long, long time. "But I'd like to stick around long enough to be best man at your wedding.''

This time it was Ethan who had trouble finding the right words. ''I'm not certain there's going to be a wedding,'' he admitted at last.

Jeff frowned but didn't take his eyes off the road again. ''I may not be too bright when it comes to a lot of things, but I can tell when a man and a woman are in love with each other. What went wrong?''

''Love isn't always enough,'' Ethan said, and his voice was harsh with the effort he made to control it.

''Yes, it is,'' Jeff said quietly. ''Katie and I loved each other. I know what I'm talking about now, even if I didn't realize it myself until it was too late.'' He was silent a long moment. ''Don't let Chris get away, Dad. Ask her to marry you. Now. Today. As soon as we get back to Bonaparte.''

''In point of fact I've already asked her to marry me. Twice.''

''And she turned you down?''

''She . . . asked me for more time. That's not the problem,'' Ethan said, and smiled mirthlessly. ''She also asked me to marry her. I turned her down.''

''Why the hell did you do something like that?'' Jeff asked, astounded.

''She asked me the night of her daughter's wedding.''

Jeff slapped his palm on the steering wheel. ''That was the day I told you I wanted to take the kids to California with me.''

''It was almost immediately after . . . our discussion,'' Ethan confirmed.

"Hell, I'm sorry, Dad."

"Don't blame yourself, son," Ethan said with a laugh that was more a groan. "I'm perfectly capable of ruining my own life."

"Since this happens to be our night for heart-to-heart talks," Jeff said with a smile, "I might as well get my two cents' worth in."

"Advise away," Ethan said, laying his head back against the seat. "I need all the help I can get."

"I'll leave the details to you. You're the strategist in the Connor family. But whatever you do, don't let that lady get away."

CHAPTER SEVENTEEN

"I THOUGHT I might find you out here," Ethan said, coming up behind Chris as she stood by the Riverwalk railing, watching Keith and Tiffany fly a kite on the sloping riverbank at the base of the low, grassy bluff behind the courthouse.

"I'm playing hooky," she confessed, turning to him with a welcoming smile, her tone as light and sunny as the spring day. She was determined not to let her nervousness show. She'd watched him coming toward her after he'd left the courthouse steps, his long strides eating up the distance between them, his footsteps echoing faintly on the wooden walkway, and she'd had time to get her heartbeat and her voice under control. "Keith and Tiffany came by and talked me into it. They said I looked pale as a ghost and needed an hour in the sun."

"Those two make quite a convincing pair."

"Convincing, and very plainspoken," she agreed with a chuckle. "How did you find us?"

"Tiffany left a note with Mrs. Baden telling me Keith had come by to bring her here to fly her kite. When I found your office door locked I put two and two together and assumed you had joined the party."

"As an interested bystander, nothing more. But Keith and Tiffany are right about one thing. It is much too nice a day to stay cooped up inside." Chris lifted her face to the warm sun, watching a fleecy cloud drift by high overhead.

"How was your day?" Ethan asked politely, looking out over the water, not at her.

"Busy," she replied, equally polite. There had been no time to talk this morning when Ethan and Jeff had returned with the van just moments before Chris had bundled Tiffany and Ashley into her car to take them to school.

"Did you get a chance to rest?"

"I slept on your couch for a few hours after I dropped Keith off at home."

"I'm sorry. It's not very comfortable."

"I didn't mind." She turned her head to search his face for signs of fatigue. "Did you find time today to rest?"

"No, but I feel fine."

He dismissed her concern with a smile that kicked her pulse rate into high gear once again.

"I appreciate your staying at my house with the children last night," he went on. "Getting them off to school was above and beyond the call of duty."

"Was it, Ethan?" Was he trying to hurt her on purpose, relegating her actions to the role of friend and not loved one, lover? Or was it only that he was as nervous as she?

"Some people would consider that it was." He rested his forearms on the railing and leaned forward to watch as Keith and Tiffany attempted to launch the kite once more. He'd shed his suit jacket and tie before reaching the Riverwalk. His broad shoulders strained the material of his white shirt. His skin looked bronzed and healthy, and she longed for the touch of his warm, strong arms around her.

"There it goes. They did it!" he said with a laugh. "How many times have they tried to launch it?" he asked Chris as the red-and-blue diamond-shaped kite caught the breeze and lifted high above the river.

"Twice," Chris replied, with a wave for the successful fliers.

"Good work, Tiffany. Keith," Ethan made a megaphone of his hands and called down the bluff.

"Grandpa!" Tiffany waved harder than ever and nearly lost hold of the string attached to her kite.

Keith made a dive for it and handed it back after righting the kite, which had dipped dangerously close to the water.

"Everything must be going well at the plant if you were able to get away so early in the afternoon."

"I've learned that leaving the plant an hour early once in a while doesn't mean everything will automatically grind to a halt."

"But you still don't like doing it often, do you?" Chris asked, tilting her head, smiling as he looked over at her with a rueful grin raising the corners of his mouth.

"No. I haven't changed that much. Actually, we started negotiations on a new labor agreement with the migrant workers' union and the growers' association today. There are going to be some long hard bargaining sessions coming up over the next couple of weeks, but I think we can strike a deal that will be fair to everyone."

"I had some news today, also," Chris said, watching an early season boater race by along the far bank of the river, a white wake spreading out behind him in the muddy brown water. "About the program."

"Do you want to tell me about it?"

It was easier for him, too, Chris realized, to talk about their jobs than the more important private issues still unsettled between them. She didn't even know if he and Jeff had come to an agreement over the children's future. She was afraid to ask, afraid to find out she might be losing Tiffany and perhaps Ethan, as well.

"It seems my fund-raising efforts for the program have been so successful that our United Fund allotment is being cut. I'm going to have to come up with an extra fifteen hundred dollars of operating capital on my own this year."

"That's what being one hell of an executive director will get you. You'll think of something," Ethan assured her. "You always do."

"Bowling," Chris said with a smile.

He lifted one foot to rest on a railing and straightened, resting his weight on his hands. "Bowling?" He looked at her with a faint frown between his eyes.

"Bowling," Chris repeated. "I'm going to have a bowling tournament. The teams will sign up sponsors to back them for so much money per pin. With any luck I can make up the difference. Of course I'll need lots of cooperation from the business community. And I'll need corporate sponsors, as well."

"You can count on Castleton's for all the support you need."

"Thanks." Chris looked up at Tiffany's red-and-blue kite, now very small and far above them. She looked at the boat wake arrowing toward shore. She watched her son and Ethan's granddaughter and didn't look at him again. How long could they go on discussing such mundane matters? How long before they had to face what was between them? And could she manage such a private conversation in so public a place? She couldn't bring herself to talk about them. Instead she asked the question that was next in importance in her thoughts.

"Did you reach an agreement with Jeff about the children?" They had all been so rushed this morning—the children hurrying off to school, Chris with appointments scheduled early in the day and Mrs. Baden hovering in the background, well-meaning but curious about the night's adventure—there had been no time to talk. Ethan had swept the girls into his arms for a quick hug and kiss as they rushed to the car, but that was all. He had exchanged a few words with Tiffany, but she had only been able to tell Chris that her grandfather had said everything would be all right, muttering that her plan was starting to work.

"Yes," he said, holding out his hand, waiting quietly for her to place hers within the comforting warmth of his palm. "We talked a lot. All the way home, as a matter of fact. Jeff is still determined to go to California, but the children will be staying here."

He pulled her a step closer, a step nearer to the haven of his arms. "I'm glad, Ethan. Tiffany will be so happy. She wants this so badly. She had a plan, you know. All of us living together in your house, one big, happy family, like a television show or a Disney movie."

"I want her to have what makes her happy. So does her father. Maybe we'll never be as close as most fathers and sons, but at least we've solved this problem without dragging the children into it, making them pawns in a battle that one of us had to lose."

"I know that both of you love the children enough to put their best interests first, no matter what problems there are between you."

"I'll remember that. You have more faith in me than I have in myself sometimes," he said in a wondering tone. "Later, maybe Jeff will come back to Bonaparte, or if he doesn't, the children will be older, better able to choose for themselves. Maybe by then I'll be able to accept their choices if they want to be with him. In any event, for now we're staying here. All of us. Does that plan meet with your approval?"

"Yes. But what about Castleton's plans for your future?"

"Being in charge of the company's major renewal project is all I'm interested in doing right now. Later?" He released her hand and slipped his arms around her waist. "I can't predict the future, Chris."

"I know that. I just want to be where you are. If it means leaving Bonaparte someday, we'll cross that bridge when we come to it."

His hands molded the curve of her waist and the warmth of his skin penetrated the thin layers of her skirt and slip. She looked up into his eyes, saw the love and uncertainty there, and suddenly felt very strong and sure of her love, of herself. If they were going to get their life together started anytime soon, she was going to have to ask him to marry her... again.

She was torn between amusement and nerves. This man and his grandchildren had turned her life topsyturvy and she would not have it any other way. He had

made her feel young again, taught her to love again,
to give of herself wholeheartedly, not merely from the
surface of her concern. She could identify with small
children now, as well as with teenagers. She could understand better the concerns of her Littles' parents, as
well as her volunteers. She could laugh and cry and
feel, experience life to the fullest. She had no intention of letting Ethan Connor or his grandchildren slip
out of her life. Not if she had to ask him to marry her
a hundred times before he said yes.

"Ethan," she began, smiling just a little as she saw
that he realized what she was going to say. "Will—"

"No, Chris," he said, lifting his finger, silencing her
with a gentle pressure against her lips. "It's my turn.
I'm not asking you again. We're just going to do it. I
know we can't wait for our lives to be perfect, for your
children to be settled and on their own, for my son to
grow up and take stock of his life. We're going to get
married now. As soon as possible."

"I—" He didn't let her continue.

"We're standing in front of the courthouse. It's 4:20
p.m. We have forty minutes to apply for a marriage
license. Come with me."

"Yes," Chris said simply and with complete con-
viction. "Yes, let's do it now. No more waiting. If we
start the paperwork now we can be married this
weekend. Is that too soon?"

"It's not soon enough." He pulled her close, un-
heeding of watching eyes from the courthouse windows and from the riverbank below. "I love you,
Christine Baldwin."

"I love you, Ethan Connor. I love you all."

"KEITH! Look! My grandpa is kissing your mother right in front of everyone!" Tiffany said, awed at the sight. "Do you think my plan's worked already? Do you think that means they're going to get married?"

"I sure hope so. Half the town must be watching that clinch," Keith said irreverently.

He didn't sound as if he was making fun of them, Tiffany thought. Her grandpa had Chris in his arms, was kissing her, holding her as if he never wanted to let her go.

"Whew," Keith said, whistling through his teeth. "Get a load of that! Your grandpa's no slouch in the kissing department."

"It's so romantic," Tiffany whispered, as if Ethan and Chris might be able to hear her, even up there on top of the bluff.

"It's embarrassing," Keith said, making a dive for the kite as Tiffany's grip on the string slackened.

"No, it isn't!" Tiffany rounded on him, ready to do battle, only to find him smiling down at her as though he knew everything in the world and she didn't. She gave the kite string a yank. It broke and her kite took off like a bird, trailing its string for a hundred feet behind it. "Oh, dear," she said, but she didn't really care that much. "I've wished and wished for Chris to be my new...grandmother," she said, settling on that description.

"I think you'd just better keep on calling her Chris," Keith advised, rolling up the string on the spool so it wouldn't make a mess on the riverbank. "I don't think she's ready to be called Grandma just yet."

"That's true," Tiffany said with a happy sigh as they started toward the wooden stairway leading up to the Riverwalk. "She's much too young and too pretty to be a grandma." She skipped ahead of him for a few steps, then turned and stopped with one foot already on the staircase. "Does this mean that she can't be my Big Sister anymore?" She couldn't see Chris and her grandfather from this angle and she was in a hurry to be with them. She started climbing before Keith answered her question.

"Slow down, squirt," he ordered. "At least wait until they are done kissing to bust in on them."

"Okay," she said breathlessly, slowing her headlong pace. "But does it mean Chris can't be my Big Sister anymore?"

"Probably. You'll have two parents. That means you don't qualify to need a Big Sister."

"Oh." Tiffany stopped with her head just level with the Riverwalk. Looking sideways, she could see Chris's legs and her grandfather's, too. They were still standing very close together. "Oh, well."

"I suppose you could say Erika is going to be your big sister from now on," Keith said, coming to a halt himself just a few steps below her. He looked a little puzzled, as though he were having trouble figuring out the new alignment of families himself. "Or will she be your stepgreat-aunt? Oh, hell, it'll take a lawyer to figure this family out from now on."

"Keith! You should watch what you say around little kids like me," Tiffany cautioned with her nose in the air.

"Pipe down, squirt." He reached out and ruffled her short black hair.

"I don't know Erika well enough to be her little sister," she said a little bit sadly.

Keith sighed, as though he were making a great big sacrifice. "I suppose if you really want to be some-one's little sister I can be your big brother from now on." He stuck one hand in the back pocket of his jeans and held out his other hand for her to take.

Tiffany looked up at him and smiled before she be-gan climbing the last few steps to where Chris and her grandfather were waiting for them. "Good," she said, because that's exactly what she'd wanted him to say. "That will work out just fine until I grow up."

"What's going to happen when you grow up?" Keith asked, stepping unsuspectingly into her trap.

"Then," she said with all the certainty in the world before she rushed forward to be swept up into her grandfather's arms, "I'm going to marry you and I won't be your little sister any more. I'll be your wife."

HARLEQUIN SUPERROMANCE®

Books by Marisa Carroll

BSMC

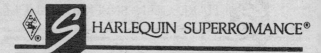

COMING NEXT MONTH

HARLEQUIN®

Temptation®

Rebels & Rogues

Trey: He lived life on the edge . . . and wasn't about to be
tamed by a beautiful woman.

THE RED-BLOODED YANKEE!
By Ruth Jean Dale
Temptation #413, October

All men are not created equal. Some are rough around the
edges. Tough-minded but tenderhearted. Incredibly
sexy. The tempting fulfillment of every woman't fantasy.

When it's time to fight for what they believe in, to win
that special woman, our Rebels and Rogues are heroes at
heart. Twelve Rebels and Rogues, each month in 1992,
only from Harlequin Temptation. Don't miss the
upcoming books by our fabulous authors such as Janice
Kaiser and Kelly Street.

WELCOME TO

The quintessential small town, where everyone
knows everybody else!

Finally, books that capture the pleasure
of tuning in to your favorite TV show!

Join your friends at Tyler in the eighth book, BACHELOR'S PUZZLE by Ginger
Chambers, available in October.

*What do Tyler's librarian and a cosmopolitan architect have in common? What
does the coroner's office have to reveal?*

GREAT READING...GREAT SAVINGS...
AND A FABULOUS FREE GIFT!

Each book set in Tyler is a self-contained love story; together, the twelve novels
stitch the fabric of the community. You can't miss the Tyler books on the shelves
because the covers honor the old American tradition of quilting; each cover
depicts a patch of the large Tyler quilt!

And you can receive a FABULOUS GIFT, ABSOLUTELY FREE, by collecting
proofs-of-purchase found in each Tyler book, *and* use our Tyler coupons to save
on your next TYLER book purchase.

HARLEQUIN®

I N T R I G U E®

A SPAULDING AND DARIEN MYSTERY

Amateur sleuths Jenny Spaulding and Peter Darien have set
the date for their wedding. But before they walk down the
aisle, love must pass a final test. This time, they won't have to
solve a murder, they'll have to prevent one—Jenny's.
Don't miss the chilling conclusion to the SPAULDING AND
DARIEN MYSTERY series in October. Watch for:

#197 WHEN SHE WAS BAD by Robin Francis

Look for the identifying series flash—A SPAULDING AND
DARIEN MYSTERY—and join Jenny and Peter for danger and
romance....

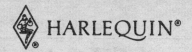

THE TAGGARTS OF TEXAS!

Harlequin's Ruth Jean Dale brings you
THE TAGGARTS OF TEXAS!

Those Taggart men—strong, sexy and hard to resist...

You've met Jesse James Taggart in FIREWORKS!
Harlequin Romance #3205 (July 1992)

Now meet Trey Smith—he's THE RED-BLOODED YANKEE!
Harlequin Temptation #413 (October 1992)

Then there's Daniel Boone Taggart in SHOWDOWN!
Harlequin Romance #3242 (January 1993)

And finally the Taggarts who started it all—in LEGEND!
Harlequin Historical #168 (April 1993)

Read all the Taggart romances!
Meet all the Taggart men!

Available wherever Harlequin books are sold.